# KAREN M. DILLON

# THE IMMORTAL SOULS

## MAGIC & CHAOS
## BOOK TWO

# THE IMMORTAL SOULS

## GUARDIAN VAMPIRE

*For Josh (AKA: Stranger Danger)…*

*… the reason that my mam didn't want
me to go on the internet*

# CHAPTER 1

The fluorescent bar lights shone into her eyes; she closed them tightly against the glare. As she closed her stinging eyes, images burned behind the lids.

A face with skin like smooth alabaster covered in blood and eyes with draining colour staring back with an expression of betrayal.

Sam opened her eyes and stared down at her shaking hands, which clutched a glass of clear liquid. Her eyes watered slightly, though she couldn't tell if it was because the lights were too bright or if she was crying.

She sipped her drink.

The liquid burned as it made its way down her oesophagus. She didn't wince against the pain. Instead she embraced it. A small amount of pain was the least she deserved for what she'd done.

Sam sat on the barstool in discomfort, wishing with all of her being that she could go back and stop herself. The exacts of what had happened skittered along the edges of her memories, if she tried she knew that she could piece everything together, but the full details were not something that she wished to reminisce. Though it didn't take too much effort to figure out what had transpired.

When she'd opened her eyes to find a body with its throat torn apart and the taste of freshly spilled blood on her lips, she *knew*.

She would have staked herself through the heart the moment she'd opened her eyes, a penance not even close to what she felt she deserved for the life she'd taken, but she couldn't bring herself to do it.

No matter how badly Sam felt that death was all she deserved she just couldn't do it. Her survival instincts outweighed the guilt of her conscience.

Which was why she had searched for hours for a specific scent, and then followed it here.

To where she would find someone else to exact her punishment.

She peered over her shoulder as a woman walked past, lightly brushing her hand along Sam's back as she did. The woman stopped at the door and turned, looking directly at her as she smiled invitingly.

It was obvious from the flirtatious way she held her body that she was inviting Sam away with her. The woman appeared to be making an effort to convince Sam that it was because she liked her, or at the very least lusted after her. But Sam knew why the woman wanted *her* and not someone else.

Sam stood, psychologically preparing herself for what was about to come; she finished her drink in one go, then followed the woman out of the bar.

Outside the air was cold and fresh, which was a nice change from the stale smell that contaminated the air inside. Once the bar door had swung shut behind her, the woman threw herself into Sam's arms and kissed her as if they'd been flirting all night.

Sam's senses were assailed by the sweet aroma of the woman's blood. The scent pulsed through her skin and rolled off her in overwhelming waves of heat. She pushed the woman gently to get her to back off; if Sam wasn't careful she would tear this woman's throat out here and now.

"Why don't we go back to your place handsome?" the woman said, batting her eyelashes. She swayed in Sam's arms, moving as if she were drunk. And if not for Sam's heightened senses, which couldn't detect the slightest scent of alcohol, she would have believed that this woman was completely wasted.

"It's too far," Sam said, barely recognising the sound of her own voice as she spoke. "Why don't we find somewhere closer?"

The woman's expression grew slightly irritated. "No," she said quickly, before she recovered herself and gave Sam a dazzling smile. She grabbed onto Sam's shirt, twisting her hand in the fabric as she stood on her toes and leaned in too close. "I'd like to go to your place. I don't mind the walk."

Sam shrugged as she removed the woman's hand from her shirt; she turned and led the way home, not needing to look behind to know the woman was following.

Sam wondered why she had been so insistent on going to her house, surely anywhere private would do? But perhaps she needed to check to see if Sam lived with other Vampires or not. Lucky for this woman, Sam lived alone, as she had for the majority of her undead life.

It took almost an hour for them to get to the house. They walked the whole way there in complete silence, the woman no longer feeling the need to keep up the lustful pretence. If

Sam were any other Vampire, this woman would have been bled dry by now. They had been in an isolated area for the better part of an hour and Sam could sense that the other members of her hunting group were so far from them that if Sam had felt the inclination for murder, this Hunter would have been dead before the others would have known what happened.

"Are we going inside there?" she asked once they'd arrived at the house. She stood a few steps behind Sam, not taking a single step past the line of trees that surrounded the building. Her arms wrapped around herself tightly as she shivered. Sam felt a slight bubble of guilt seeing her body shake; she'd been so preoccupied in her own thoughts that she hadn't thought to check whether the woman was alright walking so far in the cold while being so scantily clad.

But then, what did it matter what the woman felt? She would be killing Sam soon so why should she make any effort at niceties beforehand?

Sam turned her gaze up to the trees that surrounded the house and remembered the runes that had been carved into them. The woman couldn't step any further without an invitation.

She turned her back to the woman and stepped onto the porch; she opened the door. "Come in," she said, hoping the verbal invitation would be enough. Spells and potions weren't something she had the necessary skills to perform, so hopefully words were all she needed.

The woman slowly stepped away from the trees and walked towards the house, looking around in confusion as if she wasn't sure why she hadn't walked forward earlier.

Sam held the door for her. The woman stepped inside the house and Sam followed, closing the door on the way.

As it slammed shut, she caught her reflection in the mirror

and froze as she saw Jamie's face looking back at her.

# CHAPTER 2

$\mathcal{J}$amie stared at himself in the mirror for a moment; an image in the corner of his eye had caught him off guard as he'd walked past. But as he stared at the mirror the only thing he saw was his own reflection, and behind him the reflection of the Vampire Hunter.

She was watching him with a slight gleam of curiosity in her expression. Their eyes met in the reflection and she smiled at him seductively, still pretending that she wasn't here to kill him. Jamie let his lids drift shut and sighed before turning to face her. "So how do you want to do this?"

The woman stared at him, one eyebrow raised in confusion. "What do you mean?"

Jamie sighed with impatience; he was hoping to get this over and done with as soon as he possibly could. The longer he stayed alive, the more apprehension he felt at the thought of dying. "Look . . . I know what you are, you know what I am, so let's just cut to the chase. I'd like to get this over with as soon as possible."

"What *I* am?" the woman asked incredulously.

"I'm a Vampire," he said. "And you're a Hunter, I can smell it on you."

"You knew that and you still brought me here? That explains why you didn't play along anyway. When you didn't ask my name I just thought you were really *really* hungry," she said while laughing nervously. She looked around as if she thought she had walked into some kind of trap. "It's Lucy by the way, and I'm not alone! There's a group of us!" She spoke loudly as if trying to make sure anyone hiding would hear.

"We're alone," Jamie stated. "I'm the only one, and this isn't a trap. I brought you here so you could kill me."

Lucy's eyes widened as she stared at him. "What? You *want* me to kill you?"

"Yes."

Lucy cocked her head to the side and gazed at him in confusion, as if she'd never expected a Vampire to say anything like that. "Why? I mean, were you just Turned or something? Or is it that you've been alive too long?"

"Neither," Jamie replied. "I did something bad, something for which the only acceptable punishment is death, so I need you to kill me."

"I can't," she said, shaking her head. "I'm just the bait, I don't do the killing."

"Are you trained?" Jamie asked. "Surely they wouldn't send you in here completely defenceless."

"I took a potion," she said, as she slowly took a step away from him. "My blood is poison to you."

Jamie stepped towards her. "What if my plan wasn't to drain you, but to kill you? There are a lot of ways I could do it you know?"

"You wouldn't—"

"I could stab you, break your neck, rip your heart out with my bare hand, did you know that there's a moment before your body falls that your brain registers the fact that you're dead? It's quite horrible."

"Stop it," she said as she backed away from him. Jamie could smell the fear emanating from her.

He didn't back down, instead he advanced. "I could feed you my blood and watch that poison in your veins burn you up from the inside . . . that might be amusing for me."

The woman stopped so suddenly Jamie froze in surprise. "You won't hurt me," she said with a smug smile. "I know that because you're so desperate to be killed for what you did wrong. A monster with a conscience isn't going to do anything too bad."

"Tonight I killed a girl for no reason!" Jamie yelled. He took a deep breath to try calm himself but it was no use. His head was frantic as he naturally tried to remember, and then his desperation exploded when he hit the same mental block. "I don't even remember it!"

"Okay, just—"

"How could I not remember killing her?"

"Calm down!"

"How can I not remember? It's not like she was nothing, she mattered, and now she's dead because I killed her and I don't even know why!"

"It's what you are!" Jamie stared at the woman as she spoke. "It's what your kind does. You kill and you destroy and you don't care!"

"But I—"

"No!" she interrupted, taking a step towards him with an expression of unadulterated fury. "You don't remember it because it's *not* important to you, killing isn't your second nature, it's your first and only nature! You and your kind . . . you're all just *monsters!*"

"Then kill me," Jamie whispered.

Lucy considered him for a moment, then a slow smile crept onto her face. "This girl you killed, did you love her?"

Jamie nodded his head. "Yes."

"And you killed her?"

Jamie couldn't bring himself to speak so instead he simply nodded.

"Does it hurt? Is your heart broken? Are you suffering?"

"Yes."

Lucy leaned forward, invading his personal space before saying, "Good." She shoved past him and walked towards the door.

"If nothing else," he said, before she could walk out of the house, "do it for the money."

"What?" Lucy turned to face him, her expression half amused, half curious. *Humans are all the same,* Jamie thought, *they all think they're better than everything until you offer them money or something they desire.* "You'd pay me to kill you?" She paused as she seemed to consider it, then asked, "How much?"

Jamie shook his head. "A man named Kraven wants me dead. I'm worth about a million. If you don't believe me then do whatever you need to do to check it out."

Lucy stood there and looked at him for a moment as if trying to assess his sincerity. Then after a minute said, "Wait here, I'll be back in a couple of minutes . . . if you're telling the truth."

# CHAPTER 3

*J*amie sat on the ground outside his house. He watched the forest that stretched out before him with blind eyes, the world blurring into shadows as his mind wandered.

He had been sitting there for over an hour, listening to the group of Hunters deliberating on whether or not to kill him. *'He wants to die.' 'Let him live and suffer under the weight of his own conscience.' 'He could be lying so that we let him live.' 'Just kill him.' 'Agreed, he's a Vampire, he has to die.' 'He's worth a bounty.' 'We wait 'til we know for sure before we kill him.' 'What if he's worthless?' 'We should kill him anyway.'* – blah, blah, blah.

The conversations had been going on for so long that Jamie tuned out, no longer caring to listen. He wished they'd just get on with it already. Just kill him, help him end his misery and give him what he deserved. Jamie looked down at his legs, which were crossed in front of him. He clenched his jaw and squeezed his hands into tight fists. The ring he wore on his right hand dug into his skin so hard he was sure it would cut through his flesh. He let out a breath and brought his shaking hand up to his face, looking at the ring that Sam had given him. He hadn't taken it off his finger since the day she'd gifted it to him.

Slowly, he pulled the ring from his finger, no longer feeling he deserved to wear it. He held it between his thumb and forefinger, watching as the different shades of blue danced around each other inside the gemstone.

Jamie dropped the ring as he was struck by a sudden thought.

*Magic.*

Sam's Magic was capable of doing anything; she had hundreds of spell books. Surely there must be some kind of resurrection spell in one of them that would be capable of reviving Sam. He just needed to find the right spell and the right person to cast it.

Jamie looked up as he heard footsteps approaching.

The Hunters.

He snatched his ring up off the ground and ran through the woods in the opposite direction to where the Hunters were. He heard shouts in the distance as they noticed he was no longer where they'd told him to stay.

Right now, he had no time to deal with them. Right now he had to find something to help Sam. And he knew just who could help him do it

# CHAPTER 4

The street was dark.

Jamie stared at the streetlamp outside Sam's house in silent contemplation. It was odd, that the light was off. From what he *could* recall, earlier that night the light had been working perfectly well.

If it were just the one darkened light, it could have been something he would scarcely have noticed; what was worrying was that not one, but all of the streetlamps on the road that stretched before Sam's house were in complete darkness. Not a single beam of light fell from any of them.

It was as if something had come along and syphoned all of the light.

Usually Jamie was indifferent to the dark; he had never been bothered by it. But right then, a cold chill made its way down his spine as he felt a bubble of fear pop within him.

The dark here was not right.

And the more that Jamie watched it, the more he felt it.

He took a breath to calm himself and tried to focus on what he was here for.

Closing his eyes to block out the world, he stretched his senses outwards, focusing his energy on the house next door to Sam's.

Within the house he felt the presence of two humans.

Both female and both sleeping.

Jamie zeroed in on one female in particular, trying to gauge which part of the house he could find her in. He opened his eyes and jogged across the street, then walked around to the back of the house, his feet leaving behind footprints in the soggy grass.

He stood by the back door, reached up, grabbed hold of the wooden frame above it and pulled himself upwards. Pushing his feet against the door, leaving muddy imprints on the white paint as he climbed up to the top bedroom window.

Jamie tried to look inside, but the curtains were blocking his view. As far as his senses could tell, this was Jade's room. He leaned one hand on the window ledge, keeping his arm straight to hold himself up while he used his other hand to tap lightly on the glass. Hoping it was loud enough to wake her, but soft enough that her mother wouldn't hear.

There were no sounds of movement from inside the house. He sighed, *if I knock any louder I might wake her mother.* Jamie closed his eyes again and stretched his senses outwards, searching for Jade's mind. It was trickier than usual to find a connection because his attention was split between Jade and trying not to fall. But because she was asleep and dreaming her mental guards were down, leaving her open to hear his call.

<*Jade!*> Jamie yelled as loud as he could inside the mortal's head. <*WAKE UP!*>

Jamie heard a groan and what sounded like a mattress

creaking.

"Who's there?" Jade whispered in a groggy voice.

*<It's Jamie>* he stated, feeling a welcomed relief at the sound of her voice. *<I need your help>*

"Jamie?" She seemed confused. "What the hell are you doing inside my head at four thirty in the morning?"

*<I'd come back at five thirty but it's an emergency>* he replied, his tone sounding more sarcastic than he'd intended.

He heard Jade stand up and take a few steps around her room. "Where are you hiding?" she asked, sounding annoyed and very tired. Jamie didn't blame her, he too would be irritated if someone had woken him during a peaceful sleep and had invaded his mind to do so.

He lightly tapped on the window again.

The curtains shot open so fast it almost startled him into letting go of the window ledge. Jade stood on the other side of the window, glaring at him as if he'd committed a serious crime by daring to wake her. She threw the window open and looked down at him, then with her thumb she pointed over her shoulder to the room behind her, indicating for him to get inside.

Jamie shook his head. "Forgive me," he said, apologising in advance before he grabbed a hold of Jade and jumped from his perch, keeping one hand over her mouth to stifle her scream.

She slapped at his hands as they landed in her backyard. Jamie placed her down so that she could stand. She hit him in the arm and kicked him in the shin. "Not! Funny!" she shouted.

"Shhhh!" Jamie shushed her, doing a quick scan of the neighbourhood to make sure no one was watching. From what he could tell, her shouts hadn't disturbed any of the neighbours. "Do you *want* your mother to wake up?"

Jade folded her arms and glared at him, her green eyes saying 'if I could shoot lasers with these things I'd use this look to kill you'.

"I'm *sorry*," Jamie said. "I just really need help and I don't know anyone else."

Jade sighed and unfolded her arms, letting them drop to her sides. "What's wrong?"

"It's Sam."

Jade looked at Jamie, her eyes filled with worry. "What happened?"

Jamie let his gaze fall to the ground, eyes staring at the damp grass, which had taken on a slightly bluish hue in the moonlight. He chewed on his lip as he thought. *I can't tell her what happened. She might not help me.* Slowly, he allowed his eyes to meet hers, he took a breath. " . . . *something* attacked her," he said, while nervously pulling at the end of his sleeve.

Jade seemed confused. "*What?*" she asked. "What attacked her? When did this happen?"

Jamie sighed. "I don't know. I—"

"Did you see it?" Jade interrupted. "What did it look like? Did it look human shaped or animal shaped? Was last night a full moon? Did you see any strange lights?"

"I don't *know*," Jamie replied, feeling helpless. "I didn't see it. I was outside, and then . . . "

"Then what?" Jade prompted after a moment of silence.

"She was . . . *dead.*" Jamie's voice cracked as he spoke those words out loud for the first time. He had to try with all of his strength not to cry. "She was so weak and sick when I saw her," he continued. "I doubt she would have been able to defend herself."

"Dead?" Jade's voice was barely a whisper as she spoke. She turned her back to Jamie, looking over the fence at Sam's house. "I can't . . . " She shook her head. "What makes you think I can help?"

"Because you *knew* something," Jamie said. "On Halloween, when she was faint, you were asking her questions about spells, it sounded like you knew something, so I thought maybe you could say some sort of spell — do some sort of Magic to fix her."

Jade laughed humourlessly and shook her head. "I don't know any Magic," she said, looking over her shoulder at Jamie. "I'm one hundred percent human. I can't do anything."

Jamie grabbed Jade by the shoulders and turned her around to face him. "You *have* to do something," he said, feeling desperation swell inside him. "Or at least you have to know someone who can!"

Jade chewed her lip as she thought. "Jack would know what to do," she said quietly. She turned to look over at Sam's house again. "I need to see," she said as she took a shaky breath. "I need to see her."

"I don't think you should —"

"If you saw her I want to see her too!" Jade yelled. The volume of her voice caused some dogs to start barking from somewhere Jamie couldn't see. Jade stormed off. Her bare feet leaving imprints on the grass. Jamie followed close behind her. *When she sees the marks on her neck she'll know it was me.* Jamie sighed. *One hundred percent human,* he thought, *she should be easy to control if I need to.*

Jade climbed over the fence between her garden and Sam's, and walked up to the door. Jamie paused when he saw her push it open.

Last he remembered, he'd run out so quickly that he'd left the door open behind him.

Slowly, he stepped forward, following Jade inside the house.

Inside the lights were still on, which only helped to

illuminate the crime scene within the hallway. He expected to see a look of horror on Jade's face, expected her to turn and give him an accusing glare.

But instead, when he stepped inside, he saw a look of confusion sweep across her features. "Where was she?" Jade asked as she stared down at a pool of blood that stained the hard wood floor.

"Right there," Jamie said, pointing down to the bloodstain. He knelt beside it and stared at the empty space in bewilderment. "She was right *here*." He looked at Jade, his face now mimicking her expression of confusion.

"Are you sure she was dead?"

Jamie nodded. "She had no pulse . . . she wasn't *breathing*."

Jade pointed to the floor to Jamie's right. "Are you *sure*?"

Jamie's eyes followed Jade's outstretched arm to where she was pointing.

More blood smudges.

These ones in the shape of footprints, which led down the hall towards the kitchen. "She was dead . . . " His voice wavered in uncertainty as he spoke.

Jade furrowed her brow as she thought. "You didn't try to, um . . . *feed* her when you found her, did you?"

Jamie looked at Jade in confusion. "What?"

"Well, when you found her she was dead. Um . . . did you try to bring her back?" Jamie continued to look at Jade with an expression of utter confusion. She sighed in irritation. "Blood!" she yelled. "Did you feed her your blood!"

"Oh!"

" . . . idiot," she mumbled.

"I . . . um . . . " He paused for a moment to think. Although his memories of killing Sam may have been foggy the recollection of what had happened after was etched into his brain. But he wasn't entirely sure if Jade really *needed* to know.

With a sigh, he shrugged and shook his head. "I don't remember."

"What do you mean, you don't remember? How long ago did you find her?"

"Not long," Jamie said. "But . . . I don't really remember much, I was in shock I suppose. So I could have . . . but I don't remember."

"Okay. Well from what I can see, there's blood on the floor, and only one set of footprints, too small to belong to anyone strong enough to carry Sam's dead weight, and no drag marks, so it looks like she got up and walked out of here herself . . . possibly as a Vampire . . . or a zombie . . . though personally I'd rather she was a Vampire 'cause zombies are kind of disgusting."

"Jade!" Jamie snapped her out of her ramblings.

"Right, sorry, okay. Right now, we need to find Sam. She could be wandering around outside, being dead, and possibly hungry for blood . . . or brains. Either way, *you* have to track her down."

"You're not going to help?"

Jade looked at Jamie as if the answer to that question was obvious. She gestured down her body then back up again. "Hell-*oh*? Do I look like I'm dressed for a midnight search party? . . . No. I look like a girl who should be in bed, asleep. So I'll stay here and find a way to get in touch with Jack. You find Sam and bring her back here, and we'll figure out what to do from there. Okay?"

Jamie nodded his head in agreement. *She may be only human,* he thought, *but she works well under pressure.*

# CHAPTER 5

*J*amie followed Sam's bloody footprints down the hallway, towards the kitchen and out the back door, where they disappeared on the grass. He sighed, closed his eyes, inhaled deeply and blocked out everything except for the scent he was trying to focus on.

Sam's scent.

Or more specifically the scent of her blood.

His senses were flooded with the overwhelming aroma.

As a Vampire, Jamie found the scent of blood to be intoxicating; usually it brought about an uncontrollable urge to devour whatever human the scent was coming from. Though with Sam it was different, it was like her blood didn't register as blood in his mind.

The scent of Sam's blood was simply the scent of Sam. So when he inhaled the fragrance that her blood produced, he saw a clear picture of her in his mind. Wandering through the woods, wearing the same clothes she had been wearing the last time he saw her, only this time he saw it stained with her blood. She seemed to be in a dazed state, wandering blindly between the trees, her feet barely touching the ground.

With his eyes kept shut, Jamie followed in the footsteps he pictured Sam taking. Feeling as though he were connected to her by something unseen.

After countless moments of wandering, Jamie lost the image. He opened his eyes and looked around, trying to gauge his location. He recognised the path he was on. It was the same one he and Sam had walked down before, in a time that felt like decades ago despite that fact that only a week had passed. She was on her way to the cliffs she had taken Jamie to see.

Without a second of hesitation, Jamie started to run, forcing his legs to carry him as quickly as was possible to where he knew he would find Sam.

Stones flicked over the side of the cliff as he skidded to a stop just inches from the edge. With a breathless feeling piercing through his chest, he turned, his eyes darting frantically from left to right as he scanned the area for any sign of her.

He felt his heart drop as he realised that she was nowhere to be seen. It didn't make sense; Jamie was *sure* that this was where she was heading. So with a resigned sigh he dropped to his knees and sat in the overgrown grass, waiting for her to arrive.

# CHAPTER 6

$\mathcal{J}$amie's head shot up as he heard a rustling in the trees in front of him. Warily, he watched the space where he was sure the noise had come from for a few moments. But there were no more sounds or signs of movement. He took a cautious step forward, squinting his eyes to try see what lay beyond the trees.

"Sam?" he called out softly, taking another step. He wasn't sure what kind of mental state she would be in after what happened and he didn't want to risk scaring her off by being too loud. He held his hands up, palms facing outwards to show that he meant no harm. "It's me . . . " he said, as he took a third step. "Jamie . . . are you okay?"

Jamie's entire body froze as Lucy stepped out of the trees, a revolver pointed directly at his heart. "Stay right there," she ordered. She pulled a flare gun from her belt, stretching her arm above her head she aimed it high and shot it into the air, signalling her position the other Hunters.

Jamie slowly took one step forward. Trying very hard not to get shot. "Stop. Right. There," Lucy hissed, looking him directly in the eyes.

He looked at her for a moment, assessing her. She seemed nervous, on edge. Her hands shaking slightly. She wasn't a Hunter, he remembered, she was simply the bait. From the looks of her, she had probably never killed before. Jamie smiled to himself, then looked her in the eyes. "You don't want to kill me," he said.

Lucy simply glared at him. "Try me," she snarled through gritted teeth, putting on an attitude fiercer than she actually had.

Jamie stared her down. She didn't lower her weapon. He didn't want to have to do this, but he didn't feel as though there was any other option. With a sigh he took a step towards her. She quickly moved back. "Listen to me," he ordered, not breaking eye contact. "You are going to drop your weapon, contact your Hunter friends and send them somewhere else. And then you're going to leave, and forget that you ever met me."

Jamie assessed Lucy, who kept her weapon pointed at him; he looked at her in confusion. She smirked, and with the hand that wasn't holding the gun, she reached under her top and revealed a necklace with a black stone dangling from a silver chain. "Black obsidian," she stated. "Keeps you safe from psychic attacks, your Vampire mind tricks won't work on me."

Jamie sighed irritably. *What now?* he wondered. Sam was out there somewhere, wandering around in who knew what kind of mental state, and if these Hunters got their hands on her . . .

*I can't let them hurt her.*

Jamie gazed at Lucy and chewed his lip while he thought.

But before he had a chance to come up with a plan, three men appeared, all sporting fierce looking blades and crossbows and larger guns than Lucy wielded. Without giving him time to come up with a way to escape, they ran at him. Jamie closed his eyes and turned around, moving forward with the intention of jumping off the cliff. A fall into the ocean, he could survive. An attack from Vampire Hunters with weapons made specifically to kill him ... not so much survival.

Before Jamie made it to the edge, the Vampire Hunters screamed. He opened his eyes and peered over his shoulder just in time to see them flying backwards into the forest. He turned around fully when he saw Sam standing a few feet away with her back facing him, her body swaying slightly, as though she were in a dreamlike state. Jamie reached his hand out to touch her, but didn't. Worried she might lash out at him the way she had the Hunters.

Without turning to look at him, she moved towards the trees, where Jamie could hear the Hunters getting back to their feet. She moved through the low hanging branches, her movements light. She seemed to float as if she were an apparition, her feet barely touching the ground as she glided along. She stopped when she reached the Hunters, who gazed at her in confusion. "You're not a Vampire," Lucy said breathlessly, propping herself on her elbows.

Sam's hair floated in the breeze, the normally golden strands appearing white in the darkness, reflecting silver glints of moonlight as she shook her head.

The four Hunters looked at her, their eyes wide and their mouths open, almost as if they were in awe of her. "What *are* you?" one of the men asked.

"He's not allowed to die," she replied, pointing back at Jamie. Her voice sounded strange, lighter and almost melodic.

"We don't have time for this," Lucy said, as she scrambled to her feet. She scooped the gun up off the ground, pointed it at Jamie and fired. The bullet stopped before it hit him, floating in the air as if it were stuck in something unseen. It hovered for a countless number of seconds before it fell to the ground.

"I won't allow him to die," Sam said, moving closer to Lucy, who stumbled back as she approached. "Not *again*." Sam stopped in front of the woman, her face barely an inch away. She stood up straight, making herself taller than Lucy; the Hunter had to look up to keep eye contact. "You tell *her* that if she wants him dead she has to come through me."

"What are you talking about?" she asked in confusion. "*Who?*"

Sam watched Lucy, swaying slightly in her movements as if drunk. She raised her left arm up high, magically pulling the male Vampire Hunters to the air with her Powers. "You'll meet her when you return home alone."

With that, Sam flicked her wrist, snapping the male Hunters like dolls and letting their bodies fall to the ground. Lucy stifled a scream as she looked on in horror. "Who are you?"

"That's not any of your concern," Sam said. "You have one minute to run. If I can still sense you after, I *will* follow."

Lucy didn't argue or speak. She just looked at Jamie in shock, then at Sam, before she finally turned and ran as fast as she could. Jamie stepped forward, moving closer to Sam.

"Sam?" Jamie stepped forward carefully, not wanting to startle her. The way she was behaving made her seem almost psychologically fragile and he didn't want to cause her any upset. "Sam, it's me . . . I've come to take you home."

Sam turned around sharply and looked at him, her eyes wide and confused, as if she hadn't fully realised that he was there. Though she'd spoken about him as if he could hear and pointed to him as though she knew. Yet now, she gazed at him as if just seeing him for the first time.

She opened her mouth as though she were about to speak, but no sounds came out. Jamie watched her lips move as she mouthed something. Then her body swayed and she fell to the ground.

# CHAPTER 7

$\mathcal{J}$ade jumped, knocking several things off Sam's bookshelves, as she heard a loud bang from downstairs. She sped down the staircase from the attic, through the hallway and jumped down the first few steps onto the landing. Jamie was standing at the end of the staircase; the door behind him was ajar after he had apparently kicked it open. Sam was in his arms, her body was limp and her arms dangled lifelessly at her sides as he carried her inside.

Jade took a step towards Jamie, who was now walking up the stairs. "Is she alive?"

"Can you get her door?" Jamie asked without answering Jade. She ran ahead of him and opened the door to Sam's bedroom. Jamie followed close behind her; she pulled back the duvet so he could lie her on the bed. He spent a few seconds carefully fixing her head on the pillow and brushing her hair over her shoulder.

"Is she alive?" Jade repeated.

Jamie hesitated before answering. He stared at Sam, looking a bit weirded-out. "Yes . . . " He let the sentence trail off and opened his mouth as if he wanted to say something else but didn't have the words. He sighed and looked at Jade. "She's not *right*," he said, obviously settling on the simplest form of the words he had wanted to say.

Jade looked at him, eyebrow raised, then back towards Sam. Her skin was a little pale and she was covered in blood, her legs and feet were caked in dirt and her hair was tangled, but other than that she seemed to look like a normal Sam.

"How exactly is she not right?" Jade asked. She walked over to the corner of the room where there was a chair with a pile of clothes on it. She pulled the chair away from the wall, tipping it forward to get all of the clothes off it, and dragged it to the end of Sam's bed. She sat down, crossing her arms and legs.

Jamie sat on the end of the bed and watched his knees, seeming like he was concentrating really hard on what he was trying to say. "It's difficult to explain," he said with another glance towards Sam.

"Okay . . . " Jade thought for a moment. "Well, start from the start."

Jamie chewed his lip and looked at Jade, the expression on his face making him look like there was something he really wanted — yet didn't want — to say.

"Look, you woke me up in the middle of the night and asked me for my help, so if you know something I don't care how bad it is, you tell me right now. 'Cause I can't do anything to help if I don't know everything that's going on here."

There was no reply from Jamie. Instead he just turned his head and looked towards Sam. Jade followed his line of sight.

That was the first time she *really* noticed it.

When they had come into the room Jamie had been very careful to keep Sam's neck covered. Jade stood and marched around the bed, past Jamie who was now staring at her, his eyes wide with alarm. Yet he did nothing to stop her as she moved Sam's hair away from her neck to reveal two tears in her flesh, about the right size apart to be bite marks.

A cold fury flowed through Jade as her head snapped up to glare at Jamie, who was looking at her, his expression a mix of shame, guilt and confusion. "I swear I don't remember what happened," he said, his voice barely a whisper.

Jade let Sam's hair fall back into place, she sat back in her chair and squeezed her eyes shut tightly. It was way too early to be awake. "Tell. Me. Everything," Jade commanded. Jamie sighed. "*Now!*"

"I came over to see Sam earlier," he said hesitantly, "just before sunset. She looked like she was half dead. There were two men in uniforms and they had a wooden chest. They gave it to Sam and told her it was Danny's. They said he was dead and they had to bring it to her. After Sam got them to go, she came inside, I carried the chest. She said it wasn't Danny's and that we had to get rid of it, 'cause who knows what could be inside it. So she stayed inside and I buried it out in the back garden under the flowerbed. Then I heard a noise coming from the front and I went to see what it was. There was nothing there and then . . . "

Jade waited for a moment for Jamie to continue, which he didn't. "And then?"

He let a shaky breath. "Then I was kneeling by the front door and Sam was—she was lying on the floor. And I tried to shake her but she wouldn't wake up, and—I . . . " Jamie looked like he was close to tears and Jade felt a pang of sorrow for him. "I could taste her blood," he said reluctantly, whispering it like he was hoping no one would hear, "and I knew that she was dead."

"That doesn't make sense," Jade stated. Jamie looked at her in confusion.

He shook his head. "I wouldn't hurt her on purpose, but I know it was me."

Jade sighed. "No, you missed out a part." He tilted his head sideways, squinting his eyes in thought. "The part where you *actually* attacked her."

Jamie looked down at his lap, where he was clenching and unclenching his hands. "That's because I don't remember it."

"Okay, tell me more about before."

"Before what?"

"You said you heard a noise. You went outside and then what?"

"Then nothing," Jamie said. "There was nothing there, just an empty street filled with streetlamps and shadows. And then . . . I don't know. I don't remember seeing anything else, or hearing anything else . . . I don't even remember going inside." Jamie looked at Jade with fear in his eyes. "I don't remember what happened."

# CHAPTER 8

$\mathcal{D}$anny jumped with fright, almost firing a shot in the process. He sighed in irritation, lowered his weapon and looked around the area he was patrolling. Some civilians were walking along the streets and other members of his unit were doing their patrols. Danny marched off behind one of the buildings, where he was pretty sure no one would hear him, but he whispered anyway, just in case. "What are you doing here?" he asked, glaring at Jack, who had appeared out of nowhere and scared the shit out of him in the process.

"You need to come home," Jack said.

Danny squeezed his eyes shut tightly and yawned, the heat of the air and the stuffy uniform always made him tired after a few hours. "Why? What happened?"

"Sam died," Jack said simply.

Danny's eyes shot open and he stared at Jack. Half thinking that he was over exaggerating, or making it up so that Danny would come home. "What?"

"She died. Someone killed her, I got her to say the spell and she should be recovering. But—"

"If she's recovering then everything should be fine. I don't *need* to go home. And besides, I can't just leave whenever I want to."

Jack gave Danny a sideways glance, his expression saying 'yes you can'. "Everything's not fine. Someone tried to kill her. They have a list you know!"

"If she's not dead and she's said the spell, then they can't hurt her now can they? So yeah . . . everything *is* fine."

"*You're* on their list!" Jack yelled.

"If they think Sam is dead they have no reason to come after me," Danny replied harshly; the only reason he or anyone else on their 'list' was in danger was because they were associated with Sam. If the people thought she was gone, then they wouldn't waste their time on anyone else.

"That's not why you're on their list," Jack said, almost as if he had read Danny's thoughts. "Sam's the first one to die . . . After that they go for the others. Wanna guess who's second on their list?" he said with a meaningful look at Danny. Danny rolled his eyes. "They're on their way," Jack persisted. "Lucky for you I got here first. Now get your stuff, we're going. *Now.*"

"No. *You're* going. Now get out of here before I shoot you."

"You can't shoot me, I'm noncorporeal. You'll just shoot whoever's unlucky enough to be standing behind me."

Danny sighed and turned to walk away. Jack appeared in front of him. "Please listen to me," Jack said. Danny paused; Jack *did* look pretty concerned. "If someone tries to attack you there's nothing I can do to help. And unless your gun is filled with enchanted bullets it won't do much to help either. So please just listen to me, you have to get yourself home. You'll be safer there."

Danny let a breath. "Listen, I appreciate the concern, but I made a commitment to stay here, and I can't just leave, okay. Deserters go to prison you know. And besides, they kinda need all the help they can get here."

Danny walked around Jack. He could have walked through him, but he didn't for two reasons. One, walking through someone you were having a conversation with was weird, and two he had always worried if he did Jack's soul might get sucked into his body and permanently get trapped in there.

"I have a plan B," Jack said from behind Danny. "If I can't get you to come home on your own I will use that plan."

Danny rolled his eyes. "You're a Ghost Jack, you can't do anything."

Danny heard the gunshot before he felt it hit him. He fell to the ground, his legs suddenly limp, his ears ringing, his eyes blurred. People came running over to where they'd heard gunfire. One of them knelt down beside Danny, while the others spread out, trying to find who had shot him. Jack knelt on the ground beside the soldier, who was completely oblivious to Jack's presence.

The last thing Danny heard before he passed out was Jack saying the words, "I'm a Ghost Danny. I can possess inanimate objects."

# CHAPTER 9

*J*amie stood up and walked out of Sam's bedroom, closing the door quietly so he wouldn't wake Jade who had fallen asleep on the chair next to the bed. He made his way down the stairs, where he noticed the front door was still open. He stared out at the street which was illuminated by the rising sun. The streetlamps were still off, and the road was completely empty. There was no sound but the breeze flowing through the trees making the leaves rustle.

Last night that same street had looked completely different, and somewhat terrifying. At least from what he could remember of it. Jamie looked down at the floor gazing sombrely at the dried blood. He sighed and closed the door, then walked into the kitchen and searched through all of the cupboards and drawers until he found a cloth. He held it under the tap, and squeezed it to get rid of some of the water.

Liquid droplets ran down his arm and wet his sleeve.

Jamie sighed again as he knelt down, using the wet cloth to

wipe away the smudges of dried blood from the kitchen floor, following the trail out to the hallway and to the front door. He cleared the floor of all traces of blood, and any signs that anything bad had happened.

Once the floor was cleaned he threw the blood stained rag into the bin and stood in the kitchen, staring out the window with unseeing eyes.

Sam appeared to be alive. Though he had no idea how. Last night, she'd been dead.

She wasn't right.

He could tell.

The way she moved, the way she spoke, there was even something about the way she looked that just wasn't Sam.

Jamie chewed his lip and listened hard. In the house he could hear the sound of two people breathing. He ignored the one he knew to be Jade and focused on the one that was Sam. He zeroed in on her aura, assessing it as best he could.

Her heart was beating steadily and she was breathing normally. Jamie reached out further and tapped into her mind, surprised by how easy it was. In her unconscious state there were no barriers to keep him out.

Jamie pushed against Sam's subconscious, trying to find something that didn't belong. He wandered through the tunnels of her thoughts, expecting to have to do a lot of sifting. But in her mind there was nothing.

No words.

No pictures.

No thoughts of any kind.

There was just emptiness.

An endless gulf of black, with nothing taking up space whatsoever.

Jamie frowned.

He turned away from the window and rushed back

upstairs. Crashing through the door so loudly it caused Jade to jump out of the chair she had been sleeping in. He knelt down on the floor beside Sam and pressed his hand to her head.

"What's wrong?" Jade asked, leaning over Sam.

Jamie ignored her; instead he focused completely on Sam. He closed his eyes and searched again inside her mind, hoping that the proximity would help strengthen his Powers.

Once again he was allowed to pass through with no effort. And inside, there was still nothing. He took his hand away and looked at Jade who was watching him intently. Patiently waiting for him to reply. "She's not in there."

Jade looked at him in confusion, as if she had no idea what he meant, or what he was talking about. "What?"

"Sam's mind is empty."

"What do you mean?"

Jamie sighed, unsure as to how he could word this in a way that Jade would understand. Especially when he wasn't sure he fully understood it himself. "If I were to go inside your head I'd hear your voice, I'd see images of your life in your memories. And more importantly than that, it wouldn't be easy for me to see all of that. Everyone has walls inside their mind, little sections where they lock away all of the things they don't want anyone to find easily."

"Okay . . . " Jade looked at him in confusion, as if she wasn't sure why he was telling her this.

Jamie sighed, running his hand through his hair. He cast a worried glance down at Sam's sleeping form. "There's nothing inside her head, Jade. Nothing at all. No words, no pictures, no memories. And more importantly, there's no walls."

Jade looked at Sam. "What does that mean? Are you saying she's dead?"

Jamie shook his head. "She's breathing. I saw her move and heard her speak. She's not dead, but ... " Jamie placed his hand on Sam's head once more. "I don't think she's in there."

"But she's alive," Jade stated. "So if Sam's not inside that body, who is?"

Jamie looked at Jade, his eyebrows pulled together in an expression of confusion. He had known that something wasn't right about Sam, and he knew that her body was empty of any psychic presence, but not until now had he even considered the idea that the reason Sam had seemed so off was because there was something else within her body.

# CHAPTER 10

*J*amie sat on the chair beside Sam's bed. Jade had gone home to get dressed, leaving him alone to dwell.

He sighed, deflated, and dropped his head to his hands. He felt completely emotionally and physically drained. He hadn't slept in two days and hadn't eaten in about that long either.

Although he had completely drained Sam of blood his body still craved food. Sam's blood wasn't human, so it offered him no nutrition whatsoever. The stolen blood that flowed through his veins didn't lend him strength or make him full. Instead it made every part of his body ache. It felt as though his body was rejecting the blood.

Or perhaps it was the blood that rejected his body.

Either way it filled him with a barely controllable urge to slit his veins open and allow the blood to spill out.

But he didn't set it free.

He had brought this pain upon himself. It was the consequence of what he had done.

One of them at least.

He was sure there would be more when Sam finally woke up.

. . . *If* she ever woke up.

For now though, he sat by her side with his head in his hands, trying desperately to ignore the burning in his veins. The whole time projecting a psychic message of every profanity he could think of at Jack. Hoping he would hear it and answer.

Though with each passing moment it seemed less and less likely that Jack would appear.

Jack was the only one who knew enough about Sam to be able to help.

And neither Jamie nor Jade knew how to get in contact with him.

And the only person who did know how to contact Jack was lying on her bed in a seemingly perpetual state of unconsciousness.

# CHAPTER 11

$\mathcal{D}$anny was happy to feign sleep and not allow his body to heal as they dragged him onto a stretcher and carried him into one of the hospitals.

He was content to stay paralysed as they loaded his body onto a military aircraft and carried it for several hours across the world once he'd been sufficiently stabilised.

He was more than happy to keep himself injured and allow himself to heal the human way, until he heard a doctor tell his 'brother' that there was need of major surgery.

"And just how painful will this surgery be?" Jack asked the doctor.

The doctor seemed confused by Jack's level of interest in how much pain Danny would be in. "Well, he'll be under anaesthetic so he won't be conscious enough to feel anything."

"Mmhm . . . how much pain will he be in afterwards? And don't lie doctor, you can tell me all the tiny details of how horrific it will be."

"Okay . . . " The doctor sounded completely weirded-out. "Well, he'll be in a lot of pain, but he can heal."

"Will he ever walk again?"

"The bullet *is* lodged in his spine, but we won't know just how much damage it has caused until we open him up to see if it's been severed or not."

"What are the odds?"

"I'm sorry, I don't know."

"How long will the recovery time be?"

"For injuries like this one we usually have the patients do about a year of physical therapy, but again, that would all depend on how bad the damage is."

"It *is* pretty bad," Jack said. "I made sure to sever the spine. He's completely paralysed from the waist down . . . I'm not sure you can fix that . . . can you? I would have thought you'd need some kind of witchcraft to fix an injury like that. Tell me doctor, do you practice witchcraft or just medicine?"

Danny let an internal sigh. *God, he really can go on for days when he feels like it.*

He heard the doctor shift in discomfort and rustle through some papers. "Are you sure you're his brother?"

"Yes, he's my little brother, my baby bro, my . . . " Jack paused for a moment. " . . . Some other way of saying the same thing. You get the idea. I don't need to say it. Can't you see the family resemblance? We have the same hair colour for God's sake!"

"It says here he's American . . . you don't sound —"

"Listen, Bob, can I call you Bob?"

"My name is Peter —"

"Bob, don't tell me who I am and amn't related to, I think I'd know, okay? So can you do me a favour and stop asking stupid questions and just tell him he'll die unless he does what I say? Can you do that for me Bob? . . . Can you?"

Danny tried not to laugh at Jack's ridiculousness. He knew that Jack was only behaving like this to try and get a reaction out of him. Or to try get him to use Magic. Which Danny did not want to do. But the way this conversation seemed to be heading he was starting to get the feeling that soon he would have to give Jack what he wanted.

"Barbara! Call security!" The doctor yelled. His voice sounded further away, he was probably moving closer to the door, his only means of escape.

"Don't do that Barbara!" Jack yelled to the woman, who was probably one of the nurses or the doctor's assistant. "If you call security I'm not being your friend anymore!"

"Oh for fuck sake Jack," Danny yelled, opening his eyes just in time to see the doctor jump with fright. "I'll take the damn potion if it will shut you up!" He didn't want someone else getting involved in this madness, and after listening to Jack ramble on like this for the better part of the day, he was willing to do whatever it took to make him stop.

Jack smiled victoriously. "It *will* shut me up, but you'll have to erase *his* memory too." Jack placed an arm around the doctor's shoulder making the small man seem very uncomfortable.

"Barbara!" the doctor yelled, his eyes shifting towards the closed door.

"Shhhh . . . " Jack whispered, stroking the side of the man's face, making him look even more ill at ease. "Barbara doesn't need to know."

# CHAPTER 12

*J*amie opened his eyes slowly, blinking in an attempt to get them to focus. His head was groggy from the short nap he'd taken; after so long without sleep the time he'd spent resting had done nothing but add to his exhaustion. He stretched his senses outwards to see who had made the sound that woke him, all the while knowing in the back of his mind that it would be Jade.

He rubbed his eyes with the back of his hands and stretched his arms above his head, letting a long heavy sigh before allowing them to fall back into place.

He cast a glance at Sam; she was still unconscious, lying in the same position Jamie had left her in when he'd placed her on the bed almost eight hours ago. A sharp pain erupted in his stomach, a pain which he recognised as guilt.

It was his fault that she was hurt.

It was his fault that she wouldn't wake up.

It was his fault that she lay in bed, looking more dead now

than she had last night when her heart *wasn't* beating.

The sound of the door being opened snapped Jamie out of his reverie. Jade poked her head through the small opening and looked at Jamie, smiling. "You wouldn't happen to know where Sam keeps that mystical first aid kit of hers, would you?"

Jamie took a moment to try form a picture of the item she was talking about. He had been unconscious the only time Sam had ever used anything to heal him, and he wasn't sure what she had used to patch him back together, only that it stained his bandages blue. He shook his head in reply to her question. Jade sighed. He looked her over, wondering what was so wrong that she needed a magical fix rather than a mortal one. "Why do you need a 'mystical first aid kit' anyway? What's wrong with the regular kind?"

Jade looked down at her left hand and scrunched her nose up in disgust. She turned her hand to face Jamie so that he could see the gash across the palm of her hand. "This is what I get for trying to have fruit for lunch." Jamie gripped the arms of the chair he was sitting on so hard he was surprised they didn't snap. *Your strength is depleted,* a voice whispered in the back of his mind. *How long has it been since you last ate?*

Small amounts of blood flowed steadily through the tear in Jade's hand, staining it red as it wet her skin. Jamie's nostrils flared as he instinctually inhaled deeply, familiarising himself with the scent.

Jade continued talking to him obliviously, though he could barely retain focus for long enough to make out what she was saying.

Before Jamie could take the time to gain control of himself and calm down, he was on his feet and barely an inch away from Jade with her hand cupped in his. He could already smell the fear leaking through her pores as he stared transfixed at the blood on her hand. Quickly, he brought it to his lips to taste, and just as quickly Jade brought her knee upwards, hitting Jamie, at full force, between his legs.

The pain was enough to jolt him back to reality; he doubled over, the sudden agony leaving him with a feeling of breathlessness. Jade stepped away from him, holding her hand protectively. "What the hell is your problem!" she yelled. "You can't just go around attacking people whenever you feel like it!"

"I'm sorry," Jamie said quietly, trying to hold his breath and keep his eyes cast downwards. "Get me a scissors," he ordered. "Or a knife, just something sharp."

"I'm not giving you a weapon!"

"Jade, *please*."

She sighed in defeat and stepped further into Sam's room, she walked over to the desk on the far side and grabbed the scissors. Then she put it on the floor and used her foot to slide it over to Jamie. He quickly grabbed the scissors off the floor and opened them, using the sharp blade to slice his left hand open. Keeping all of his thoughts on his own blood and keeping the wound on his hand from healing, he stood and walked over to Jade.

She backed away as he got closer, keeping her hand cradled protectively against her chest as she watched him with suspicion. As he got closer, she looked to the side, her body tense and poised to run.

Before she had a chance to escape Jamie filled the space between them and grabbed onto her hand. She clenched it into a fist, making blood drip down her wrist. Jamie exhaled sharply at the sight of it, but quickly turned his thoughts back to his own wound.

Forcing Jade's palm open he rubbed his hand across hers, allowing his blood to mingle. He took a step back to show

Jade that he was making a really good effort to *not* kill her. She relaxed a little, then looked at her hand just in time to see her skin stitch itself back together.

"Do yourself a favour," Jamie said, not taking his eyes off her. Jade looked at him cautiously. "Next time you've got a cut it might be wise to *not* show the Vampire."

Jade was silent for a moment as she looked at her now healed hand, still holding onto it. "Would you have killed me?" she asked, her voice quiet and frightened.

Jamie hesitated for a moment before answering. Jade was Sam's friend, he didn't know her very well but he liked her, and he hoped that one day they could be friends too. Which was why he told her the truth. "Probably," he said with a sigh. Jade's expression darkened. "Not under usual circumstances, I don't just kill humans at my leisure, but I'm sleep deprived and food deprived, so this time . . . probably."

Jade glared at him, her expression unamused and hostile. She furrowed her brow and pursed her lips, then quickly threw her arm out, her fist hitting him on the side of the arm.

It hurt a little, meaning she had made an effort to put her strength into it, though it didn't hurt enough for him to be angered by the fact that she'd struck him. Instead he looked at her with confusion. "What was that for?" he asked, instinctually rubbing his arm despite the fact that there was no longer any trace of pain.

"You tried to eat me!" Jade yelled. Before Jamie had a chance to correct her, or say anything at all, Jade hit him again, just as hard. "When you look at me do you just see a giant chicken leg!"

Jamie cracked a smile as the image of Jade dressed as a steaming cooked chicken leg formed in his mind. "More like a giant blood bag," he replied, trying to hold back his laughter.

Jade punched him again, looking furious when he let his

laughter slip out. "You think this is funny?" She kicked her foot at his shin. Jamie dodged her, his reflexes kicking in even though he knew she wasn't strong enough to cause him any real pain. "Don't dodge me!" she yelled when Jamie took cover behind the chair. Using it as a barrier to protect his shins and the rest of his body from Jade's attacks. "C'mere and let me beat you!"

"Jade, I'm sorry," Jamie said when he managed to stop laughing.

"Yeah, you will be!"

"Jade!" Jamie spoke loudly, also projecting his voice into her mind. Knowing that it would make her pause, which it did. He sent waves of energy in her direction, encasing her in a warm, relaxing aura. Jade took a deep breath as she relaxed.

"I'm *not* your food," she told him, her tone calm but serious.

Jamie nodded in agreement. "You're not my food."

"Try it again and I'll kill you."

Jamie didn't say anything in reply. He knew that her strength was no match for his, if she tried to hurt him she wouldn't succeed, but that didn't mean he wanted her to try. He didn't want to be in a situation where he would have to hurt Jade or puppet-master her into being nice to him.

He didn't have many friends . . . or any friends really. And the ones he *did* have, he would prefer that they were his friends because they wanted to be, not because he'd made them think they liked him.

# CHAPTER 13

$\mathcal{D}$anny jerked slightly with fright as the curtain around his hospital bed flew open. "You could have knocked," he mumbled, giving Jack his most unimpressed expression as he finished tying his shoelaces.

Jack glanced at Danny in amusement. "When have I *ever* knocked?" he asked rhetorically.

"When you were human," Danny replied, thinking that Jack must have had manners at some stage of his life, and had just lost them over the years he'd spent as a Ghost.

Jack smiled and shook his head. "I grew up in a house with five brothers ... we McKenna men don't knock. We walk where we please and if people don't like it they can fuck off."

Danny sighed and rolled his eyes. "What did you do to the doctor?"

Jack pushed the curtain back all the way and pointed to the corner by the door where the doctor was sitting bound and gagged, staring up at Jack with an expression of fear.

"Jesus, Jack... couldn't you just subdue him or something?"

"I could . . . but that's not nearly as fun," Jack replied with a creepy smile.

"You're a psycho."

"Takes one to know one."

"Let him go," Danny ordered as he pushed himself off the bed, standing—unsteadily—on his legs for the first time in over a day.

"I will," Jack said. "Once *you* erase his memory."

Danny sighed as he looked from Jack to the doctor. "Why can't you do it?"

"Because," Jack said, "you need to get over it. You're not human and you should stop pretending to be. It's okay to have Powers, and it's more than okay to use them."

"No—"

"I'm not going to do it," Jack said stubbornly, folding his arms across his chest, speaking and looking at Danny as if he were a parent who was scolding his child. "And you *are* going to do it."

"N—"

"About three minutes to wipe his memory," Jack interrupted. "About five to make a portal. So I'll give you ten."

"What?" Danny asked, wishing he had never taken that potion.

"You have ten minutes to wipe his memory and make a portal to get you home."

Danny let a derisive snort. "You can't make me."

Jack smiled his slow, creepy, ghostly smile. "I'm going to go out there and call security. You have ten minutes to clean up and get out."

"But—"

Danny tried to protest, but Jack was already gone. Dematerialising before his eyes, and moving to somewhere else in the hospital.

Danny cursed and ran to the doctor, putting his hand to the man's head, starting the process of erasing his memory. The only sound in the room was the doctor's muffled scream.

# CHAPTER 14

*J*amie's eyes shot open as he heard the front door close downstairs. The room was dark now; the sky outside the windows was a murky black, polluted by the orange glow of the street lamps.

It was night time.

Jamie stayed where he was, sitting on the floor of Sam's room with his back against the door. He could hear two sets of lungs breathing slowly in and out, meaning everyone who would come in through the front door was already inside the room.

Slowly, Jamie pushed himself up, facing straight out into the room so that he could confirm with his own eyes that Jade and Sam were both sleeping. He walked over to Jade, taking care to step lightly so whoever was downstairs wouldn't hear. He placed a hand on Jade's shoulder and gently shook her. She grumbled incoherently, rubbed her eyes without opening them, then let her hand fall to her side and continued sleeping.

Jamie sighed, he couldn't shout because he'd be heard and he couldn't shake her too hard because then she'd shout and that would make a sound. So he did the only thing he could; he used his Power to influence her.

<*Don't make a sound until I say it's okay*> He paused for just long enough for the thought to seep into her subconscious, then he shook her.

Hard.

She woke with a start, her eyes wide as she looked at him with a 'how dare you wake me' expression. She didn't speak though, and Jamie knew that she had no idea as to why she wasn't speaking; she simply wouldn't feel like it until he told her it was okay to.

<*There's someone in the house, they're downstairs*> he spoke into her head, stretching out his senses just far enough to tell that the intruder was now in the kitchen. <*I need you to be awake in case they come up, while I'm down there*>

She nodded her understanding. <*Try to be quiet*> he said, as he reached into her subconscious and pulled out the command he had left there earlier.

Jamie stood, made his way to the window, and — trusting that Jade could handle herself for a few minutes — opened it and climbed outside. Once he had himself perched on the window ledge, his body facing outwards, he jumped, giving himself enough of a push that he wouldn't hit into the wall on the way down. He landed — crouched — on his feet, shifting his weight to the top half of his body so as not to make a sound. He stayed low, looking up just enough that he could see in the window.

The lights were on inside, and he could see the living room. He moved to the far edge of the window, getting himself at the right angle to see into the house through the living room door. That was when he saw a man, youngish looking with blonde hair, walk through the hallway and up the stairs.

Jamie jumped to his feet, climbing up the side of the house as fast as he could. He pulled himself in through Sam's window. Jade grabbed onto his hand and helped him inside. "Anyone?" she whispered.

Jamie nodded his head moving towards the doorway. "He's coming upstairs." Jamie didn't know anything about other supernatural creatures, so he didn't know how to sense if someone was human or something else. He didn't know if the man had Magic and was here to hurt Sam, or if he was just a human who was trying to burglarise the house. Before Jamie had enough time to decide whether he would go at the man with his full force or not, there was a knock on the door.

Jamie froze at the sound of the noise. Confused as to why anyone who had broken into a house would bother to knock before entering. The doorknob turned and the door opened slowly, allowing light to spill in from the hallway. Without wasting time by figuring out what the man wanted Jamie pulled the door open and grabbed the man by the front of his coat, about to slam him to the ground when—to Jamie's surprise—the man fought back.

He twisted out of Jamie's grasp, and pushed against his chest in one swift movement, hitting him with enough force that it threw him backwards. He hit Sam's wall with a loud bang. Jamie steadied himself and lunged at the man just as Jade flicked the lights on. He grabbed the man again, this time not holding back on his strength, and before the man had a chance to fight him off, Jamie had him on his back, with his knee placed firmly on his chest.

"Jamie stop!" Jade screamed, before Jamie had a chance to punch the man so hard it would knock him out.

"He broke in!" Jamie yelled defensively, looking at Jade

who was watching him.

"Excuse *you*," said the man, sounding very aggravated, "but I live here." He turned to look at Jade. "Can you please put a leash on your Vampire?"

Jade folded her arms across her chest. "He's not *my* Vampire. He's Sam's."

The man rolled his eyes and grumbled something that didn't sound too friendly. Whoever the man was, Jade seemed to know him so, reluctantly, Jamie let him up. "Crazy day," he said while straightening out his clothes. He stood up. "First I get shot by a Ghost, then rugby tackled by a Vampire."

"Shot by a Ghost?" Jamie asked curiously.

At the same time Jade yelled, "Jack shot you?"

"Yes," he replied. "And who the fuck are *you* anyway?"

Jamie opened his mouth to speak, but someone else did it for him. "He's Jamie." Jamie turned towards Sam's bed where Jack was now sitting. The mattress didn't sink under his weight, instead it looked as though he was hovering just a millimetre above it. "That's Danny." Jack pointed to the man.

"Oh." Jamie smiled when he recognised the name. "You're Sam's brother."

Danny replied with a grunt; folding his arms across his chest, he gave Jamie a look of annoyance. "And you are?"

"Uh . . . " Jamie paused, wondering what the correct answer to that question was.

"He's my replacement as Sam's BFF," Jade replied, Jamie glanced at her, and she gave him a knowing smile before she turned to Danny and continued, "Not even gone yet and I'm already replaced."

"Mmhm . . . " Danny glared at him as though he wasn't convinced. He turned his head towards Sam for a brief moment. "Why, through all this noise, has Sam not woken up?"

"I already told you," Jack said with a sigh. "She died, she spelled, she's healing."

"And *how* did she die?" Danny asked without taking his eyes off Jamie. Danny was watching him as if he *knew*, though Jamie wasn't sure how he would know. Jack hadn't been here when it happened, and Jade was the only one he'd told. So there was no way he could possibly know.

"Long story," Jack said, once again saving Jamie from answering. "If we're going to go through it we should do it downstairs. I want to make sure Sam doesn't overhear."

"She's unconscious," Jamie stated. "I checked, and there's nothing—"

"Downstairs." Jack didn't stand up, instead he just vanished.

Jamie let a breath to calm himself. It had been about three months since he'd found out about the existence of other supernatural creatures, but after two centuries of not knowing or believing that anything else existed, he still had a hard time seeing anything unnatural and being okay with it.

He turned and followed Jade out the door, Danny stood by the doorframe watching him, waiting for him to leave before going downstairs. After Jamie walked out of the room Danny followed, closing Sam's door behind him. Keeping her protectively sealed inside.

Jamie walked down the stairs slowly, wondering about Danny's sudden appearance. As far as Jamie knew, he was supposed to be overseas somewhere with the military. Sam had said nothing about expecting him home.

And then there were the letters.

Jamie cast a glance at the table in the hallway, where he knew for a fact was a drawer filled with unopened letters from Danny. Thinking about it made Jamie feel overwhelmed by curiosity, and he wondered what exactly had happened to cause such a great amount of animosity between the two of them. So much so that Sam refused to speak to him, or even acknowledge his letters.

Jack was standing in the living room and Jade was seated on the sofa. Jamie walked inside and took a seat next to her. Danny stayed standing in the doorway, leaning his body against the doorframe. Jamie didn't need to turn around to know that Danny was staring at him, the prickling sensation on the back of his neck told him that he was being watched.

"Okay," Jack said with a loud clap of his hands. "Now that everyone's here there are some things I need to say, so please hold your questions 'til I'm done.

"Firstly, Sam's okay and yes Jamie, I know she's empty —"

"What do you mean empty?" Danny interrupted.

Jack glared at him. "Don't interrupt!" Danny sighed. "Her soul has vacated her body so that the body can heal. She'll be fine once the regeneration has completed. It usually takes a bit over twenty four hours, so she should be awake soon. Which is why we're having this family meeting. I don't want any of you to tell her what happened. Nothing at all. Anything you know, keep it to yourselves, don't say anything in front of her. I want to see how much she remembers, and how her memory has been affected by the healing process."

"*Will* her memory be affected?" Jamie asked, secretly hoping that it would be. He didn't want Sam to remember what happened. He didn't want to see how she would look at him knowing what he'd done to her.

Jack shrugged. "Maybe . . . it's why I want to check. She might be . . . *different.* And I need to know how different, so I don't want her polluted by outside sources of information."

"You never told me how she died." Danny said.

Jack let a sigh. "There was an entity —"

"An entity?"

Jack nodded his head. "I don't know what it is, but Sam has been seeing it for months now. I never saw it, but she said it looked like a shadow, and it made her feel scared."

Jamie furrowed his brow. His mind vaguely recollecting the 'entity' that Jack was speaking about. "You've seen it?" Jamie looked up to find Jack watching him. "Because that looks like the expression of someone who knows what I'm talking about."

"Last night," Jamie said slowly, hesitating in his speech because he didn't want anyone to know what he'd done. "I don't really remember though, but there was a black puddle on the ground outside . . . I thought it was oil or something and then . . . "

"It jumped at you?" Jack asked. Jamie shrugged, keeping his head down as he tried not to focus too hard on the blurred memories. Jack sighed. "What's the last thing you *do* remember?"

"I was sitting by the front door, and Sam was—"

"I *knew* it!" Danny interrupted. Jamie didn't turn to face him, he stared at the hard wood floors, trying to gain control over his emotions before he broke down in tears. "Whenever anything non-human is around it's always to kill Sam. Mystery solved! Kill that guy and we're safe."

"Shut the fuck up Danny!" Jack yelled. "Jamie *did not* kill Sam. Something else did."

"Oh, something else did?" Danny mocked.

"Fucking right something else did. The entity that he saw just before he blacked out. Or do you really think that an evil genius murderer would just sit around and pretend to have amnesia after murdering someone who would kill them as soon as she healed?"

"I never said he was smart."

"Okay, do you both want to shut up?" Jade interjected. "He

told me everything he remembers and I believe him. Mostly because ... well look at him. He's confused and scared because he has *no idea* what happened. So either be helpful, or shut up."

Jamie gave Jade a grateful smile. He could see why Sam enjoyed her company. "I woke up covered in blood and Sam was dead and I'm pretty sure I killed her," Jamie said, not feeling any better after saying it out loud. "But I don't remember doing it," he added quickly, glancing around at the faces of the people that surrounded him.

"That's because you were possessed by an unidentified entity."

Danny snorted as if he disagreed. Jack responded with a glare.

"So we need to find out what this entity is, and then find out how to get rid of it?" Jade asked. Jack smiled and nodded.

"Yes, our top priority is now to identify the unidentified entity. And hope there's a way we can get rid of it easily." Jack turned to Jamie. "Do you remember it jumping into your body?"

Jamie took a moment to gaze in the direction of the TV. He pressed his lips together tightly, hoping it would look as though he were attempting to think about what had happened, when in fact he was really trying hard *not* to think about it. On some level he knew that remembering what had happened was important, but he couldn't bear allowing those memories to roam freely through his mind.

With a sigh, he shook his head.

"Do you remember it coming out of your body?"

Jamie thought again, that was a memory that already sat on the surface of his mind, and it was something that didn't bother him too much to think about. "I think I saw black smoke just after I woke up. But, I thought it was just my eyes going funny."

"Okay, that's something!" Jack declared, seeming happy as if Jamie had given him some vital piece of information. But he couldn't see how any of the details he'd given would be in any way useful.

"So, what do we do —" Danny's question was cut off by the sound of a scream. Everyone turned to look towards the stairs at the same time. Jamie was the first on his feet, and the first up the steps. Though he was pretty sure that Jack would get to Sam first.

# CHAPTER 15

Sam checked her watch for the seventh time in ten minutes. It was five minutes to midnight, which meant that she could finally start closing up the library.

She hated working the night shift. The only time anyone would come in after eight was during times when there were exams to study for and projects to finish. Other than that the library was quieter than a cemetery at this time of night.

And during the night, there was something *wrong* about it.

It was always colder, always darker . . . even in the emptiness Sam felt like there were a thousand eyes upon her. Watching her every move. The thought that she wasn't alone filled her veins with ice and sent shivers through her body.

With a breath to calm herself, she switched the computer off and quickly grabbed her bag from the floor, before she stood and made her way straight for the door. Being sure to slam it shut quickly once she'd turned the lights off.

Outside the rain was pouring down, typical for this time of

year. When she turned her face towards the sky she noticed the black clouds, and without spending too much time thinking about it she knew that a storm was coming. Sam pulled her coat around herself tightly, as though the material would shield her from whatever was coming. Storms like this were always a prelude to something awful, that one undeniable truth she had learned in her life.

She ran to her car, thinking that she would call Michelle and suggest they keep the library closed if the storm was still going by tomorrow morning.

At the car, she rummaged through her bag for her keys, but paused, when she felt something missing.

Her glasses.

With an irate sigh she realised that she must have left them on the desk.

For a moment she stared at the distorted reflection of the old gothic building in the car window, a feeling of dread gnawing at her insides. She closed her eyes and took a deep breath to calm herself. *I am a grown woman,* she thought, *not a child . . . I shouldn't be afraid of the dark.*

Sam squared her shoulders, before she turned and jogged across the parking lot to the library doors. The ends of her jeans being soaked in the rain. As she approached the door she pulled her keys from her bag and unlocked it, ignoring the apprehension she felt as she pushed it open and stepped inside.

The bells on the library's clock began to chime just as the door swung shut behind her, she winced at the sound of the tolling bells echoing in the emptiness.

She reached out a hand and flicked the light switch beside the door.

Nothing happened.

She let a sigh, and flicked the switch again and again,

feeling herself become more and more agitated as, once again, nothing happened.

Sam closed her eyes in annoyance, and reached into her pocket to pull out her phone, using the light from the screen to provide a small amount of visibility to lead her to the desk. She ran to it, feeling slightly breathless as she frantically began to search the tabletop for her glasses. Finding it difficult because of the dark.

After a moment, her hand hit into what felt like their leather case. She pointed her phone at it, allowing the screen to illuminate the spot, just to make sure. Relief flooded through her when she saw that it was in fact her glasses, and she shoved them into her bag, looking around at the darkness as she did.

She turned, about to make her way out of the library when she heard a noise coming from the back room.

The sound of a creak in the darkness caused her to jump with fright, and slowly she looked over her shoulder, her heart racing within her chest.

*It's nothing,* she told herself, *it's probably just a rat or something.*

Sam took another step towards the door when she heard the noise again.

All of Sam's instincts were shouting at her to run. To get into her car and to get home as quickly as she could. But there was also this little voice in the back of her head that urged her to go and see what was making that sound.

Against her better judgement, Sam carefully made her way behind the librarian's desk to the back room. She held her keys in her hand to unlock the door, but when she came to it she found that it was already open.

She was sure she had locked it earlier.

Slowly, she reached out and pushed the door open, walking

in to the narrow hallway where there were two other doors. Both of the doors were closed and back here she could hear no more noises.

Sam exhaled with relief, laughing at herself as she thought that she had probably imagined the whole thing.

She turned, about to head back outside where her car was waiting to take her home, but paused when she heard a click. The noise would usually have been a quiet one, but in the dead silence of the library the almost inaudible sound was amplified to a point that it echoed. The sound sent chills running down Sam's spine, because she knew it was the sound of a door being unlocked.

Sam turned slowly, shining her phone at both of the doors in an attempt to see if she could determine which one of them the noise had come from. Her heart clenched in her chest as the handle on the basement door turned and slowly, it began to open.

For a moment she simply stared at it, not sure what else to do.

Black mist seeped along the floor, crawling out of the open doorway. Fear taking over, Sam turned to run, no longer caring where the noise had come from. But the only door that she could escape through slammed shut as she turned to face it, keeping her trapped.

Sam reached for the handle, noticing for the first time the bandage wrapped around her hand, and spending barely a second wondering where it had come from.

She yanked at the door with her bandaged hand and twisted as hard as she could, though it was no use. The door was locked. Not even the energy projections she attempted to blast at the door would make it budge. She jerked around to see where the Shadow had gone, her heart pumping nothing but adrenaline.

It was still there, floating along the floor behind her, its form building in height as though it was preparing itself for the attack. Sam ran past it to the other door, knowing that it was just a bathroom and that there was no window to escape through, but thinking that maybe if she could lock herself inside for long enough she could call for help or think of a way to escape.

But that door was locked too and no matter how hard she tried she couldn't get it to open.

The Shadow jumped at Sam and she let a scream as she was encased in darkness. She felt a cold rush as the Shadow forced itself inside her body. Distantly she felt herself fall to the floor as her body started to twitch violently.

And within seconds, she felt nothing at all.

Once the body had been secured, she slowly got to her feet and walked into the basement with no hesitation and none of the fear she had felt just seconds before.

Down the wooden staircase, in the centre of the basement, was a circle of candles. The light from the dancing flames gave the room an ominous glow. Sam dropped her bag in the corner and slid her coat from her shoulders, allowing it to fall to the floor. Afterwards she removed both her sweater and the t-shirt she wore beneath it. Leaving her clothes lying in a pile by the bottom of the stairs, she made her way to the centre of the candles where an athamé lay waiting for her.

A thousand Shadows filled the walls, watching her as she bent and took the dagger in her hand using it to carve an X over her heart. Ensuring the wound wasn't deep enough to kill the body, but *was* deep enough to draw the required amount of blood.

Once she had finished, she dropped the athamé and walked to the far corner of the room. Pressing her fingers into the slit in her skin, feeling the warmth of the blood spilling onto her hands. She used it to draw runic symbols on the walls, not stopping until there wasn't an inch of the stone wall that wasn't covered with an ancient symbol.

Sam walked back to the centre of the circle and knelt on the ground, using the athamé to carve runes into the skin on her stomach as she chanted, "*Enim eb ydob siht tel. Swodahs htiw luos eht dna soahc htiw traeh eht llif. Ydob siht evah em tel. Ssyba eht otni luos siht tsac.*"

At the last word she thrust the blade through her heart, killing the body almost instantly. Blood dripped from Sam's heart onto the athamé, to her hands, to the floor. The Shadow looked around the room through Sam's eyes, wondering why it was in pain.

The body was numbed, so the Shadow couldn't scream. Then, before another moment could pass, Sam blacked out and fell to the floor, both her soul and the Shadow being cast out.

Six people walked out of the darkness, seeming to appear from nowhere. Two men and four women, all of them looked unsettling, though the Shadow knew that they were no danger to it; they had been claimed long ago.

All six of them stood around the circle of candles and joined hands, humming and chanting, opening the portal to the Chaos dimension so the little Shadow was free to return home safely.


A few miles away, Sam woke up, and screamed.

# CHAPTER 16

*J*amie burst through the door, pushing it so hard that it slammed into the wall behind and left a dent in the plaster. Sam was sitting up in her bed, her eyes tightly shut, her mouth open wide as she screamed a piercing scream.

Jack was kneeling on her bed, half bent over her, gripping her arms tightly as she struggled for freedom. "Sam!" he yelled, trying to get through to her.

Jamie walked over to her slowly, not sure what he should, or even could do to help.

Danny and Jade barged into the room behind him, but they both stood in the doorway. Watching Sam with worried eyes.

"Sam!" Jack yelled again. Shaking her hard as she kicked at him with her legs. Half wrapping them around him, getting him in the back, though he hardly seemed to notice or to care.

"How can I help?" Jamie asked, his voice coming out quiet compared to the volume of Sam's screams.

"She's going to wake up the neighbours!" Danny yelled.

"They'll probably call the police!"

"I'm trying to wake her up!" Jack shouted, his voice projecting angrily above the noise. He spoke to Danny without turning to face him, his attention focused one hundred percent on Sam.

"Sam!" he yelled once more.

Jamie stood there uselessly, watching Jack's futile attempts at calming Sam. He watched for countless moments, his mind going numb from the sounds of the screaming and the shouting, until finally, he managed to snap himself into action.

He closed his eyes, blocking out the surrounding noises and the other people in the room. He scarcely noticed Danny shove him aside as he moved to help Jack. Jamie focused on Sam. Casting out a psychic net, attempting to reach her in a way the others couldn't.

*<Sam?>* Jamie called to her inside her head. Gaining entrance to her mind was simpler than usual, but he found comfort in the fact that it wasn't as easy as it had been this morning. And inside her mind there were colours, glittering images that appeared as though they were just beginning to form.

*<What are you doing in here?>* He heard her voice inside his head and felt a surge of relief wash over him at her responsiveness.

*<Sam, you need to wake up>*

*<What do you mean?>* she asked, her voice sounding as though it were coming from directly behind him. *<I am awake>*

*<No Sam, you've been unconscious for over twenty four hours>*

*<Why are you being so weird?>* she asked with a laugh. "And why are you talking in my head instead of out loud?"

Jamie's eyes shot open. He sucked in a breath as he looked

around slowly, taking in his surroundings, instantly recognising the cliffs where he stood despite the fact that it looked different.

Trees that stretched on for what seemed like an eternity lined the space at his back. The grass at his feet was cut short, and was a healthy green, appearing as though it was regularly maintained, which Jamie knew for a fact it wasn't.

The sky was a colour unlike any Jamie had seen before, well . . . unlike any shade he'd ever seen the sky before. It was a bright, luminous blue, with billows of glittering purple and green dust swirling around like clouds.

Sam was sitting on the ground, her feet dangling over the edge of the cliff. But in front of her, instead of an endless ocean, was a city.

It looked like it was at least a thousand years old. Small buildings nestled around a large castle, the whole thing surrounded by what appeared to be a wall that was made of Magic.

A few metres to his right was a rope bridge that connected the cliff to the island kingdom.

"Sam," Jamie said, kneeling down so they were at eye level. "You have to wake up . . . this isn't real."

Sam looked at him and smiled. "*Really?*" she asked, thumping her hand down on the grass beside her. "It *feels* real." She plucked a fistful of grass from the earth beside her and held it out to Jamie. "Dare you to," she said with a devious smile. "Tell me if it tastes real."

"Sam *seriously*, you need to wake up. I don't know what's going on. I *need* you to wake up."

Sam sighed and frowned as she turned her face away from him. "This is what it used to look like, you know?"

"What?"

"This place," she said, directing around them. "Over a

thousand years ago . . . would have been around the year seven hundred . . . that's when the world forgot."

"What did they forget?"

Sam looked at him. Her eyes seemed sad, and somehow wiser than her years should allow. He'd never noticed that about her before. "They forgot that Magic is real."

"That's because it's a secret," Jamie explained. "Humans aren't supposed to know."

Sam shook her head, her hair floating in the cool breeze. "A long time ago everyone knew. Nothing was a secret." She turned to Jamie and smiled fondly, as if she were recollecting the world as she'd known it, which she couldn't be, because Sam hadn't been alive in the year seven hundred. "Humans, Witches, Warlocks, Vampires, Lycanthropes, Faeries, Valkyries . . . even Gods. Everyone knew about everything. People travelled between dimensions. This universe was connected. But then . . . then the war started. And everybody left, so now this world belongs to humans, because they don't remember that it's supposed to be shared."

"Sam—"

"This is before," she continued, indicating to their surroundings. "The war hasn't started yet."

"Then let's go before it does," Jamie pleaded with her, gazing at her with imploring eyes.

Sam looked at him as a slow smile spread across her face. "Asking me to run away with you? As if you haven't done *that* before."

Jamie opened his mouth to answer her, but before he could speak a word, the world around them crumbled and everything went dark.

# CHAPTER 17

"*J*amie!" He opened his eyes to find himself on the floor, with Jade standing over him. "What the fuck happened you idiot! What did you do?"

"I . . . " Jamie blinked his eyes to get them to focus. He pushed himself off the floor and into a sitting position. "I tried to go inside Sam's head to wake her up . . . how did I get on the floor?"

"Um . . . " Jade looked up towards Jack before answering.

Jamie followed her line of sight. Jack was sitting on the edge of Sam's bed with Danny, and behind them Sam sat with the duvet wrapped around her legs and her hand pressed to her cheek. "Yeah . . . Sorry about that," Jack said to Jamie. "That was my bad."

"Don't apologise to *him!*" Sam yelled, wearing an expression of indignation. "He's not the one you punched in the face!"

"You were having a fit!" Jack yelled in his defence, turning to face her. "*And* you refused to wake up."

"So how does that explain how I ended up on the floor?"

"You were in Sam's head," Jack explained. "You had a psychic link with Sam's subconscious, meaning you were in a trance. And when I woke Sam up, it broke the link, taking your psychic projection and throwing it back at you . . . I already said sorry and I'm not doing it again."

"Well," Jamie said with a sigh. "At least she's awake now."

Jack nodded his head.

"What do you remember?" Danny asked Sam, ignoring everyone else and wasting no time before beginning his interrogation.

Sam looked at him. Her expression suddenly going blank, as if she was trying with all of her efforts to mask any feelings she may be having. "Shifters," she said. "They brought me a box. Jamie buried the box out back. He rang the doorbell about an hour later. A Ban Sídh screamed. His eyes went all shadowy, then whatever was puppeteering him killed me. Then Jack woke me up and forced me against my will to say a spell, and then I went into regeneration mode, and then Jack punched me in the face . . . and now I'm here. The end."

"You sure he was possessed?" Danny asked, with a meaningful and very hostile glance at Jamie.

Sam rolled her eyes. "I'm sure."

"I think she'd know if she was murdered by her own boyfriend."

The room seemed to go quiet, and everyone stared at Jack. "What?" he said, his expression seemed confused. "Is there something on my face?"

"He's not my boyfriend," Sam said, at the same time Jamie said, "She's not my girlfriend."

Jack rolled his eyes and shook his head. "Seriously, are we still playing this game?"

Sam glared at Jack and shook her head.

"Why are you all for this?" Danny asked. "Last time a boy looked at Sam you tried to murder him."

"He was human," Jack said dismissively. "And let's be honest . . . how awesome would it be if Sam's babies were half Vampire? I've never seen a baby that was born Vampire, do you have any idea how *rare* that is? We could all be famous!"

"Vampires can't have babies," Jamie said at the same time Sam yelled, "No one is having Vampire babies!"

Jamie looked at Sam curiously; she sighed and turned away. Jack laughed a little. "Vampires can only have babies with other non-humans, and since Sam is about as powerful as non-humans can be, I figure she could carry a Vampire child. It would be awesome, and we would call it Jack."

Jamie laughed. "What if it was a girl?"

Jack rolled his eyes as if the answer to that was obvious. "Then we'd call her Jackie . . . obviously."

"There will be no Vampire babies!" Sam yelled. "So everybody shut up about it and for the love of all that is holy can someone *please* get me some food! I feel like I've been starved for weeks."

"Your body is still adjusting," Jack said, giving her an empathetic smile.

Jade crossed her legs and sat down on the carpeted floor beside Jamie. "I don't think there's anywhere to get a pizza at this time. It's about three am."

Sam's head dropped to her hand as she let a whimper. She sulked as she scratched at her duvet.

"Okay, I'll take the orders," Jack said with a resigned sigh. Sam smiled widely as he pointed to her and asked, "Pepperoni?" She nodded, then Jack turned his finger toward Jade. "Barbeque chicken, green peppers and red onions?"

Jade smiled. "Yup."

He turned to Danny. "Do you even eat pizza anymore."

Danny rolled his eyes. "Pineapple and ham."

"I know *you* don't eat pizza," Jack said, looking at Jamie thoughtfully. Jamie opened his mouth to speak, but Jack held up his hand to stop him. "I'll get you something else."

Before anyone could even blink, Jack was gone.

Jamie let a breath and looked down at the cream carpets. *I'll never get used to that.*

"I'll get some drinks," Jade said as she stood. "Danny." He looked at her curiously, Jade indicated towards the door with her head.

Danny looked from Jade, to Jamie, to Sam who was staring off into the distance, her mind elsewhere. "You know where the fridge is," he said stubbornly as he turned back to Jade.

Jade scowled at him and folded her hands across her chest. "Don't be an ass and come help me."

Danny sighed as he reluctantly got to his feet. Glaring at Jamie as he walked past him and out the door. Jamie turned to see Jade close it behind her.

"What do they need the door closed for?" Danny asked from outside.

"Shut up," Jade replied, her voice sounding over footsteps moving down the hall.

Jamie turned his attention back to Sam, she was staring at the wall across from her, her eyes seeming as though they were barely focused.

Jamie got to his feet, and hesitantly sat himself down on the edge of her bed. She turned to look at him curiously, his movements breaking her out of her reverie. "I'm sorry," he said quietly.

She gave him a small smile as she spoke. "For what?" she asked, though it sounded rhetorical. "Being dumb enough to get yourself possessed? It's not really something you could have controlled."

Jamie sighed. "I'm sorry about lots of things," he said. "I'm sorry about almost killing you, and I'm sorry about the other night, and I'm sorry I'm so useless." He shook his head, looking at Sam through his lashes, he laughed humourlessly. "I pretty much had a complete psychological breakdown when I thought I'd killed you."

"Do you remember doing it?"

He paused for a moment, images flashing through his mind; he forced himself not to think, then slowly shook his head.

"Then why would you assume it was you?"

"Because I could . . . I just knew."

She paused for a moment, thinking to herself. "Have you guys figured out what it was yet?"

"No, we have no idea. I'm the only one who's seen it, apart from you, and I can barely remember."

"Barely?" Sam eyed him suspiciously. "A minute ago you couldn't remember at all."

"You know what I mean."

Sam half-smiled, pushing the duvet off her legs. Her skin was still covered in dried dirt and blood. "I *will* go inside your head."

Jamie sighed. "I *don't* remember."

Sam moved herself so close their faces were less than an inch away from each other. She was so near that he could smell the scent of the blood and dirt on her skin, the smell of sweat on her clothes, and the scent of the fresh air that lingered on her hair. "If you couldn't remember anything you'd be in denial about what happened, not feeling so guilty. So *tell* me," she said, "what do you *really* remember?"

Jamie hesitated for a moment, his eyes staring right into hers. The familiarity of the sight of her, alive and awake, was the most comforting thing in the world. Which was why, despite his better instincts and the pain it caused him to go past the mental block he had built to protect himself, he decided to tell her the truth.

" . . . I remember *everything*."

# CHAPTER 18

*J*amie descended the staircase slowly, following the voices to the kitchen, where Jade and Danny were sitting at the table with Jack standing next to it holding three pizza boxes in his hands.

They all looked up as he entered the room. "Where's Sam?" Jack asked.

"He probably murdered her again," Danny mumbled.

Both Jade and Jack glared at him, though he didn't seem to care.

"Sam said she felt disgusting so she was going to have a shower, and to tell everyone that if anyone looks at her food the wrong way she'll eat them for dinner," Jamie informed them, relaying what Sam had told him.

Jack watched him assessingly for a moment, "No, that wasn't a convincing Sam at all."

Jamie shrugged. "I paraphrased slightly to remove a lot of the profanities and inappropriate sentences."

"Ooh, whole sentences of profanities? That sounds more like it," Jade said with a laugh.

Jack set the boxes down on the table. "Well I'm glad she's decided to shower *before* the food. I didn't want to say anything in case it upset her, but she looked like a train wreck, that had been bombed, then acid rained on, then —"

"We get it Jack," Jade said, cutting him off before he could go on much longer.

"Anyway," Jack said, dropping a bag that Jamie hadn't noticed before. "While she's in there we need to have a talk."

"About what?" Jamie asked, as he pulled the wooden chair beside Jade out from the table and sat down.

"Sam," Jack said, handing the bag to Jamie. Jamie looked at him curiously for a moment, before he hesitantly took the bag from Jack. He opened it and looked inside, relieved to find two flasks from his storage back home.

"You and Sam are *way* too comfortable breaking into my house," he said, taking out one of the flasks.

"You're welcome," Jack replied.

Jade eyed him curiously. "What —"

"Don't ask," Danny cut her off, shaking his head as he looked at her. "It's better if you just pretend it's coffee or something."

"Ah." Jade nodded her understanding.

"Anyway," Jack said. "Sam . . . There's something close to home that's trying to kill her, so I don't want her left alone, *ever*. So, Jade, you're on friend duty, permanent sleepover 'til I say so."

Jade shrugged. "My house sucks anyway."

"That's the attitude I was looking for," Jack said with a smile. "Danny, you're on research with me. Also, go around the town, reintegrate and keep your eyes and ears open for anything weird."

"I don't see wh—"

"Wrong attitude Danny, I can use guns, remember?"

Danny sighed and nodded his head. "*Fine.*"

"What do you need me to do?" Jamie asked.

Jack smiled. "Glad you asked. You're Sam's daytime chaperone."

"Okay, so I walk her to school, hang around, then walk her home?"

Jack shook his head. "No, you'll walk her to school, walk her to class, stay with her *in* class, and walk her home when school is over."

Jamie stared at him for a moment, unable to tell if he was being serious or if he was joking. "You want me to go to school?"

Jack nodded. "Yes. Me and Danny are too old to fit in, Jade graduated last year, so that leaves you. No one knows you—"

"I've had conversations with people there!" Jamie interrupted.

"Then we'll erase their memories of you," Jack said sternly.

"You'll be the foreign exchange student," Jade said. "I thought Vampires loved to do that stuff."

"You watch too much TV," Jack said.

Jamie stared at her in confusion. "Why would I want to go to school? I already went almost two centuries ago. I'm not sure there's anything new to learn."

"*You* went to *school*?" Jade asked incredulously. "I thought people back in your day didn't go to school."

"A lot didn't," he told her, taking a few sips from his flask. "I did."

"You posh bastard," Jack said, giving Jamie a half smile.

Jamie laughed a little.

"I don't get it," Jade said.

"Only the well-off went to school in *his* day," Jack

explained. "I bet you went to university too." He shook his head. "Posh bastard."

"Actually I never got to go to university. I was Turned just before, I did get accepted though."

"Wait," Jade said, turning her gaze towards Jamie. "So, if you're rich, then do you wanna buy me a Porsche? Black, convertible, preferably diamond encrusted."

"I'd love to," he said. "But my house was kind of burned down in eighteen-twenty, and all of my belongings were inside at the time."

"If you have no money, then how do you live? How do you buy clothes? How do you pay rent?"

"I never said I didn't have money. I just don't have enough to warrant buying you an expensive car."

She shook her head. "And I thought we were friends."

Jamie laughed. "If that's what friends do then why haven't you bought *me* a diamond encrusted car?"

She smiled. "Touché."

"Okay," Jack said with a smile. "So . . . school, go learn something useful."

Jamie sighed. "Fine . . . but I'm not happy about it."

Jack shrugged. "You don't have to be happy about it, you just have to do it."

Jamie jumped, looking over his shoulder towards the living room when he heard the sound of a door closing upstairs. Jack turned his head to look in the same direction. "We never had this conversation," he muttered hastily when Sam's bedroom door opened.

"What do you mean—"

Jamie's question was cut off by the sound of Jack shushing him. Jamie gazed at him curiously. He mouthed the words, *'Never happened.'*

"You know how I know you were talking about me?" Sam

said as she stepped into the kitchen, dressed in a pair of light blue shorts and a grey t-shirt. "It's the sudden silence . . . but what *really* gives it away is when Jack shushes people as loud as he possibly can because for some reason he thinks I'm deaf.

"So," Sam walked over to the table, pulled out the chair next to Jamie's and sat down, "what are we talking about?"

"It's a secret," Danny said. "And Jack says it never happened."

"I *will* shoot you again!" Jack yelled at Danny.

Sam looked at Danny curiously. "Jack shot you?"

Danny nodded his head. "That Ghost of yours is a real bastard."

Sam opened the pizza box and took out a slice. "Did it hurt?" she asked nonchalantly as she bit into it.

Danny laughed humourlessly. "Like hell."

"Good."

Jamie gaped at Sam, unsure as to how she could say something like that to her own brother.

He turned towards Danny who was leaning back in his chair, his arms behind his head. He smiled slowly as he watched Sam. "Wow, Sam . . . It's nice to see you too."

Sam didn't respond. She just sat in silence and continued to eat her pizza. Jamie opened his mouth to ask what exactly it was that happened between Sam and Danny to cause so much animosity. Though he stopped himself, when he caught sight of Jack in his peripheral vision.

Jamie turned to face him, and Jack shook his head. A silent indicator that whatever it was that had happened, it was something that they didn't speak about.

# CHAPTER 19

$\mathcal{S}$am was lost in her thoughts.

Dying was different than she'd imagined it would be, and becoming immortal hadn't been as simple either.

She always assumed that she'd die and that would be the end of it. She didn't believe in the afterlife. She knew too much about the way the universe worked to believe that there was a separate plain simply for the dead.

Of course, she did know about Limbo, but that was just because of what Jack had told her. Even so, Jack was the *only* Ghost there was. She'd never been to Limbo, so she didn't know what it looked like. She didn't know if there were other Ghosts there or not. And if there were, why was it that Jack was the only one to walk between dimensions?

When Sam had died, there had been nothing. No afterlife, no existence, there was just nothing. At least, that was what she remembered of her death.

And after she'd come back . . . it was like she was here, but at the same time she wasn't. It was like her consciousness was living in a pocket at the back of her mind, in a world of her own creation. It had been strange. While she was there, she felt something else, like a second consciousness living in her mind, fighting for control of the body, pushing Sam to the very back of her own subconscious, trying to completely take over.

Ever since Sam had woken up properly, she'd been probing. Projecting psychic energy, the way she would into someone else's mind, into her own. Searching for something that didn't belong. What worried her was the fact that she found nothing . . . even though she *knew* that there was something there.

# CHAPTER 20

$\mathcal{J}$amie watched Sam intently. "Does anyone else notice that she keeps doing that?" he asked. Sam didn't seem to hear him, and if she did she didn't speak or move.

"She's adjusting," Jack said, barely glancing in Sam's direction. "It might take a few days for her to be back to normal."

"I wonder what she's thinking," Jade said. "What was in her head when you went in?"

"Uh . . . " Jamie turned to look at her. "It was strange. It was like she made a little world in there, and when I went in she was sitting on the cliffs and there was this ancient city —"

"That would be the Witches' Kingdom," Jack intervened.

"So it actually *was* there?" Jamie asked, his voice sounding as surprised as he felt. He hadn't truly believed any of the things that Sam had told him about it. It wasn't that he didn't think Sam was a reliable source, if she had been conscious when she'd said it he would have had no problem believing every word she spoke. But they had been inside her subconscious, a place fuelled entirely by her imagination.

"*Is*... " Jack said. "It is there, but... not. Didn't Sam explain how dimensions work?"

"Sam did what?" Sam said, the sound of her name being called snapping her out of her trance.

"You never taught him about dimensions," Danny said. "You're a sloppy tutor."

"I brought him to Tír na nÓg... " she said to Jack, completely ignoring Danny. "That counts, right?"

"Did you explain how it worked?" Jack asked. "Them being there and us being here."

" ... no."

Jack laughed. "Then it doesn't count."

Sam sighed tiredly. "We live in a universe, and in this universe there are a bazillion dimensions. Tír na nÓg is one of them —"

"Vampire Kingdom," Jack interrupted. "Limbo, The Underworld, The Witches' Kingdom, even my home is in an alternate dimension."

"Why is everyone in separate dimensions?" Jamie asked.

"That could take a while to explain," Sam stated.

"Three Witches went insane for power and fucked up the universe because they wanted all of the power," Jade said simply.

Jack smiled. "Or Jade could summarise an entire millennia into one sentence... Tell us about the Romans?"

"Some guy went insane for power and killed a shit load of people to take their countries so that he could have all of the power."

"You should write books... " Jack said with a ridiculously serious expression. "History as told by Jade."

"Plot twist, the Romans and the Witches go to war with

each other . . . everybody dies in the end, nobody wins the power."

"Okay," Jamie muttered, thinking to himself for a moment. It made sense when he thought on it; if he were living in a world that had been taken over by a power hungry dictator he would probably want to move elsewhere too. "By the way," he said, turning to Sam. "I forgot to ask, what were you screaming about?"

"She wasn't conscious Jamie," Jack said.

Sam looked in his direction for a moment, then back to Jamie. "I had a bad dream," she said. "It was pretty freaky. I was in the library, and then I got jumped by a Shadow and it made me kill myself. And there were people around who were chanting at it."

"You went crazy over that?" Danny asked.

"You try having a vivid dream where you get a knife to the heart!"

"But you weren't conscious enough to have a dream," Jack said, wearing an expression of utter confusion.

Sam shrugged. "Obviously I was, since I had one."

Jamie had no idea if it was possible for Sam to have dreams in the psychological state she had been in. So he did what he always did when he wasn't sure, he scanned Jack's expression for indicators that what Sam was saying could have been possible.

When he found Sam she had been embedded so deeply in her own subconscious that she thought where she was, was real. He didn't think that being that far inside her own head she would have been capable of dreaming and having physical reactions while still unconscious.

And from the expression on Jack's face, it was clear that he wasn't the only one who thought that there was something more going on.

# CHAPTER 21

Waking up early in the morning was something that Jamie didn't think he would ever get used to.

When he first met Sam, he'd made an attempt to readjust his body clock to better suit hers. It was difficult at first, and over time it had become less difficult than it had been, though it still wasn't something that he did easily.

It would be the equivalent of a human attempting to sleep all day and stay awake all night, every night for the rest of their lives. Their bodies weren't built for nocturnal life, just as Jamie's wasn't built for the daylight hours.

Nevertheless, he forced himself to wake, the sound of a shrill beeping noise reverberating around his brain. With a sigh, he pushed himself out of his bed and got dressed. Picking up the bag he had arranged last night, he left his home, and went to meet Sam at her house.

It was about seven thirty when Jamie arrived, meaning he

was right on time. He walked up to the front door, about to ring the bell, when he heard shouting from inside and hesitated. His hand hovered just in front of the doorbell as he listened to the voices inside.

Barely a second after he *didn't* ring the bell, the front door flew open. Sam stood on the other side, glaring at Jamie, though he could tell that her anger wasn't aimed directly at him. The glare was simply a by-product of her current mood.

"Morning," he said with a smile.

She sighed and rolled her eyes. "Hi,"

"Where the fuck are you going with *him!*" Danny yelled, appearing in the hallway behind her.

"*Fuck! You!*" she screamed, turning around to face him. "You can't just come back here and tell me what I can and can't do!"

"Yes I can! I'm your legal guardian and I own this fucking house, you wanna live here you'll do what you're told!"

"I'm *eighteen!*" she yelled. "And if you don't want me here then I'll just move out!"

"And where the fuck are you going to go?"

"Maybe I'll go live with Jamie!"

"*Fuck off* are you going to live with *him,* he's not allowed in this house or anywhere near you!"

"You fuck off!" Sam turned abruptly and walked out the door, slamming it shut behind her. "Move," she ordered, grabbing onto Jamie's arm and pulling him away from the house.

Jamie turned his head, looking back over his shoulder when he heard the front door reopen. "Why do you always have to behave like such a *child!*"

Sam turned herself around to face him, walking backwards. "Why do you always have to behave like such an *asshole!*"

Danny bit his tongue and gave Sam the finger. Jamie looked

at her and saw that she was wearing an expression of suppressed rage, very similar to the one Danny wore, and she gave him the finger with both hands.

Before Danny had a chance to say anything else, or to make any more hand gestures at Sam, she turned on her heel and stormed off, grabbing onto Jamie's arm and dragging him along with her.

"You shouldn't talk to him like that, you know," Jamie said, once they were far enough away from the house for Sam's pace to slow.

She turned her head and glared in his direction, though from the expression on her face, he could tell that her heart wasn't in it. She seemed tired and distracted. Ever since she'd come back she'd been distant. Well, more distant than usual. "Why not?"

"Well, he's your brother."

"*So?*" Sam said, staring off into the distance. An action that had become somewhat of a regular habit for her. "No he's not," she said with a sigh. "Not really."

"But—"

"He's never been like a brother to me," Sam said, cutting him off. "He's hated me since the moment I intruded on *his* family. He blames me for everything bad that's ever happened ... He *hates* me and he never did a thing to make me think any different."

"I don't think he hates you," Jamie said in an attempt to comfort her. From his experiences with Danny, it seemed as though he behaved like a brother to her. He even glared at Jamie any time he got too close to Sam, treating her protectively, which was something that older brothers tended to do with their sisters.

"You don't know," Sam mumbled.

"Then tell me."

Sam sighed, and turned her gaze towards him as she shook her head. "I don't wanna talk about it."

Jamie sighed. "Okay . . . by the way, did Jack take care of people's memories?"

"Was he supposed to?" Sam asked.

Jamie groaned; he was already feeling apprehensive about his role in Jack's plan, he really didn't need the stress of not knowing whether or not Jack had done his part.

Sam laughed a little. "If he said he would, I'm sure he did."

"Are you *sure*?"

Sam shrugged. "Pretty sure."

"*Great*," Jamie said with an irritated sigh.

He watched her as she walked down the road, looking up at the grey clouds that floated across the sky as if she could see something more in them. "Sam." She turned to look at him, the sound of his voice snapping her out of her thoughts. "You know, if you really don't want to stay at home, you're welcome to stay with me. If you wanted to," he said. "I mean, I *do* only have one bedroom, but you're welcome to it, um . . . I could—" Jamie turned to face her when he heard her suppress a laugh. "What?"

"Are you really *that* uncomfortable with the thought of sharing a bed with me?"

"Well . . . I just, I mean . . . " He let a flustered breath and ran his hand through his hair. "After the other night I just thought that—"

"I don't want you anywhere near me?"

"You ran away from me," he said, trying very hard not to let the memory form as he spoke about it. "Crying. And I still have no idea what I did wrong."

Sam let a sigh, and turned her face away.

"Did you not *want* to?"

"If I didn't want to it wouldn't have happened."

"Okay, well, what then? I mean, you weren't a . . ."

"A what?" she asked with a smile that let him know she already knew what he was going to ask.

"A . . . virgin?"

She snorted. "No . . . do I look like a fourteen year old?" she asked rhetorically.

"No," he answered slowly. "Were you really fou —"

"Do you really wanna have that conversation?"

Jamie paused for a moment. "Maybe some other time."

Sam nodded along, though it appeared as though she was only half paying attention to him.

"Just tell me what I did," he pleaded, his voice sounding as desperate as he felt.

Sam let a sigh and chewed her lip. Glancing at him sideways. He could tell that she was reluctant to answer, which didn't make him feel any better about it. "I wanted sex," she said.

"Um . . . okay?"

"And you made it weird."

"Weird?" Jamie stopped walking. "How did I make it weird?"

Sam paused for a moment, and looked at him over her shoulder, indicating with her head for him to keep moving. He followed her as she continued down the road. "You said I love you, and that made it weird because I don't want you to love me." She spoke without making eye contact, keeping her tone level and as emotionless as he'd ever heard her speak. "I don't want you to have *any* feelings for me. Like I said, I wanted sex, and I didn't think that you felt *more*, and then when you said that I felt awful so I left."

"I see," said Jamie, trying to keep his voice as unemotional as hers. "Can you *honestly*, look me dead in the eyes, and tell me *honestly* that you feel *nothing* for me?"

Sam turned, standing right in front of him, blocking his path so he had to stop walking. She looked straight into his eyes, and keeping her expression neutral she said, "I feel *nothing*."

Jamie let a frustrated breath and clenched his jaw. "Say 'I don't love you'."

Sam shook her head. "Why?" she asked. "What exactly will that accomplish?"

"I want you to look me in the eyes and tell me that you feel nothing for *me*, not that you feel nothing. I want you to look me in the eyes and tell me that you don't love me, that you don't care about me at all."

"*Why?*"

"Why not?"

She let an exasperated sigh and stared at him, the irises of her indigo eyes crackling with sparks of purple. Showing a sign of the Magic that lived within her. "Even if I told you, would you believe me?"

Jamie let a half smile, despite the fact that he didn't *really* feel like smiling. "I'd only believe it if I didn't know it was a lie."

Sam scoffed. "And you *know* that, do you?"

"Yes," he said simply.

"And *how* exactly would you *know* that?"

"Because," he said with a smile. "We've been having this conversation for almost five minutes, and you still haven't told me that you don't love me."

"I still haven't told you I do either," she retorted, before she turned and started walking. "You're going to make us late."

Jamie followed her, walking less than a step behind. "Just because you haven't said it, doesn't mean you don't," he said, just loud enough for her to hear. She said nothing in reply. Instead, she kept walking forwards, staring into the distance, once again lost in a world of her own.

# CHAPTER 22

$\mathcal{S}$am looked to the desk where Jamie had made himself comfortable. He had his legs stretched out in front of him and was leaning back in his chair, playing a game on a Nintendo DS, not paying any attention to the teacher's ramblings or to the people around him. And none of them paid any attention to him. They acted as if he was sitting there taking notes, or paying full attention. Sam stretched her senses out slightly; she didn't need to push too far to catch the scent of Magic in the air. And she knew immediately that it was Magic that belonged to Jamie.

Vampire Magic didn't have the same aura as regular Magic. Because technically it wasn't regular Magic, it was more of a psychic wave of energy. Regular Magic always made the air feel either light or heavy, depending on the type that was used, however, Vampire Magic felt completely normal.

It didn't change how the air felt, except sometimes in the moment the Vampire released the thought that influenced the minds of other beings. Everyone had the potential to be affected by Vampire mind tricks. The only reason Sam held an immunity was because of the sheer amount of Power she possessed.

The only way anyone else would know that a Vampire was playing mind tricks was to either have a will strong enough to try resist it, or to have heightened senses that enabled them to sense when Power had been used.

Sam sent a burst of her Magic into the air, an invisible shield that would protect her from sight. A perception filter of sorts that would make it appear as though she were sitting in her seat taking notes. Which she assumed was the same image Jamie was projecting into everyone's heads.

"What are you doing?" she asked, not making any attempt to hide her irritation at his presence.

"Playing Zelda," he replied, not taking his eyes off the game while he spoke.

Sam rolled her eyes and sighed internally. "I meant what are you doing *here*?"

"Had to be me," he stated, chewing his lip while trying to talk to Sam and concentrate on his game at the same time. "Danny's been here before, Jack looks too old, Jade graduated last year and no one knows me, so I was the only one who could do it."

"Why do you *have* to be here at all!" Sam yelled, instinctively turning to see if anyone had heard her even though she knew they hadn't.

Jamie paused his game and set the console down on the desk. He turned to her, biting his lip, looking as though he was deciding whether or not to tell her something. After a moment of silence, he sighed, his shoulders dropped, and he ran his hand through his hair, a gesture Sam had come to understand as him making an effort to think of some words.

"Because . . . " he started, eyeing her intently. "You weren't *you* when you woke up."

"What are you talking about?" she asked, her expression showing her confusion. "Everyone was there when I woke up and I'm pretty sure I was me, if I wasn't I would remember it."

"Exactly," he said. "You *don't* remember it. You were awake the night you . . . " He chewed his lip again and hesitated before continuing. "*That* night you were awake. It was maybe two, three am, I was out in the woods, surrounded by Vampire Hunters, then you showed up, your clothes covered in blood. You killed three of them and sent one home with a message, and then you looked at me and you were . . . you looked *different*. You sounded different and . . . "

Sam was listening to what he was saying, coming to the conclusion that she must have woken up in a state of shock or something, then wandered off. "And what?" she prompted.

He gave her a look that was somewhere between confusion and trepidation. "You called me James." He spoke quickly, as if he needed to get the words out before his brain had too much time to process what he was saying.

Sam raised an eyebrow, not sure why calling him by the wrong name while she was half unconscious was such a big deal. Obviously she hadn't been thinking straight and got the words confused and blurted out whatever name she could think of at the time. Not that she could know for sure what her thought process had been considering the fact that she still had no recollection of this whatsoever.

"Um . . . *sorry?*" she said, wondering why he looked scared and confused by what she'd called him. Was he worried she had a secret boyfriend or something? Knowing Jamie, that was probably it. "You can't hold me responsible for calling you the wrong name when I was half unconscious and in a state of shock. *And* by the way, I don't remember any of this."

Jamie smiled a little, his fearful expression now holding a hint of amusement. "You weren't wrong."

"What?"

"For all legal intents and purposes my name *is* James. What's strange is that *you* didn't know that, yet somehow you did."

Sam shrugged. "Well, I must have heard you say it, or maybe I saw it written down somewhere," she rationalised, trying frantically to think of where she'd heard or seen it.

Jamie shook his head. "I haven't gone by James since before I was Turned. That was almost two centuries ago. The *only* place it is written down is my grave, which I highly doubt you've ever been to. I never told you, and I wouldn't have considering I haven't used it in so long. But that's not the part that worries me, the part that worries me is that the person who spoke used your body, but it wasn't *you*. I could tell Sam, until the moment you regained consciousness you were empty."

"What do you mean empty?" Sam asked louder than she'd meant to.

He sighed, running his hand through his hair again. "It's difficult to explain," he said. "When I got you home I went inside your head to make sure you were okay. When you go into someone's mind there's walls, and noises, and —"

"I know what it's like inside someone's head," Sam interrupted.

Jamie nodded. "If I tried to go into your mind right now, there'd be nothing but a steel wall, and behind that an electrified fence that surrounded another steel wall, you're full of barriers, you're closed off, even when you're sleeping —"

"And you know that *how*?" Sam interrupted again, eyeing

him suspiciously.

"My point *is*," he continued without answering, "not only did you not have any barriers, you had no sounds, or words, or pictures. There was nothing in there whatsoever. It was like . . . " He paused for a moment to think. "It was like you were a body with no soul inside."

"But, I'm fine *now*," Sam declared, despite the fact that she didn't feel completely sure of that fact. Ever since she'd woken up she'd felt different, though she wasn't entirely sure in what way, she just knew there was something off.

Jamie gave her a sceptical look, indicating that he also wasn't completely convinced that she was fine. "Are you *sure*?" he asked. "Where do you keep going?"

Sam tilted her head in confusion. "What do you mean? . . . I've been with you the whole time."

Jamie tapped on the side of his head. "Up here, where do you keep going? You've been zoning in and out non-stop since you woke up."

"I haven't been *completely* zoned out," Sam protested.

Jamie raised a sceptical eyebrow at her. "The other day, everyone had a conversation about you while you sat right there. Do you know what the conversation was about?"

Sam scoffed. "You're lying, that *so* didn't happen."

"We were talking about how you keep zoning out," Jamie said. "And what confuses me is how I seem to be the only one who thinks that it's *not* just a normal readjustment symptom."

"Who said it was?"

"Jack did."

Sam smiled confidently. "Well *then*, if Jack says it's normal, then it must be."

Jamie sighed in defeat, picked up his Nintendo and unpaused his game. "Whatever you say."

# CHAPTER 23

$\mathcal{S}$am hurried to her regular table, the one in the corner of the cafeteria at the very back. She walked towards it, trying her best to pay no attention to the people who stared at her as she moved past. Well . . . they weren't really staring at *her*, but rather at the 'new kid' trailing along behind. She didn't need to turn around to know that he wasn't paying any attention to them. He was doing the same thing he'd been doing all day. Playing a game on his Nintendo.

Sam sat in her regular seat and slammed her bag down on the table in front of her. Jamie took the seat across from her. "Someone's in a bad mood," he stated without taking his attention away from his game.

Sam didn't dignify him with a response, instead she opened her bag, removed her notebook and her lunch, and ignored Jamie as he'd been ignoring her for most of the day so far.

Jamie leaned forward and looked down at her notebook. After a few seconds, he sighed and sat back in his chair. "You should rewrite it," he said.

Sam glared at him. "*Why?*"

He pointed to one of the words on her notebook, without even looking at what he was doing. "Irregardless is not a word, it's a double negative and it cancels itself out."

"You're not a word," Sam mumbled.

"Actually it is," he said with a smile. "And it has two variations."

Sam gave him an unimpressed look. "I *will* kick you," she warned. "Stop being annoying, and stop correcting my homework."

Jamie smiled. "I'm being helpful."

"No . . . you're being irritating, there's a difference."

"How many non-humans at this school?" Jamie asked, changing the subject, his eyes sifting past all of the tables slowly, assessing every person he could see.

"Why?"

"I'm trying to teach myself to sense the difference."

"If you were to guess?"

Jamie looked around the cafeteria. His eyes settling on the table closest to the door where Madison sat with her group of friends. "Well . . . at the very least there's the two of us."

"What's so special about that table?" Sam asked, following Jamie's line of sight.

"It's disturbing over there," he said, his eyes squinted in concentration.

"How?"

He shrugged, and with a sigh turned back around to face Sam. "It's just *off* somehow. I'm not sure who it's coming from though, it could be anyone there."

"Madison is a member of the Coven," Sam said. "So is Elle. Madison is half-Warlock, Elle is human but she thinks Magic is cool so she practices . . . well, she tries anyway."

"So it's Madison then?" Jamie asked, glancing at her over his shoulder.

"I'm not so sure. I've known Madison since I got here, the creepiness is new." Sam leaned across the table, so that she was closer to Jamie and no one would hear. "See that guy talking to Kami—"

"Who's Kami?" Jamie asked.

"The girl with the brown hair . . . the Asian girl."

"I don't know why you didn't start with Asian," Jamie muttered, looking briefly in the direction Sam had directed. "There are three brunettes at the table and only one of the group is an Asian girl. It's completely illogical to begin the description with hair colour."

Sam glared at Jamie for long enough that he smiled and sighed. Getting back to the point he said, "Okay, so *that* guy."

"That's Elliot," she said. "I have *no* idea what he is . . . but I get this weird vibe off him. Like, scary . . . *creepy* weird."

"Did you?" Jamie pointed to his head, asking if she had checked inside.

Sam rolled her eyes. "Of course I did . . . I didn't dig too deep, what I saw made me want to gouge my brain out. It was filled with regular male perverted creepy."

"So he registers as human?"

Sam shrugged. "More or less, yeah. Apart from the disturbing vibes, he's human."

"Maybe it's something else then," Jamie said, watching Elliot over his shoulder.

"Like what?" Sam asked curiously.

"That thing that possessed me, it was . . . I don't know, it felt terrifying, but when it was in me did I register as anything other than Vampire?"

Sam took a moment to think about it. As far as she remembered, Jamie had seemed slightly off, but she hadn't known he wasn't him until the moment he attacked her. "No," she said. "You were just you . . . but a bit off."

"So, what if he's him but a bit off because there's an evil Shadow living inside him?"

"Jamie," Sam whispered. She let her eyes go quickly to the table. Elliot was now staring in their direction, a curious expression on his face.

Jamie's expression went suddenly serious. "He heard me say that?"

Sam broke her gaze away from the table where Elliot was now grinning wolfishly at her. She nodded her head. "Yeah."

"From all the way across a crowded room with over a hundred people?"

Sam nodded her head again.

"I'm a genius," Jamie stated, before he went back to playing his Nintendo. "You should do your homework," he said. *<Let him think we don't care>* he spoke inside her mind. *<We'll watch him, see if he does anything weird, hopefully he can lead us to whoever is doing the possessing>*

*<Jack will be thrilled>* Sam replied. *<We found a link to his mystery monster>*

Sam watched Elliot from across the room, half zoned out as she remembered the first time she'd seen him walk into class and known there was something wrong with him. Though she hadn't sensed it then, not in his head at least, and when she pushed now she still couldn't sense it.

Elliot looked at her and grinned, as though he knew what she was doing — what she was thinking — and didn't care in the slightest. If he knew what and who she was he wasn't scared. His expression said as much.

She reached out with her senses, deciding this time she would push past the disgustingness on the surface of his mind and dig deeper, knowing that if she did she'd find something in there.

She had just about made it through, when a crash from across the room broke her concentration.

At first Sam wasn't bothered looking for the source of the sound, assuming it had just been someone dropping a lunch tray . . . which it was. She'd found out as much when the yelling started. *That* was when she looked.

Down the end of the lunch line there were two guys, Sam didn't recognise them . . . but then, she didn't exactly make the time to get to know the faces of *everyone* in the school, just those she shared classes with.

One of the guys, presumably the one whose lunch had dropped, shoved the guy in front of him, causing his tray to fall to the floor too. Before they could exchange any words, the second guy threw his arm up and punched the first guy in the face.

Some of the students nearby gathered around, seeming giddy and encouraged them to fight. Sam sighed and rolled her eyes.

Boys were so stupid sometimes.

Jamie was watching them too, though he hadn't left his seat, and his expression looked confused rather than intrigued or excited. "Did you see that?" he asked without turning away from the fight.

"See what?" Sam asked, her attention already back on her notebook where she'd scribbled out most of the paragraph around the word irregardless.

"Something attacked those guys."

"Yeah," Sam said with a laugh. "They attacked each other."

"No." Jamie shook his head, his eyes now scanning the entire cafeteria crowd. "It looked like a Shadow."

Sam felt herself go cold as she looked towards the fight. Which seemed to be spreading like an infection to anyone gathered around it. It was no longer just two guys in a fist fight; there were now at least ten people involved. It was starting to look like less of a fight and more like a mosh pit gone wrong.

"What the fuck?" Sam mumbled, as she sat forward slightly, watching as the light in that corner of the cafeteria flickered before switching off entirely.

She turned to look in Elliot's direction; he was the only person still *not* watching the mob of thrashing bodies. Instead his eyes were fixed on Sam. He watched her with an expression of amusement, the way an adult would watch a child attempt to do something they were too little to figure out.

"We have to clear everyone out," Sam said suddenly, turning to Jamie. "We need to get everyone out before more people get involved."

"*How?*"

Sam chewed her lip and looked around the cafeteria, trying to think of a way she could get everyone out quickly.

There wasn't a fire alarm anywhere in sight, so she couldn't pull it to get people to leave.

"Can you start a fire?" Jamie asked, his head tilted upwards where there was a fire sprinkler.

"Not in public."

"No one's looking," Jamie said, casting a quick glance around. He was right, no one *was* looking, everyone was too busy gawking at the fight or jumping in the middle of it.

Sam took a breath, and without wasting another second — in which she could have been swayed by her better judgement — she conjured up a ball of purple fire in her hand, and threw it upwards.

The Magic exploded at the sprinkler and within seconds water splashed out. Some people screamed and ran for the door, where teachers were running in to break up the fight.

Jamie grabbed Sam's arm and pulled her with the crowd, taking her notebook in one of his hands, while she grabbed hold of her bag. They pushed their way through the crowd and out to the hall, she could hear Elliot snickering quietly as she walked past his table and she resisted the urge to look at him or to call him out right there and then.

Once they were in the hall, Jamie rushed forward, dragging Sam with him into the chem lab. As soon as they were inside, he slammed the door shut behind them. "What are we doing in here?" Sam asked, once he'd let go of her arm.

"They're not leaving," he said distractedly.

"I noticed. Apparently they're immune to water."

Jamie walked over to the teacher's desk and pulled it open, removing a key from the drawer.

"What are you doing?" Sam asked, frowning as Jamie took the key to the chemical storage cabinet and unlocked it, taking out bottles of liquid.

"Starting a fire," he said simply, as if that was something that she didn't need to be worried about.

"We could just pull the alarm."

"No," Jamie said. "This isn't a normal situation, those Shadow-creatures attacked those people, and I don't think that a loud noise will scare them . . . but a fire might. Do you want to turn on the Bunsen burners?"

"How many?"

"All of them."

"Do you even *know* what you're doing? Did they even have chemicals in ye olde ancient times?"

"Hey," Jamie cried. He stopped pouring chemicals into glass beakers for a moment to look at her. "I *almost* went to university you know. Mathematics and science . . . not that you asked. Do you know what that meant in the eighteen hundreds?"

"That your parents weren't that closely related so you could add two numbers without getting too confused?"

Jamie scowled. "Bunsen burners!" he ordered.

After Sam lit all of the flames, Jamie ran around the room placing beakers on each of them, starting at the back of the room and working his way back to the door. He moved quickly, as if he didn't have a lot of time to waste.

"What are you burning?" Sam asked curiously, as he grabbed her by the arm and pulled her out the door, slamming it shut behind him. The sounds of the fighting students could be heard from the hallway.

"Carbon disulphide," he said, dragging Sam down the hallway and around the nearest corner. Sam heard an explosion from behind, and turned just in time to see a whirl of flames and a plume of black smoke. The air was instantly pierced by the shrill ringing of the fire alarm.

"Did you just find the most flammable chemical you could and then burn it?" Sam asked in disbelief.

"No . . . I found the most *volatile* and burned it. That will spread fast." Jamie leaned forward and peered into one of the classrooms. Sam followed his line of sight. Through the classroom she could see a giant crowd of people pouring out of the cafeteria's emergency exit. "How much do you want to bet someone poked their head out the door, saw the fire, then screamed?"

"Wow . . . " Sam said, watching the self-satisfied grin on Jamie's face with some amusement. "I never realised what a psychopath you were."

Jamie shrugged, then started walking swiftly down the hall. "We should go, like I said, that will spread fast."

Sam looked behind her, where there was a growing black cloud of smoke. Without wasting more time she turned and followed Jamie to the front of the school.

"Wait," Sam said, as they walked past the principal's office.

"Sam . . . there's not really time for waiting."

"Elliot," Sam said pointing at the office. "They'd have his address in there."

Sam looked behind her. She could hear the crackle of flames from the other end of the building, but the smoke that trailed along the ground was light, it wasn't thick enough to warrant missing an opportunity like this one.

Jamie sighed. "I'll get it, you go outside."

Sam opened her mouth to protest, but Jamie put his hand up to silence her. "I need less air than you do."

Sam nodded her agreement and watched as Jamie disappeared into the principal's office. When the door shut behind him, she ran at the front door where she waited on the steps outside for Jamie, hoping that he knew fire was one of his weaknesses.

# CHAPTER 24

$\mathcal{K}$ami screamed when the sprinklers went off, as did all the other girls who sat at the table. Not that Elliot paid much attention to the other girls, and he really couldn't have cared less about what the guys were doing. But he found the fact that she screamed to be amusing and before he could control it, a smile spread across his face.

Elliot was so distracted by his amusement that he barely noticed the Witch walk past him with the herd of students who fled to escape the wet.

The people at his table all scrambled to collect their belongings before they too made their way towards the door.

With an irritated grumble, he grabbed hold of Kami, who had just started following the others. She froze when he placed his hand on her arm, and her head shot around to stare at him, her mouth open as though she was surprised. "The building's on fire!" she yelled, attempting to pull away from him . . . or perhaps she was trying to pull him with her.

He couldn't be sure what she was attempting to accomplish. Either way, he gripped her tighter. "Just wait a minute," he said. And with a quick energy projection he stopped the artificial rainfall.

"I saw some kid pull the alarm," he said with a smile as he let go of her arm. "Probably trying to break up the fight." Elliot let his eyes wander in the direction of the fighting students. A devious smile formed on his lips as he saw that not only was it still going, but the infection had spread. He turned back to Kami. "Apparently the idiots didn't know that angry people don't give a fuck about—"

His sentence was cut off by the sound of an explosion, followed by the shrill ringing of the fire alarm.

Curiously, he turned his head in the direction of the door, and saw that black smoke was forcing its way through the crack at the bottom. He scowled, knowing that the fire had something to do with the Witch and the Vampire. They knew he wasn't human and they were — *literally* — trying to smoke him out.

Kami screamed again, and this time the sound of her voice irritated him.

Elliot got to his feet so quickly he knocked over his lunch. Usually an action like that would have been something people would notice and mock, however, everyone else at the table — and most of the people who had been in the cafeteria — were already gone.

With an irate grumble, he grabbed onto Kami's arm and pulled her from the cafeteria. Releasing the twenty or so fighting people from his spell, after taking a moment to consider whether or not he would let them burn out of spite for the Witch.

The fighting stopped suddenly, and those involved seemed to be dazed for a moment, before they noticed the smoke and ran for the exit, pausing to help those who were more severely injured.

Elliot rolled his eyes at their pointless actions. He, personally, didn't see the point in helping others . . . what was the point in living your life being good for the sake of other people? When it came to life you were better off living for yourself.

What was the point in wasting your time caring?

Didn't the idiots realise that everyone dies in the end?

He and Kami were some of the last to evacuate the cafeteria. They came out into the fresh air, and Kami immediately started to shiver. He smiled at her, then sighed once again at his own inconsistencies.

It always happened when she was around; one minute he found her endearing to the point that it caused him physical pain and the next he found her presence to be so irritating he wanted to cause *her* physical pain. The back and forth that she caused was starting to wear on his nerves and once again, he considered the thought of simply killing her to take her out of the equation.

"It's *freezing* out here!" she declared, wrapping her arms around herself as though that would keep her warm.

The obviousness of her statement caused Elliot to roll his eyes. "What do you expect? It's November and we're soaked."

If she was bothered by his sarcasm she didn't let it show. Instead she continued as if he hadn't said a word. "I wonder where Madison is." She stood on her toes in an attempt to see over the crowd of people.

"Who *cares*?"

She sighed and turned her head in his direction. With any other person the sigh would have indicated that they were about to glare, but when Kami turned her head to him she was smiling. "I care," she said simply. "I want to make sure everyone's okay."

Elliot let a sigh, something Kami caused him to do quite frequently. Locating the group was simple due to the fact that one of the members possessed magical blood. "There," he said, pointing straight ahead where the students who shared his table stood.

Kami stood on her toes and leaned to the side, following his finger to the group. She smiled then started to walk towards them. Elliot wrapped his arm around her waist to pull her back. "What?" she asked, looking at him curiously. "You don't want to go?"

Elliot gazed at the group of students with a cold disinterest. Usually he wouldn't care one way or the other, but the Witch and the Vampire were still unaccounted for. They had staged the fire to get him outside and he didn't feel like waiting around for them to find him.

He smiled, using his head to indicate towards the parking lot. "Let's go."

She turned to face him, laughing. "Go where?"

He shrugged. "I don't know where *exactly*, but what I do know is that I'm soaked, you're soaked, and it's cold outside. Do you know what that says to me?"

He gathered, from the coy smile she gave him that she knew what it said to him, but she didn't say as much. Instead she moved towards him, gazing at him from under her eyelashes. "What does that say to you?"

"That we should go somewhere more private where we can get ourselves out of these clothes."

With a smile, Kami walked past him towards where his car was parked. Elliot followed her quickly, not pausing to look when he sensed the Vampire walk out of the building.

# CHAPTER 25

*I*t took over three days for Lucy to get in contact with *her*. At least she assumed it was the 'her' the Witch had been referring to.

She made her way through an old Victorian house. All of the windows were completely blacked out with heavy burgundy curtains. Lucy stepped into the parlour with some hesitation, feeling anxious about the fact that she was about to meet with the leader.

Vampire Hunters didn't work the same as other Hunters. Hunters worked in small groups, usually families, each one headed by a matriarch who was in charge of organising assignments.

With Vampire Hunters, Lucy had always thought that there was no leader. Some people were raised into it, some people found their way to it and others were recruited to it by others.

It wasn't until recently that Lucy had discovered that all she thought about Vampire Hunters was a lie. And not only was there an overall ruler who manipulated the Hunters from behind the scenes, but that the woman who led them, was also a Vampire.

"Lucy," the Vampire spoke as Lucy stepped into the room, gazing up at her from her place on an overstuffed, faded red arm chair.

The woman was striking, not overly beautiful, but otherworldly in appearance. Her pale skin showing blue veins beneath, her dark brown eyes reflecting the flames of the candles that adorned the room. "Sit down," the woman said with a slow smile. "Make yourself comfortable."

Lucy hesitated, then slowly perched herself on the edge of the sofa closest to the door behind her.

The woman smiled, clearly amused by Lucy's discomfort. "My name is Bethany," she said. "I hear that you have a message for me."

"Apparently so," Lucy said quietly. She was still having a hard time getting over the fact that she was expected to sit there and have polite conversation with a Vampire.

"Come now," she said, with a smile that flashed sharpened canines. "I promise not to bite."

"This is bullshit," Lucy said. Bethany looked taken aback. "Who the fuck put you in charge? We're supposed to kill your kind, yet there *you* sit. Demanding answers from me as if you have a right to!"

Bethany's smile was slow and calculating. "Oh dear," she said. "And I *had* hoped we could do this the civilised way."

"My blood is poison to you leech!" Lucy said as she stood, glancing over her shoulder for just a second to calculate the distance from here to the door.

"Draining you . . . " Lucy jumped and whipped her head around, Bethany was standing right in front of her. So close that her coldness seeped into Lucy's skin, sending chills to her bones. "It's not the only way to kill you."

With a speed that Lucy couldn't match, Bethany reached her hand out and snatched the amulet from Lucy's neck. Stealing her only form of psychological protection. Barely a second later she could feel the Vampire's presence in her brain, pushing and probing at her memories. Violating the sanctity of her mind.

Lucy felt herself fall to the cushioned couch as Bethany laughed with glee. "You found him!" she declared. "I can't believe it, after two centuries, you finally found him! You genius child!"

"What are you talking about?" Lucy asked, putting a hand to her head which was swimming with the after-effects

"The heir to the throne," Bethany said as if the answer had been obvious. "Don't you realise how long I've been searching for him?"

"A long time?" Lucy sat up, regretting the action immediately after, her head was throbbing with the beginnings of a migraine.

"A *very* long time," Bethany said, sitting herself on the sofa too close to Lucy. "I'm a Vampire Hunter," she said. "I have been since I was thirteen . . . I also happen to be a Vampire. I want to kill the heir to the throne, kill the king, and then guess what?"

Lucy groaned. "What?"

"Then the Vampire throne belongs to Vampire Hunters. Then we know how to get to their dimension. And then . . . " Bethany let the sentence trail off, eyeing Lucy expectantly.

Lucy thought for a moment, her eyes growing wide as her mind came to a sudden realisation. "We can completely wipe them out."

"Exactly," she said with a smile. "You don't think I'm a

Vampire for *no* reason, do you?"

Bethany handed the amulet back to Lucy. "Now," she said as she stood. "Show me where you found him."

# CHAPTER 26

"Learn anything interesting?" Jack asked. He was in his corporeal form. Sam could tell because people glanced at him curiously as they walked past, on their way home early after the school had done a roll-call to make sure everyone who was present today had gotten out safely.

Which they had.

No one died, and the only ones injured were those involved in the cafeteria fight.

"Today I learned that Jamie is the oldest person alive who owns a Nintendo DS," Sam said as she stepped closer.

Jack frowned thoughtfully for a moment, pushing himself away from the wall he had been leaning against. "I don't think that's true."

Sam smiled. "I've seen him play it."

"No," Jack said disbelievingly. "There *must* be someone older."

"Who's the oldest person you know?" Jamie asked Jack,

who was gazing thoughtfully at the red bricked wall of the school.

"Atropos . . . I *think* she's the oldest of the three . . . " He shook his head. "I don't think she plays, the Moirai aren't really the gaming type. Anyway, he's just a kid, of course he has a Nintendo."

"I'm at *least* eight times your age," Jamie said.

"I know that physically I look like a damn sexy twenty-six year old, but I'm actually a damn sexy forty-five year old," Jack said with an amused smile. "And unlike Vampires, we Ghosts actually continue to age psychologically once we cease to age physically."

"What are you talking about?" Jamie asked, at the same time Sam said, "You're so *old*."

"Vampires don't age psychologically, it's why, no matter how long you live you'll always behave like a kid."

"Firstly, I'm actually two hundred and seven . . . secondly, physically I'm nineteen. *Neither* of those ages are anywhere near *kid*."

Jack smiled and shook his head. "Exactly what a kid would say . . . I rest my case."

"Well I beg to differ."

"You'll beg *no* differ!" Jack spoke loudly, eyeing Jamie as if daring him to attempt to speak. Some students walking out the gate turned to look in Jack's direction, before they giggled and walked away.

Sam laughed when she saw the thoughtful expression on Jamie's face as he attempted to think of something smart to say. "Don't even try," she said. "There *is* no comeback for that."

Jamie sulked. "So's your face," he mumbled to Jack who was smiling triumphantly.

All he said in response was, "*Kid*."

"I don't know why you sent him," Sam said, pointing towards Jamie. "He hated school so much he burned it down and he was only there for a day."

"That was *you*?" Jack asked, giving Jamie a look of astonishment. Though he seemed more impressed than anything else.

Jamie shrugged as if it were nothing. "People were acting strange, being possessed, I distracted them with explosions."

"Possessed?" Jack furrowed his brow and looked in Sam's direction.

"We found a link to your mystery monster," Sam said. "Well . . . Jamie figured it out."

"I knew I liked you for a reason!" Jack declared, spreading his arms wide. "Hug me!"

"I'm okay, thanks," Jamie said with a laugh.

"Don't be a bastard." Jack wrapped his arms around an uncomfortable looking Jamie, and squeezed him for a moment, then patted him on the back as he released his grasp. "There," he said. "Your reward for doing your job."

"What have you been making Jade and Danny do?" Sam asked, as they walked out the school gates. "Have they been busy bubble wrapping the house while I was out?"

"No," Jack said. "Good idea though, they can get started on that tomorrow."

"If I come home tomorrow and the house is filled with bubble wrap I *will* run away."

"You can't run away from me Sam," Jack said, his voice calm even though his eyes showed signs of worry. Almost as though he thought her running away was a possibility. "Firstly, I'm a Hunter, I'm trained to track people. Secondly, I'm your guardian, therefore I have special ways of always knowing where you are."

"Ways?" Sam asked sceptically.

"Tracking devices?" Jamie asked. "Spy cams?"

"No Mr thinks he lives in the CIA," Jack said with a laugh. "Ghostly ways."

"Like for example?"

Sam eyed Jack suspiciously. "Did you plant runes on me?" she asked, thinking back to all of the things that Jack had given her. Which consisted of the stuffed bunny that had shared her bed for as long as she remembered, and the amulet she hadn't removed from her neck for the past three months.

"*No,*" he said. "I'm sick of these questions, forget I said anything."

"I don't think —"

"Okay, so where's the link to my U.I.E.?" Jack cut Sam off before she had a chance to finish.

"What's a U.I.E.?" Jamie asked.

Jack rolled his eyes and sighed dramatically. "Unidentified Entity . . . *obviously,*"

Jamie stared at Jack blankly for a moment, as if he couldn't quite understand what Jack was saying. "You *do* know that unidentified is one word, right? So that would make it a U.E., not a U.I.E.."

Jack glared at Jamie. "Why are you trying to ruin everything I care about?" he asked. "It's a U.I.E. because I say so . . . Any more questions?"

Jamie laughed and shook his head.

"Good! So where's my link?"

"He left when we did," Sam said.

"He?" Jack asked excitedly. "So it's someone in the school? Why didn't you say so sooner! We should've followed him!"

"Relax," Sam said. "Jamie got his address from the principal's office."

Jamie reached his hand into the pocket of his jeans and pulled out a yellow Post-It. "I committed a crime to get this.

I'm expecting regular visits if I end up in prison."

"No problem," Jack said as he snatched the Post-It out of his hand. "Sam, conjugal visits every other weekend."

"I believe he asked *you* for those visits," Sam said with a glare in Jack's direction.

"Yeah, but what he really wants is my permission to have you. Which he has." He turned his head in Jamie's direction. "She's your problem now . . . you're welcome."

"Hey!" Sam punched Jack in the side, he laughed. "You're not funny."

"This isn't too far from here," Jack said as he read the address on the Post-It. He looked around for a moment, assessing their surroundings. "About ten . . . fifteen minutes? We could go there now. If we run we might even get there before he does."

"No," Sam said. "Be smart Mr 'I'm the greatest Hunter ever'."

"I never said that," Jack said. "It's true though. I am the greatest that ever lived. It's a fact . . . an *inter*nationally known fact."

"You should go lurk around tonight," Jamie said. "He's heard me and Sam talking about him so he'd notice one of us, but he doesn't know you and you can go invisible, so he'll never know you're there."

"*Obviously,*" Jack said with a snort. "I'll observe, get to know his schedule. Then when the house is empty, we can — what the fuck is going on over there?" Jack asked, squinting his eyes at a crowd of people that were blocking the street about a minute down the road.

Sam stopped in her tracks, taking a moment to assess the crowd. She recognised a lot of the people ahead from school, meaning that they hadn't been there too long. But the longer Sam observed the more she noticed that something was horribly wrong. Despite the fact that it was November, and the air held an icy pre-winter chill, it was colder than it should have been. The air was so cold that it sent shivers through Sam's entire body, the fine hairs on the back of her neck stood on end as her body registered an unnatural presence.

Without wasting more time, Sam took off running down the street, pushing her legs as fast as she could, with Jamie and Jack at either side of her. She shoved her way through the crowd of people, propelling herself forward, through the library gates and the yellow police tape that had been put up as a barrier between the library and any passers-by.

"Miss!" a policeman called, extending his arm in front of Sam to keep her from going any further. "I'm sorry," he said, stepping forward to push her back behind the police line. "This is an active crime scene. You can't come through."

"What happened?" Jack whispered, once the policeman was out of earshot.

"A murder," Sam said. "Someone was killed." She eyed the crowd for a familiar face, hoping to find out which of the two librarians had been killed.

Her eyes settled on a tall woman with mousy brown hair, her eyes red from her tears. "Jessie," Sam said with a sigh. "Jessie's dead."

"How do you know that?" Jamie asked, following her line of sight. "How do you know it was a murder?"

"Because . . . " Sam paused as she saw Hayley step forward and wrap an arm around Michelle. She looked over her shoulder at Sam and smiled a slow, disturbing smile. A smile that she had seen before, one that she knew didn't belong to anything human, or anything good. And then, in a flash, it was gone. Hayley watched Michelle sombrely, as if she'd never given Sam *that* look.

"Sam?" The sound of Jack calling her name snapped her out

of her thoughts.

"Because," she said again, taking a breath to calm her racing pulse, "I saw it happen."

# CHAPTER 27

$\mathcal{J}$amie walked through the crowd at a brisk pace, following closely behind Jack who was dragging Sam away from all of the people. They walked along the pathway beside the stone wall that surrounded the library to the back of the building where it was isolated.

"What do you mean you saw it?" Jack asked, releasing Sam's arm from his grasp once he'd stopped walking. "When was this?"

"Um . . . well . . . I didn't really *see* it, it was more like I dreamed it."

Jack let a sigh. "When?"

"Before I woke up, I had this dream where I was in the library at night, and then I went down to the basement and was attacked by one of those Shadow things I saw before, remember?" she paused and glanced at Jack, who nodded his head. "And then, I don't know, it was weird . . . it was like, *me* but not me. And there was a ritual, runes written on the walls with blood and these people—"

"What people?" Jack asked. "What did they look like?"

"Four women and two men, I didn't really get a good look at them."

Jack nodded his head, his expression somewhere between concentration and worry.

"We need to get inside," Jamie said. "We should see if everything looks like it did in Sam's dream or if it's different."

Jack nodded his head. "He's right, it *may* be different."

"What if it's the same?" Sam asked. "Am I psychic now? Because I don't want to be psychic now, not if my visions are going to be like that one."

"Visions are a common thing with Magic users," he said, his eyes wandering over Sam in a silent assessment.

"But those are forced through spells or rituals."

Jack let a frustrated sigh. "I don't know then," he said with a shrug. "Someone could have gifted you with it."

"Gifted me?"

"I've heard stories of powerful psychics being able to gift people with visions. Was there anything in the dream that would indicate it may have come from someone?"

Sam's expression went distant. She chewed her lip as she thought. Jamie watched her expectantly, as did Jack. He noticed her eyes grow wide, before she scowled as in her mind she seemed to remember something of importance. "A bandage."

"What?" Jack asked, his tone confused, his expression puzzled.

"A bandage!" Sam repeated loudly, her voice filled with rage as she spoke. "A ratty looking, blood covered, disgusting old bandage. Covered in red and black blood, wrapped around my hand."

"Um . . ." Jack watched her for a moment. "Does that mean

something important?"

At the mention of the bandage, Jamie's mind went immediately to Tír na nÓg, where he had spoken with that girl. The one whose veins were filled with poison that couldn't be cured by Vampire blood.

"Effie," Jamie said, remembering the small girl's name.

Sam seemed to get angry at the mention of her. "I *knew* there was something off about her," she said, looking at Jamie with an expression of ire. "I *told* you there was something off with her and *you* didn't believe me."

"Well Sam, I don't think —"

"Don't try to *defend* her!" she cut him off.

"Sam," Jack said, the tone of his voice was kind, which appeared to be the tone he used when he was attempting to reason with Sam when she was being difficult. "I don't think someone who gifted you with a vision is your enemy. It's someone who's trying to help you."

"*Why?*" Sam asked. "Why would someone who doesn't know me try to help me?"

"You'd be surprised," Jack said. "A lot of people out there, who've never met you, do all sorts of things to help you."

Sam snorted in disagreement.

"At least eighty percent of the Hunters refuse to help capture you."

Sam looked at Jack with an expression somewhere between disbelief and shock. "What?"

"The bounty was put on you when you were two days old, they refused to hurt a baby. And once they saw what those bastards were capable of, they refused to hunt you altogether."

"I get shot at by Hunters all the time!" Sam argued.

"That would be the twenty percent who are assholes, and have no moral standing. We're not serial killers," Jack said.

"We have society and rules, and morals. One of the rules is we don't hurt people who we *know* to be innocent. And a baby who's been alive for two days isn't guilty of anything. Everyone was horrified that someone even dared ask them to hurt you."

Sam looked completely unconvinced of what Jack was telling her. Jamie had only encountered one Hunter, other than Jack. And he had been murderous, almost psychotic. He attacked Sam outside, in a place where humans could have come in at any moment, for anyone to behave in such a way they'd have to be insane.

Jamie *knew* Jack, and Jack wasn't psychotic. He was kind . . . he was protective . . . he was the polar opposite of the other Hunter. Having seen the difference between the two was why — despite Sam's disbelief — Jamie found Jack's claims to be believable.

"I don't think Effie is dangerous," he said with a sigh. "I think, if she *is* the one who gave you that vision, that she did it to try help you."

Sam scowled at him and folded her arms across her chest. "Whose side are you on?"

Jamie let a frustrated breath. "The same side I'm always on . . . *yours.*"

# CHAPTER 28

*T*he sun set before the clock struck six, as it always did this time of year. Jamie sat on the roof of Sam's house and watched as the streetlamps flickered to life one at a time.

"She does like to be difficult," Jack said as he materialised beside him.

Jamie didn't move at Jack's sudden presence. Surprising himself by his non-reaction, he must have become more accustomed to Jack's ability to appear and disappear than he'd realised.

"She really does," he mumbled, letting out a long, heavy sigh, his breath coming out in a mist as the heated air from his lungs mingled with the cold.

"She gets it from her mother," Jack said. "She was an *extremely* difficult woman."

"You knew her mother?" Jamie asked out of curiosity. Sam never spoke about her family. Not her birth parents or her adoptive parents. It was like Madison had told him, she would speak to you for however long you wished to have a conversation, and she would talk about any subject you wanted to talk about. Unless of course, that subject was about her in any personal way.

Jamie had always been curious about her life before. But he never asked, because he knew that her reaction would be to shut down, turn off the conversation, and it would take a while for her to feel like talking about even trivial matters again.

In fact she avoided personal subjects to the extent that she had never even asked Jamie anything about himself. Like exactly how old he was. Where he was from. How he came to be a Vampire.

If he hadn't known Sam as well as he did, he would have found her lack of interest offensive.

"I knew her," Jack said, gazing up at the starless sky. "I was supposed to, basically, arrest her and deliver her to the Elder Witches'." He laughed. "She *was* difficult though."

Jamie smiled. "You arrested Sam's mother?"

Jack laughed again and nodded his head. "Before I was dead, obviously. Back when I was a Hunter."

"So she was like Sam?"

"Oh yeah," he said. "She was stubborn as a mule. It's why they put a bounty on her, she refused to join ranks, wanted to stay independent. They threatened her, killed her family, but she wouldn't budge. Went into hiding ... She had this *ridiculous* plan that if she stripped herself of her Magic, and became human that she could blackmail the Elder Witches into staying away from her. They'd let her live because she had information that could destroy them, and they wouldn't bother her because she was human."

"I take it that didn't work?" Jamie asked.

Jack smiled and shook his head. "Actually it did ... for a

while. When they found out she'd given birth and her Powers went to her child, they hunted her and the father down. They hid Sam. They were both tortured for her location."

"They didn't get it?"

Jack shook his head. "They died to keep her safe."

Jamie paused for a moment. He couldn't imagine what it would have been like for someone to suffer torture and withstand it all, just to protect a child.

But then, that child had been Sam. And if it came down to it, he knew that he'd do the same to protect her.

"What was her father like?"

Jack went silent for a moment, his body suddenly still. Then he let a sigh and said, "He was just some idiot who was always getting in the way, screwing up people's plans. A lot of people think he's the reason that Sam's mother was killed, but..." Jack shrugged. "She was the one everyone wanted, the special one everyone either wanted or wanted dead ... I mean, *I* wanted her dead ... and he was just kinda *there*. Very run of the mill, he wasn't anyone important ... not *really*."

"Was he a Witch too?"

Jack laughed and shook his head.

"Well, what was he?"

"Like I said ... " Jack looked at Jamie with a rueful smile. "He was no one important, he was just some guy and now he's just not here anymore."

Jamie let the subject go, seeing Jack's reluctance to continue to speak about it. He watched Jack as he pulled at a loose thread on the ends of his jeans. Jamie looked on with curiosity, chewing his lip as he contemplated asking Jack about something that had been bothering him for the past few months.

"Jack ... " Jack looked in Jamie's direction expectantly. "Do you mind if I ask you some things about you?"

"Um . . . sure," he shrugged. "Why not?"

"What are the marks?" he asked, looking at the exposed skin of Jack's hands and neck where the intricate red marks were visible.

Jack looked down at his hands for a moment, then pulled up his sleeves to reveal that the marks did not just cover his hands, but his arms as well. "I've got them everywhere," he said. "Everywhere but my face really. They're the marks of the Hunter. We all have them. The men anyway. No one is entirely sure if they have a purpose or not, it just seems to be that all of the men are born covered in these marks. It's a species thing I think."

"Only the men have them?"

He nodded, pulling his sleeves back down. "Yeah. The men are covered all over. The women have only one mark on their bodies. The family crest. Each Hunter clan has a different mark, some of which get combined through mating and things, but generally, a child is born with the mark of their mother's family. We're all mammy's boys. The only time a child would have the mark of the father's family would be if the mother was not a Hunter. Which is rare because mating outside of species is frowned upon. Like you can get disowned and kicked out and shit."

"That seems a bit drastic."

"Yeah," Jack shrugged. "It's a bit harsh, but that's just how it works."

Jack turned a little and lifted his shirt up slightly to reveal his back. He pointed to a specific mark on his skin; within the swirling lines that were the rest of his marks there was a symbol just slightly to the left of his spine. A crescent moon with a star nestled close by.

"That little one there is the mark of the McKenna's."

"Hmm," Jamie looked at it for a moment, wondering if the

marks meant anything special. If they granted Hunter's any special skills the way Sam's mark seemed to power her Magic. Jack allowed his shirt to fall back into place and turned to look up at the sky once more.

Thinking of Jack as anything other than what he was now was difficult. And Jamie found himself wondering about what it was like to be a Ghost. How different was it really to life as anything else?

"Do you ever sleep?"

Jack laughed. "I'm a *Ghost* . . . Ghosts don't sleep."

"Okay, so where do you usually go when Sam is asleep?"

He frowned for a moment, his expression thoughtful. "Depends on whether or not there's things to be done. Sometimes I go gather information, sometimes I just hang around."

"Do you ever get hungry?"

Jack laughed. "What's with all the strange questions?"

Jamie shook his head and looked away. "Just some things I've noticed that don't really make sense."

"Oh?" Jack seemed confused. "Like what?"

"Well . . . I've noticed that your clothes change."

Jack laughed. "No, they —"

"They *do*," Jamie cut him off before he could deny it. "They look the same but they're not, every now and then the colours will be slightly off, if I didn't have heightened eyesight I probably wouldn't even notice it. Sometimes they're creased, and other times they're not. Almost as if they've been ironed or washed. Your jeans get worn over the course of a month, then all of a sudden they're brand new."

"But . . . " Jack looked down at the ends of his jeans, which were frayed, then turned his gaze back to Jamie. "No," he said, shaking his head. "These are the clothes I died in. I've been living in them for *years*. Maybe when I go corporeal they

130

seem a bit scuffed and then when I'm non-corporeal they're fine again. Maybe that's it."

Jamie shook his head. "Your hair gets longer, then again, at the start of every month it's back to its normal length, as if it's been cut."

"It's impossible!" Jack yelled, glaring at Jamie angrily as if he didn't want to hear what he had to say. "I don't know what you're talking about, or what the fuck you're accusing me of but you can—"

"I'm not accusing you of anything," Jamie said calmly, assessing Jack's expression for any hints of his thoughts. But he simply looked scared and confused, and slightly livid.

"Good, because we can't talk about this . . . what you're trying to say, we *can't* talk about it."

Jamie paused for a moment, allowing his brain to come to the conclusion that had been floating within his thoughts for weeks now. "If you were in your corporeal form, and I were to listen carefully, would I hear your heart—"

"Stop it," Jack whispered. Looking as though it pained him to think about what Jamie was implying. "I'm here for Sam. And if you keep saying things like that I *will* be sent away."

"But *why?*"

"We just can't," he said sternly. "So don't say another word about it . . . *ever.*"

Jamie let a sigh and nodded his head. "Okay."

"And don't say anything to Sam either."

Jamie considered Jack for a moment, wondering what exactly he was trying to hide. And more importantly, why was it something that needed to be hidden from Sam? He didn't speak his thoughts though, instead he simply nodded, letting Jack know that he wouldn't speak a word of their conversation to Sam.

His shoulders sagged as he relaxed. "Good," he said. "We

should go now." He stood up, balancing perfectly on the slanted roof, as though he barely noticed that he was almost three storeys off the ground. "The library should be vacant now. I'll get Sam and Danny, you go get Jade."

Jamie gave a curt nod, then stood and—with no hesitation—jumped off the roof, landing lightly on his feet, barley making an imprint on the grass.

He jogged across the lawn and hopped over the fence that separated the two properties. He wasn't even at the door before it swung open. Jamie slowed his pace, before stopping completely, standing at least five steps from the front door.

A middle aged woman, with dark hair that fell to her shoulders and a complexion a few shades darker than Jade stood at the door, staring stonily at him from inside the house.

"Hello," Jamie said with a smile. "Could I see Jade please?"

Hayley simply glared at him for a moment. Then she folded her arms across her chest. "Do you know how long this town has been under Coven rule?"

"Um . . . " Jamie stared at her blankly for a moment, before he shrugged, indicating that he didn't know, and wasn't completely sure why she was asking.

"A lot longer than you've existed. Do you know the protocols for other supernatural beings who wish to reside in a town that is already under rule?"

Jamie shook his head.

"You are supposed to find the Coven leader . . . which would be *me,* and notify them of your presence and any plans you have. Then you are to await their decision on whether or not you have *permission* to live here. Yet here you are *Vampire,* in a town run by Witches, living and feeding as if the rules don't apply to you."

"If it makes you feel better, I technically live *outside* of town, so—"

"You think breaking the laws is funny?"

Jamie shook his head again. "I wasn't aware that there were any laws. And besides, as far as I know Vampires are a neutral party and can live where they want," he said. Even though what he was saying weren't things that he knew for a fact, he *did* know that there was a war between Witches and Demons, and that Vampires were neutral. So that would mean that he didn't have to abide by Witch's rules. At least, he thought that's what it meant. "So if you don't mind," he continued. "I would like to speak with Jade now."

Hayley didn't reply, instead she took a step back and slammed the door shut. Jamie stood there for a moment, watching the door with confusion, unsure as to what he should do next. He had just decided to get Sam and have her collect Jade, when he heard a sound. Jamie looked around in confusion, trying to find the source.

The words, "Back here idiot!" came in a low whisper from behind the house. Slowly, Jamie stepped to the side, and then, keeping an eye out for Hayley, made his way to the back of the house.

Jade was hanging from her bedroom window, her back to the yard, her hands clasped on the window ledge, her feet pressed firmly to the side of the house.

"What are you doing?" Jamie asked, keeping his voice low.

"Oh, I'm just getting some fresh air," she whispered, her voice sounding sarcastic despite the fact that she was speaking quietly. "What does it look like I'm doing?"

"Trying not to fall?"

Jamie took a step closer to the house, standing more or less under where Jade was hanging. His body tense as he prepared to catch her if she fell.

"Catch," she called, laughing as she let go of the window ledge, kicking at the wall with her feet to push herself away from the house.

Jamie rushed back slightly, and caught her in his arms. He stumbled backwards, holding onto her awkwardly as he tried to regain his balance.

"Nice catch." She grinned as Jamie set her down on her feet. "Next time I'll do a back flip in the air and you can catch me over your head, Dirty Dancing style."

Jamie laughed. "I don't think I can do that."

Jade rolled her eyes. "Well *obviously* you won't get it the first time. We'll practice though, and one day you'll get it right."

"We should go before your mother realises you're missing."

Jade nodded her head and sighed dramatically as she led the way to Sam's house, climbing over the fence and keeping her head low so as not to draw attention to herself.

"Is your mother always so scary?" Jamie asked as he pulled himself up over the fence.

"Pretty much," Jade said. "She's been like that for a while now. Around the time Sam's grandmother died she got really weird." Jade shook her head and let a sigh. "I can't really stand to be around her."

Jamie nodded, he didn't blame Jade for not wanting to be around Hayley for too long. He had barely spent five minutes with the woman and even that had been too much. It wasn't just her attitude either, or the way she glared at him, but there was something off-kilter about her in general. Something that gave him a feeling of unease, and made Jamie want to keep his distance.

The garage door opened as they got to the front of the house, and Sam popped her head out, waving them over with her hand. Jade hurried ahead of Jamie, into the garage where there was a sleek, shiny black car with windows tinted so darkly they blended into the paint.

Jamie paused, taking a moment to stare at it in confusion, then peered over the roof, expecting, even though there was hardly the space for it, to see another car beside it.

"Go on," Sam said as she opened the back driver's side door. Jade slid herself into the car, to the seat furthest from where they stood.

Sam eyed Jamie expectantly, waiting for him to get inside. "What happened to *your* car?" Jamie asked as he got in, and moved to the middle seat beside Jade.

Sam got in beside him, and closed the door behind her. "This *is* my car," she said as she put her seatbelt on.

"Did you get a new one?"

Sam smiled and shook her head. "I barely use it," she said. "But I didn't want to risk it being recognised, so I made it different."

"You mean, you use Magic?"

She nodded as Danny yelled, "Seatbelts people!"

"So, if it's your car then why aren't you driving it?"

Sam let a sigh and rested her chin on her hand, her elbow propped up on the door handle. "He grabbed the keys and ran for it . . . apparently he has to drive because he's old and this is the only joy he gets in life."

"No Sam," Danny said from the front. "I said I get to drive because I'm older than you, so I win."

"Okay!" Jack shouted, shutting Sam up before she had a chance to say anything else. "No fighting, let's just go."

# CHAPTER 29

$\mathcal{B}$ethany allowed Lucy to drive. Usually she wouldn't allow anyone else to drive her car; she was the sort of person who enjoyed relying on only herself. But in this case, she felt it would be better for Hunter morale if she allowed Lucy to lead the way. Deciding against the idea of stealing every thought from her tiny brain and draining every ounce of crimson liquid from her veins.

It was easier to remain in control if she restrained herself from murdering the help.

"How much longer?" she asked, her tone bored as she watched the rapidly moving landscape through the tinted windows.

"We're almost there," she said. "I don't really remember the way to his house, it was warded."

"Warded?"

Lucy nodded. "He knows a Witch, who I assume was the one to put the wards all around his house. Runes for protection and misdirection. I couldn't get within twenty feet of the front porch without a verbal invitation."

"Was he living residential?" she asked, though she already knew the answer would be no; Jamie never had enjoyed residential living. As a child he'd lived in a manor house in the middle of the country, and as a Vampire he tended to stay out of the way of humans.

"It was in the middle of the woods."

Bethany nodded her head. "So where are we going then?"

Lucy let an exasperated sigh. Bethany half smiled in amusement; Lucy didn't seem to fear her the way a lot of the other Hunters did. If nothing else, she seemed to be annoyed by her general existence. "We're going," she said, with an irritated tone, "to the place I met him ... you can track him from there, right?"

Bethany sat forward slightly as the scene outside became less crowded by trees. "In town?"

Lucy nodded. "He was at a bar getting wasted."

Bethany turned her head in Lucy's direction, glancing at her curiously. "Really?"

Lucy scoffed. "Yeah," she said. "That's where we find a lot of Vampires, they lurk around bars where people come out drunk and uninhibited."

Bethany smiled. "I'm aware of that ... it's just surprising that you should find *him* in a bar ... not *lurking* but getting drunk."

"Do you *know* him or something?" Lucy asked.

Bethany shook her head, smiling fondly at her memories despite herself. "Apparently not as well as I thought."

# CHAPTER 30

$\mathcal{I}$t took less than five minutes for them to drive to the library, which made Jamie wonder why they had bothered to take a car at all.

"Camouflage," Sam said, as if reading the unspoken question in his mind. "We needed to *not* be seen on the way here."

She opened her door and stepped outside, pushing it all the way, leaving space for Jamie to step out after her. Jade opened the door on the other side and stepped out, stretching her arms over her head. Jamie turned to face the wall that surrounded the library, and listened carefully, stretching his senses outwards as he scanned their surroundings for signs of life.

He let a sigh of relief and his shoulders relaxed at the silence. "It's empty," he said to everyone. They had been standing around him, patiently waiting for him to check that the coast was clear.

Jack stepped forward first, running at the wall, then jumping at it, using his feet to push himself up high enough that he could grab onto the top and haul himself over. He turned when he reached the top—perched in a crouching position—and smiled down at them. "Who's next?"

"There's a gate, you know?" Sam said sarcastically, before mimicking Jack's movements perfectly, and sitting next to him on top of the wall.

"That's on the other side of the library, Sam," Jack said with a roll of his eyes.

"Yeah," Jade said, shaking her head. "I can't do that . . . I must have missed the ninja classes at school."

Jack laughed, and leaned forward, balancing on his toes as he extended his arm. "You lift," he said to Danny. "I'll pull."

Jade opened her mouth to protest, but was silenced almost immediately when Danny grabbed her from behind, wrapping his arms around her waist, lifting her high enough that she could reach Jack's outstretched hand.

"I am not okay with this!" she cried, as Danny carried her closer to the wall.

"Shut up and hold on," Jack said. He wrapped his hand around her wrist, as Jade did his. She pressed her feet to the wall and hung awkwardly for a moment before Sam grabbed onto her other arm.

Danny bent his knees and put both his hands on her backside and pushed her upwards. "Hey!" she yelled.

"It's okay," he said assuringly. "I'm not enjoying it."

"I think," she said breathlessly as she turned and sat on the wall between Jack and Sam, "that that's slightly *more* offensive."

Danny laughed before he jumped at the wall and pulled himself up, crouching beside Jack as he looked at the library with eyes squinted against the darkness.

Jamie could feel Sam watching him despite the fact that he was busy gazing at the empty space behind him. There was something about this place that wasn't right, though it could have been nothing more than bad energy produced by the murder, proving — at least — that Sam had been right about it being supernatural. The stench of it hung in the air, causing Jamie to feel uneasy.

"Last one to the door goes in first!" Sam declared before jumping from the wall.

Jamie smiled, as he ran forward and leapt over the wall in one movement, landing gracefully on his feet before he sped around the building and to the large front door, leaning against it casually, as if he'd been there for hours. Which he easily could have been, since he was already standing there by the time anyone else rounded the corner.

Jack laughed when he saw Jamie, staring at his fingernails as though he'd been bored while waiting for so long for the others to join him. "And that's why you *never* challenge a Vampire to a race."

Sam was the first to the door; she stood beside him and looked over her shoulder waiting for Danny and Jade. "Technically, Jade is last," Danny said as he walked forward at a casual pace, moving slowly so Jade wouldn't be left alone. "I'm only fourth because I had to help her off the wall."

Jade punched him on the arm as he laughed. "I am *not* going in there first!" she said. "This place is creepy."

"I'll go first," Jamie volunteered. He hadn't honestly expected that anyone else *would* go first. Out of everyone present, he was the best candidate for it. "I have better night vision anyway."

He opened the door, ducked under the crime scene tape and stepped inside. Sam walking so close behind him he could feel her breath on his back, which sent shivers running down his spine. Once he was standing inside, by the first of the tables that were set out for the library users, he paused, taking a moment to look around and gauge the surroundings.

Sam stepped in front of him. He reached out to stop her from going too far alone, but paused when he saw a purple glow emanating from her arm. He looked down and saw that the mark on her wrist was glowing. The light shining brightly in the dark room.

Sam flicked her wrist, moving the light from her arm to her hand, then without wasting a second, threw a ball of light into the air. It exploded like a firework and rained down cascading sparkles of light, which fell endlessly and seemed to be coming from nowhere.

Now that the room had a source of light it looked less terrifying, the purple beams of Magic even made the room feel warmer.

Jamie stepped forward and made his way across the room and behind the librarian's desk to the narrow hallway beyond. Both doors were open. He turned to his left, where he remembered the basement to be and stepped through the doorway heading towards the stairs, moving carefully but without hesitation despite the fact that his insides felt frozen with fear.

Sam whispered something behind him, something that sounded like a warning or a protest, but he hardly heard it. He rushed down the stairs, the magical lights following over his head. He stopped dead in his tracks when he reached the bottom of the stairs, the scene before him locking his muscles in place.

He'd stopped so suddenly that Sam crashed into his back, the force of her body against his caused him to waver slightly. "What the hell!" she yelled, stopping everyone behind her.

Jamie gaped at the room. On the floor was a circle of cream

coloured candles, pools of dried wax spilled around them, most of it stained with splashes of dried blood. The walls were covered in strange markings, painted in red. He didn't need to get too close to know what it was. The moment his brain registered it, his senses were swarmed by the recognisable stench.

The blood was nearly three days old, meaning that the librarian had been long dead before her body was discovered.

"Is this what you saw?" Jamie asked, his voice quiet yet somehow sounding loud in the empty room. Sam pushed past him and stepped forward. He tried to grab onto her arm to hold her back, but she pulled away, moving to the centre of the room inside the circle of candles.

She turned around slowly, her eyes scanning everything in the room as she did. Finally she answered. "This is it," she whispered. "This is what I saw."

"Exactly as you saw it?" Jack asked. Jamie turned to look at him and saw that he was standing in the centre of the staircase, leaning against the wall, his arms folded across his chest.

He could just about see Danny and Jade at the top of the staircase, Jade slightly behind Danny as they peered in the doorway; they didn't come in any further.

"Yeah," Sam said. "Exactly the same."

"This happened days ago," Jamie said to Jack, keeping his voice low. Somewhere in his mind he imagined that if he spoke too loudly, or made too much noise he would disturb whatever evil had done this. Because even though he couldn't consciously feel anything right now, there was still this feeling, creeping around in the back of his mind, that there was something else here with them.

Jack nodded his head. "Probably happened while she dreamed it."

"Don't people usually get visions of the future, not the present?" Jamie asked in confusion. What good would it do anyone to see something bad happening in their dreams if there wasn't a chance that they could stop it?

Jack nodded again. "Usually."

"It wasn't the future," Sam said as she took a step towards one of the walls. Slowly, she reached out her hand and lightly touched it to the blood covered bricks. "I was seeing it as if it was happening to me, *when* it was happening to Jessie. Just like with you—"

"What do you mean with me?" Jamie took a step towards her, careful not to tread on anything that might disturb the crime scene.

Sam looked at him, her eyes wide, her expression startled. "What?"

"You said, just like with you. What about me? Did you have a vision of me?"

"Maybe," she said with a shrug. "It's kind of fuzzy."

"When was this?" Jack asked, unmoving from his post on the stairs.

"Um . . . "

"Before or after you woke up?"

"Before," Sam said. "After I said the spell and went unconscious. It's fuzzy though, I barely remember it. There was a woman, she was a Hunter and I . . . *he* left with her. After that it just gets blurry."

"Did that happen?" Jack asked Jamie.

Jamie nodded. "That was about an hour or so before I found Sam in the woods, she killed the Hunters who were trying to kill me, sent the woman home with a mess—"

Jamie jumped as his head started to violently throb and started to sting. He turned to find Jack standing right behind him, glaring down at him with an expression of unmasked rage. "Why are you *that* stupid!"

"Did you just hit me?" Jamie asked in confusion. Jack could hit extremely hard for a Ghost . . . or whatever he was.

"Yes!" he yelled. "Of course I hit you! You wandered off with a Vampire Hunter while I was sick with worry, trying to keep Sam alive, find your sorry ass and get Danny home."

"I'm—"

"Not *only* that," Jack said, cutting off Jamie's apology. "But you let one of them get *away*!"

"But I—"

"The woman wasn't even a Hunter, was she? *No*, she was the *bait*. And *you* let her run off to the other Hunters! Do you think she *won't* come back with more?"

"I didn't really think about it," Jamie argued in his defence. "I was too busy, being confused about how Sam was alive and behaving like she's possessed by a completely different person."

Jack opened his mouth to respond, but Jamie didn't give him the chance. "I don't care what you say . . . she's *not right*. Her body was *empty* yet she was walking and talking. And what I don't understand is why *everyone* is just pretending like it didn't happen!"

"You think I'm not right?"

Jamie turned to face Sam, who was looking at him with an expression as close to hurt as he'd ever seen her look. "You're not," he said gently. "You have to know that there's something wrong."

"There is something wrong," she said. "There's something very wrong. But I think that we should really prioritise right now, don't you guys? There's something *very* evil out there, and it's killing people. The air in here is tainted, can't you feel it?"

Jamie took a breath to calm himself. She was right, and he

*could* feel it. The air in this room was cold, and heavy, and sick. It felt like it was poisoned.

"There is something wrong here," she continued, "and it's not me."

# CHAPTER 31

*I*t was dark by the time they arrived in town. Not as dark as it could have been, but enough for Bethany to feel comfortable. They parked the car a few blocks away and were making their way through the town on foot.

Lucy offered to start off their tour as close to the Vampire's house as she could remember, but Bethany didn't care much for that idea. She felt it would be better for them to begin their search where Lucy's night had started. And that was at the bar.

Lucy stepped through the door first, and Bethany followed behind her. Inside the bar was quaint. But then, small town establishments always were. It was filled with warm colours, the walls painted a dark cream — not that you could see much of the wall behind all of the framed pictures of what appeared to be people playing sports — all of the furniture was made of a dark mahogany wood, and any fabrics present, like the leather that covered the stools and chairs, was a deep burgundy.

Bethany inhaled deeply, an action which was customary to her upon entering new places. Breathing in the scent of the air allowed her to calm herself, and to get a good sense of the place she was in.

The air was filled with the smell of alcohol, beer mostly, and something warm and spicy that came from the door set into the wall beside the bar.

The kitchen.

"This is where you found him?" Bethany asked, a smile curved her lips as she tried to imagine him sitting at the bar with a drink in his hand, and failed.

"Yeah," said Lucy. She pointed to one of the stools that was placed at the centre of the bar. "He was sitting right there."

"How did you know there was a Vampire in town? Had he been caught feeding?"

"No," Lucy said, with a curious expression on her face. "We actually weren't hunting that night. We were just having some drinks."

"Celebrating?"

"Yeah." Lucy shifted uncomfortably as she eyed Bethany. "We just came from a hunt. We were over there." She pointed to one of the tables in the far corner.

Bethany walked to the table Lucy pointed to, which was currently empty of people. She pulled out one of the wooden chairs and sat herself down, her back to the wall, looking in the direction of the bar where she had a clear view of the stool he'd been sitting on.

"He just walked in," Lucy said, taking a seat next to her. "Sat down, minded his own business."

"And you thought," said Bethany as she glanced over the stiff laminated menu that was in the centre of the table, "that while he was there, inebriated and less able to defend himself, that you'd just, what? Lure him home and kill him?"

"Yes," Lucy replied, her jaw set stubbornly. "We could tell he was a Vampire, so why wouldn't we kill him?"

Bethany let a sigh. She hated having conversations with the newest generation of Hunters, none of them seemed to understand anything, or have the ability to see past the now. Bethany had learned long ago that it wasn't the now that was important . . . it was the future.

A boy dressed in a black shirt, black trousers, with a black apron tied around his waist walked over to their table, which was one of the few in the bar that actually had people sitting at it.

"Good evening," the boy—who couldn't have been any older than eighteen—said with a charming and polite smile. "Can I get you ladies anything, or would you like more time to look through the menu?"

"I'm not all that hungry for food," Bethany said with a devious grin and a glance towards Lucy, who was scanning the menu. "I'll just have a glass of wine, thank you."

The boy scrawled something on his little notepad, nodding his head. "Red or white?"

"Red," she answered.

He scribbled her order on his notepad, then looked to Lucy expectantly. "I'll have some french-fries, a double cheeseburger and a coke."

The boy smiled approvingly; clearly he was the type who liked girls who enjoyed food, then he wrote down her order.

"I'll be right back with your drinks," he said as he took the menus from the table.

"Thanks," Lucy said absently.

Bethany leaned forward so she could read his nametag, she wasn't one for feeding on the job, but she liked the look of this boy, there was something about him . . . he had that certain *je* ne sais quoi that she appreciated in humans, especially those of the male gender, she smiled. "Thank you . . . Scott."

# CHAPTER 32

$I$t was just about midnight when Elliot awoke from a
fitful sleep.

The inability to get a good night's rest was beginning to
wear on his nerves. Was *one* night too much to ask for?

Apparently so.

He saw the Shadows before he even opened his eyes. Well,
not so much saw them as felt them. The link they shared was
strong enough that he didn't need to open his eyes to be able
to see that they were there.

Nevertheless, he did open them, reluctantly pushing his
tired body into a sitting position.

With a huff, he shoved the duvet away and swung his legs
around the side of his bed. Gripping the edge of the mattress
tightly as took a few deep breaths to readjust himself to the
physical world and tried as best he could to forget his
nightmares.

After he felt a little better he glared in the direction of the darkest corner of his room and asked, "What *now?*"

The voice answered inside his head, and as always it spoke in a language that no one but Elliot could understand. *<Tsal nac taht emos deen ew. Seidob erom>*

Elliot's eyebrows pinched together with confusion. *More bodies?* he thought. *Where the hell am I gonna find more?*

# CHAPTER 33

$\mathcal{S}$am's dreams were disturbed by *Propane Nightmares,* her eyes shot open when she recognised the sound of her current ringtone.

Jade grumbled beside her and shifted beneath the duvet. "Answer the phone bitch," she mumbled.

Sam sighed and forced herself into a sitting position, grabbing her phone off the bedside table. "Hello?" she said as she rubbed bits of dried eyeliner from her eyes.

"Sam?"

Sam smiled when she recognised the voice on the other end of the line. "I don't believe for one second that you've been *that* busy."

Aleczander sighed tiredly. "You have no idea just how busy I have been."

"Lycanthropes?"

"Among other things, yes."

"So, do you want to come here or should I take him there?"

"Right to the point, as always." Aleczander chuckled. "You can bring him to me, if it is not too much trouble. I am expecting someone else later on today, so I should stay here."

"Okay," Sam said. "I wasn't doing anything else today anyway."

"Is he there with you right now?"

"*No!*" Sam snapped defensively, wondering why Aleczander would think that Jamie would be with her at seven a.m. on a Saturday morning. Did he think they were always together or something? Did he think they were *together* together? And why would he even think that in the first place?

It had been a long time since she'd seen Aleczander in person, and even longer since he'd seen Jamie. So why would he think that they were spending their nights together when he didn't really *know?*

"How quickly could you get him to a portal?"

"Um . . . about an hour, give or take."

"Alright," Aleczander said. "I will see you soon."

"Bye."

Sam hung up the phone, then went to her contacts list and scrolled down to Jamie's number and dialled.

The phone seemed to ring for an eternity, in which she sat there chewing her lip anxiously as she waited for Jamie to answer.

It *was* pretty early, and it was Saturday, so he was probably lying in bed right now completely unconscious. Which, for a Vampire, meant he was more or less dead to the world. Though, something she had learned quite recently, in the times that she'd witnessed Jamie sleeping in the corner of her room, his back against her door as if he were protecting her from anything that may come in to try to hurt her — not that she really *needed* protection—was that Vampires, despite the fact that they didn't breathe frequently enough to *not* appear dead while they were still, looked strangely peaceful while they slept.

The usual waves of energy, the concealed aggression and underlying predatory way in which they appeared was nonexistent while they slept. Instead, they gave off waves of calm and peace. It was like watching a baby sleep, something that you could just sit there and do indefinitely as though time didn't exist.

Or perhaps, that was just what it was like to watch *him* while he slept.

Sam jumped slightly when she heard the sudden rustle from the phone.

"Hello?" came a groggy voice from the other end of the line. Sam paused for a moment, imagining that the noise of his phone ringing must have woken him. She could picture him in his room, completely in shadow, the heavy black curtains that framed his windows pulled shut, lying in his bed with the duvet crumpled around him and she felt—not for the first time in the past week—an immense amount of guilt, tinged only slightly with longing. "Sam?... Is everything okay?"

"Aleczander called," she said, with an intake of breath that closely mimicked the sound of a yawn.

"Oh?" He didn't sound nearly as excited as Sam had always thought he would be the moment they heard back from Aleczander. But she supposed, after waiting for so long, and with everything that had been going on lately, Jamie meeting his Sire had kind of fallen down a few notches on the priority scale.

"He wants us to meet him in an hour, you think you can get here before then?"

Jamie laughed a little. "I could be there right now if you wanted, I wouldn't be in a presentable state . . . but I'd be there."

Sam half smiled. "Okay, well you have an hour to get yourself to a more presentable state. You think you can manage that in *only* an hour?"

"Oh . . . I'm not sure . . . I might have to skip the lipstick today, but I'm sure Aleczander won't mind."

Sam laughed. "Okay, text me when you get here otherwise you'll wake everyone up."

"Are you saying I can't sneak into your house without waking everyone up?"

"No," Sam said, shaking her head even though he couldn't see her do it.

"Challenge accepted."

"That wasn't a challenge!" Sam said, then turned swiftly to look in Jade's direction when she stirred in her sleep. She whispered into the phone. "Just text me when you get here."

She hung up before Jamie had a chance to say anything in response. Then she got out of bed and started getting herself ready, careful not to wake Jade as she did.

# CHAPTER 34

The sun had barely risen and the sky was completely overcast in dull grey clouds, meaning that although it was daytime, the dullness—and the fact that it was so early—provided Jamie with just enough cover to not be seen as he climbed up the front of Sam's house.

Her window was unlocked, as she always kept it. He'd never checked the front door, but she may have always kept that unlocked too; because she had the house warded against intruders there was no real need for her to keep everything secure. Except of course, that keeping things open meant that Jamie could sneak in to her house quite easily.

He pulled himself up and peered in through a gap in the curtains where he could see Jade's dark hair spilled out across Sam's pillows. Sam wasn't there, but when he listened carefully, he could hear the sound of water falling in the bathroom.

Putting all of his effort into being as soundless as Jack when he appeared out of nowhere, Jamie pulled the window open slowly, keeping his eyes on Jade the whole time, being sure not to wake her. When the window was open just wide enough, he climbed inside, landing carefully and lightly on his feet.

Once inside, he closed the window, making it look as though he had simply materialised out of nowhere. He sat himself down on the chair by Sam's desk, with his legs stretched out in front of him, half resting on the end of the bed, his ankles crossed, and waited patiently for Sam to finish her shower.

Barely five minutes had passed when the door opened, unleashing a cloud of steam, out of which Sam emerged with a towel wrapped around her body, strands of wet hair clinging to her shoulders. Jamie looked away only slightly, he hadn't expected her to walk out in nothing but a towel and the sight of her like that made him feel a mix of things, one of which was shyness.

It took a moment for Sam to notice he was there, but he knew she'd seen him when she jumped and stopped walking, her body suddenly completely rigid, her eyes wide with surprise. After a few moments, her expression of shock turned to one of annoyance, and she pulled the towel tightly around herself, gripping the top of it with both hands to keep it secured.

Jamie smiled at her, trying not to let her see that he was taking mental photographs of her dressed in her towel. "Challenge met," he said triumphantly, uncrossing his legs and setting his feet on the floor.

"It wasn't a challenge!" she hissed, looking in Jade's direction for just a moment as if to make sure the noise hadn't woken her. Which it wouldn't have, Jamie could tell from the rhythmic beating of her heart, and the depth of her breathing, that Jade was *completely* unconscious. It would take something a lot louder than whispering to wake her up.

"Strange," he said with a smile. "Because it *sounded* like a challenge."

She scoffed, and walked forward, stopping right next to him where she pulled her closet open and starting searching inside. "Stop watching me," she said without looking at him.

"Why?" he asked, his eyes taking in the entire image of her, water droplets running from her hair onto her neck and down her shoulders, her bare arms hugging the towel so tight that she may as well have not had it at all.

"Because I'm basically naked, and it's weird to stare at someone when they're not dressed." She stepped away from her closet, with clothes thrown over one of her arms.

"I like the basically naked look on you though . . . you should dress like this more often."

Sam glared at him, but didn't respond.

He smiled. "Would it make you feel better if I wore a towel too?"

"You're not funny." She turned and walked away from him, storming across the room quickly, back into the bathroom where she gave him one last glare, before she closed the door.

Leaving him to wait for her once again.


The second time she emerged from the bathroom, she was dressed in a pair of well fitted grey jeans and a long white t-shirt. Her hair was dried and had a slight wave to it, and she wore it brushed over one shoulder, Jamie noticed for the first time that there was no longer a scar on her neck from where she'd been bitten.

"Awww," Jamie said, feigning disappointment. "I liked you in the towel."

Sam glared in his direction. He had never really noticed it before, but her glares seemed to feel more aggressive when she wore make up. Perhaps it was the black outline that framed her eyes that made the glare appear more lethal. "You're still not funny," she said as she sat, cross-legged, on the floor and slipped her feet into a pair of black ankle boots.

"I wasn't being funny," Jamie said with sincerity. "Seriously, my offer for you to see me mostly naked stands should you ever wish to call me on it."

She stopped lacing up her boots for a moment, to look at him, her mouth twitched slightly as if she was trying not to laugh or smile, or give him any kind of expression that may encourage him.

"Remember the conversation we had the other day?"

Jamie leaned back in his chair. "I mostly remember the parts of the conversation that we *didn't* have."

"Like what?"

"Well, there was the part where you basically admitted that you love me, by not admitting that you *don't*."

"Yeah, see, I mostly remember the part where I said I'm all for casual encounters and I didn't want you to make it weird. I also don't remember saying *that*, mostly because *I didn't say that*."

"Alright, then let's test it, shall we?"

Sam sighed and rolled her eyes, she stood up and walked over to him. Jamie caught his breath as she leaned forward, looking him directly in the eyes as she did. A slow smile crept across her face, as she reached behind him. Then she pulled her jacket off the back of the chair.

"How do you plan to test it?" she asked, her eyes glittering with the amusement she clearly felt at his expense as she stepped away from him. He let a breath and gazed at her.

Sam knew what he felt, and yet, the only time she ever

acknowledged his feelings was when she could use them to get an amusing reaction from him.

If Jamie didn't know her as he did, he would have found her behaviour towards him to be quite callous and vindictive. But it was because of the fact that he *knew* she did have feelings for him that he overlooked how she was. Choosing — instead of getting angry or upset about how she acted towards him — to attempt luring a confession from her.

"Just a test," Jamie said as he stood and wrapped his arm around her waist, pulling her backwards into the bathroom, closing the door once they were both inside.

Sam looked at him in confusion. "*How* is *this* a test?"

"The test hasn't started yet."

Jamie walked forward, until he had Sam pressed against the bathroom door.

Sam let a sigh and rolled her eyes. "You really do have an obsession with having me pinned to a wall, don't you?"

Jamie smiled widely. "Well, I wouldn't mind if you pinned me to the wall . . . but you never seem to try. So here we are."

He wrapped both of his arms around her waist and pulled her in closely. So closely he could feel her heart beating in his own chest, which was a sensation he liked. He enjoyed feeling the thrumming of her heart against his ribs. Enjoyed the way it beat slightly harder the closer he held her. Pressing her body to his, he put his hand under her chin and tilted her face upwards, so that they were looking eye to eye.

Her pulse sped slightly, and he smiled as she set her lips in a worried line. "I heard that," he whispered.

"I *will* punch you."

"Why would you punch me?" he asked as he moved in slowly. Taking his time in his movements, which caused her heart to thrum faster.

"Don't," she whispered. Jamie froze where he was, his

mouth barely a centimetre from hers.

"Why?" he asked, his lips brushing against hers as they moved.

Sam put both of her hands on his chest and pushed him away from her. He let his hands slide from her waist as he moved back. "Because I said so." Without waiting for another second to pass, she opened the door and stepped into her room. Pausing for a moment when she saw Danny standing on the other side of the door.

He folded his arms across his chest and looked at Sam, then moved his glare over her shoulder to Jamie, who was still standing in the middle of the bathroom.

"What are you doing in here?" Sam asked, her tone more irritated than angry.

"I'm all out of toothpaste, wanted to know if I could borrow some," Danny said, without taking his eyes off Jamie for even a moment. "It's seven thirty . . . what is *he* doing *here* . . . in *your* room at *this* time?"

"Oh my Gods," Sam said with an irritated sigh as she shoved past him, over to the end of her bed, where she'd left her jacket lying.

"Was he here all night?"

"Yes," Sam said sarcastically. "He was here all night. We were having lots and lots of outrageous sex while Jade was sleeping right there."

"Not funny Sam," Danny said seriously, then turned back to Jamie. "*You*, you're not welcome here."

"Um . . . " Jamie shifted uncomfortably. He wasn't sure if he should speak, or if doing so would just make Danny hate him more.

"Yes he is," Sam said as she zipped her jacket up halfway. Danny looked at Sam, his mouth opened as if he was about to speak, but Sam got there first. "*I* have been living in this house for longer than *you*. *I* paid the bills for the past year and a half. *I* took care of *our* grandfather, while you couldn't be bothered to come home. So *I* get to decide who is and isn't allowed in this house."

"Bu—"

"No," Sam cut him off again. She grabbed her bag up from the floor. "Come on Jamie, we're going. Toothpaste is in there." She indicated to the bathroom.

Jamie stepped out, and moved awkwardly trying to avoid any physical contact with Danny who stood there stoically, glaring at him.

Once he was clear, he moved quickly, following Sam out of her room and down the stairs.

"Where are you going?" Danny demanded. Jamie turned to find him standing at the top of the stairs.

"We're going to see Aleczander," Sam sighed with impatience as she walked down the hall instead of out the front door. Jamie followed her.

"More Vampires!" Danny yelled. "Why can't you just *try* to be normal? You know, maybe if you *tried* people would stop dying!"

Sam stopped by a door at the end of the hallway, next to the kitchen. She turned and gave Danny a stony glare, but said nothing. Jamie could tell by the expression on her face, that what he'd said had upset her, and she was trying really hard not to let it show.

She spun back around abruptly and opened the door, revealing another set of stairs which she stormed down.

Jamie turned to Danny. "That wasn't fair," he said. Danny shot him an irate glare. "It's not her fault that people die."

"No," Danny said, his voice sounding calmer than his expression looked. "It's only her fault that certain people die."

Without another word, Danny stalked back up the stairs.

Jamie stared after him for a moment, feeling slightly guilty, and helpless. Wishing that Sam and Danny could have the kind of relationship that he'd had with his brother.

# CHAPTER 35

$\mathcal{A}$dmitting to his fear was not something that Elliot was prone to do, but as he lay on the bed in his locked hotel room gazing at the ceiling with unseeing eyes, it was difficult to pretend that he wasn't freaking out a little.

Bodies were something that he was used to seeing.

He saw them when he woke and when he slept.

Both with his eyes and within his mind.

Every miniscule part of his existence was tainted.

There were very few people in the world that Elliot cared about even a little, or at all really, so maybe caring wasn't exactly what it was.

There were very few people in the world whose existence that Elliot could tolerate. And as of last night, that number had become somewhat smaller than it had been the day before.

Bodies.

More bodies.

Always. More. Bodies.

The stupid taint never seemed to have its fill.

No matter how many it consumed it was never enough.

It was never satisfied.

It always wanted more.

One more.

Two more.

Twenty more . . .

There had been so many that Elliot couldn't count them if he tried. All of their faces were the same in the end.

The blank masks of puppets. Empty shells that only served to host a portion of the taint. A heart filled with Shadows. A body without a soul or any will of its own.

All the same.

None that he would be likely to remember.

But last night . . .

He closed his eyes and shivered as he recalled the scenes of his home.

They were two faces he would never forget.

*<Od ot krow evah uoy. Gnilkrad elttil, gniod uoy era tahw.>*

Elliot gritted his teeth at the intrusion. Not opening his eyes he replied. "Well I don't really feel like it right now."

The moment he spoke a shiver shot down his spine and an icy feeling exploded within his chest. A Power unlike anything else pressed against the walls of his room.

Shadows seeped from the corners of the ceiling, darkening

the room and dimming the lights as their presence grew. Elliot sat up on the bed and pulled his legs up, his knees pulled into his chest so as to not make any physical contact with the taint which grew in volume to mirror the anger of Kon, the mind controlling the puppets.

In a voice much louder and intrusive than before, Kon snarled within Elliot's mind, *<Teluma eht em gnirb won. Eno elttil em yebosid ot ton llew od dluow uoy.>*

Elliot frowned deeply, glaring at the Shadows that swirled mindlessly around the edges of the room. Why — of all the things in the whole universe — would this almighty being want such a pointless, powerless artefact.

He was so confused by the request that he couldn't help but voice his question aloud.

The answer came in a flash of images, slow at first but speeding up every second, one after another, image after image after image.

What he was seeing — what he was being shown — was terrible; ideas and thoughts too horrible to share. Plans and schemes so dark he couldn't fathom how they would or even could benefit anyone.

His eyes grew wide when the final image came.

A complete, all consuming darkness.

But this was not the black of an empty mind.

The darkness was part of the plan.

The final act.

For the first time in his entire life, Elliot was appalled.

*<Teluma eht deen I.>*

# CHAPTER 36

$\mathcal{J}$t had been precisely one week since Malachi's encounter with Sam, and although he'd heard that she was in fact still living, he couldn't help worrying over how long that was likely to last.

Despite his attempts to keep whatever Dark Magic was inside that chest locked away, the evil seemed to have spilled out, not only causing a scenario where Sam had to use an immortality ritual to survive being drained by a Vampire, but now the town appeared to be plagued with people acting strangely. Not to mention the murder of a practicing Witch, which looked, as the police had said in their reports, like some kind of satanic ritual.

It was because of his concerns over these happenings that Malachi had agreed to meet with Madison, despite the fact that they were supposed to have the most minimal of contact.

But he supposed he owed her one after she had given him a cover story for his trip to visit Sam in person.

He'd agreed to meet her early in the morning when there wouldn't be many people around. He was at a diner in the centre of town, perusing through the breakfast menu when she walked in. He didn't have to look up to know that she had arrived. In the many years he'd been living he'd learned to sense when anyone with even the slightest amount of Power was near.

Malachi sat up straighter as she approached, looking over her shoulder as if she expected to have been followed. Which she wouldn't have been for two reasons. Firstly, when people had covert meetings they usually did it at night in isolated areas. Meeting a woman for breakfast wasn't unusual . . . especially when you had previously shared a bed with that woman.

Secondly, there were none on the side that Madison currently occupied — that of the Witches — who were aware that they had any connection whatsoever.

"Good morning," he said as she took a seat across from him. He handed her a menu.

"What . . . the hell . . . is happening?" she asked, wasting no time, she leaned in as she spoke so that she could keep her voice low.

Malachi sighed and ran his hand through his hair. "I honestly don't know."

Madison scoffed and sat back, folding her arms across her chest. "*Sure.*"

"Honestly," Malachi insisted. "I heard about Jessie."

Madison's expression went still, her mouth set in a tight line, her eyes cast down. "It was *horrible,* I saw the basement."

"You got in?"

She nodded her head. "I went when you said, but Sam was there, so I waited until they left . . . they're probably trying to figure out what's going on too."

"What was it like?"

Madison shook her head, strands of her strawberry coloured hair falling in front of her face, she huffed irritably and brushed the hair away from her eyes. "It was like nothing I've ever seen, or even *heard* of. There were runes . . . I *think* they were runes, painted all over the walls with *blood*."

Malachi nodded. He'd managed to get a look at the crime scene photos, and although he recognised the symbols as runes—as they were clearly magical in some way—he couldn't identify them either. "Did you *feel* anything while you were there?"

Madison sighed. "There was something cold, and heavy, and sick and . . . I don't know, *evil*. But I mean, the people—"

"People? What people?"

"People are acting weird. It's like they're going crazy or something, they're acting—"

Outside there was a loud crash. Both Malachi and Madison looked out the window, where there was blue car and a red car mashed into one another. The drivers both got out of their vehicles, and started shouting *loudly* over whose fault it was, and who would pay for the repairs. Before Malachi had a chance to blink, the argument broke into a fist fight.

"Like that?" he finished.

Madison sighed. "Not just that. The violence has been a *lot* worse. This is a quiet town, violence on this level just doesn't happen as often as it has been. I mean, I told you about what happened at the high school, right?"

Malachi nodded his head, he remembered clearly enough Madison's descriptions of the events from the brief phone conversation they'd managed to have earlier in the week. From what he recalled, the level of violence that had broken out among the number of people involved . . . she was right, for a town like this it was highly unusual and perhaps the events deserved closer investigation than they were currently receiving.

She sighed heavily and sat back in her chair, folding her arms across her chest. "I don't know . . . There's something wrong . . . It's like people aren't themselves anymore."

# CHAPTER 37

$\mathcal{J}$amie stepped through the portal into an immense cavern made of sandstone. There was a giant opening to his left, out of which he could see clear skies of dark blue, glistening with silver dots of starlight. Outside, there was no light pollution, so he knew without getting too close to the opening that they were somewhere far from civilisation, and he wondered, briefly, if there were only Vampires residing in this dimension or if it was shared.

Jamie turned as he felt Sam appear behind him. He didn't look at her as she stepped through the portal; using it unnerved him enough as it was and he thought that seeing someone appear from thin air might just be the thing to send him over the edge.

"You should see it from the outside," she said, following his gaze to the opening. "It's a castle carved out of a mountain."

"Really?"

"Yeah, and in this dimension it's always night, the sky

varies in shades of blue, but there is no sun."

"Huh." Jamie took a step back. "Is that why the Vampires chose to live here?"

Sam laughed slightly as she shook her head. "That's not how dimensions work," she said. "Dimensions are built by people, and they're built to certain specifications. So if someone wants a world with no sun, that's what they'll get."

"Oh." Jamie nodded his head despite the fact that he didn't quite understand. Magic was confusing, and no matter how many people tried to explain things to him his brain just couldn't grasp the mechanics of it.

"Come—" Sam paused as the air shimmered behind her and a girl with long wavy pink hair stumbled into existence. She was wearing a white dress with a full underskirt that was the same shade as her hair. Around her waist was a tightly pulled corset.

"I don't feel well," the girl said as she stood up straight, one hand on her forehead the other clasping at her stomach. Jamie stepped forward to help her but froze when he recognised her face.

"*What* are you wearing?" Sam asked, laughing at the sight of the girl.

Victoria glared at her, though the expression couldn't be taken seriously when she was wearing an oversized bow on her head. "It's called kawaii Lolita, and I look *adorable!*" she huffed and folded her arms across her chest. "What are you —" Victoria paused as her gaze slipped from Sam over to him. Her large brown eyes grew even larger as she appeared to recognise him. She mouthed something, then smiled widely, apparently thrilled to see him, then ran at him and yelled, "Puppy!"

Victoria jumped, wrapping her arms around his neck and her legs around his waist. Jamie stood rigid, his arms by his sides with his fist clenched tightly.

"Puppy?" Sam gave Jamie a questioning look as she laughed uncontrollably.

Jamie looked straight at Sam. He wasn't sure what kind of expression he was wearing on his face, but it seemed to sober her laughter instantly. She raised an eyebrow curiously, now looking slightly concerned. "Get. Her. *Off*. Me," he whispered.

"Victoria," Sam said, stepping forward. Reaching her hand out to the smaller girl. "Come on, let him go."

"No!" Victoria yelled, nuzzling her face into his neck. "He's *mine*, I missed him forever! But he came home to me!"

Jamie kept his hands by his sides, his fists clenched so tightly that his nails bit into his skin. He wanted to push her off him so badly, but didn't because he knew that if he put his hands on her once, he wouldn't stop until he knew she was dead.

"Victoria," Sam said warningly. "Let go."

"Get her off!" Jamie yelled.

Sam shot him an impatient glare. "I'm *trying!*"

Sam wrapped her arms around Victoria's waist and attempted to pull her off him, but she just gripped him tighter, squealing slightly in the high pitched voice of a stubborn child.

Jamie couldn't keep himself still any longer. "*Get off!*" A bubble of anger rose up from his stomach and before he knew what he was doing, he had placed both his hands on Victoria's shoulders and shoved her — as hard as he could — which sent her flying through the air and into the wall on the far end of the cavern.

The sandstone wall cracked where she'd hit. Jamie stared at the dark lines separating the stone, breathing hard despite the fact that he needed no air, he watched as the cracks grew and spread, small pieces of stone and dust falling to the ground.

As he watched the tiny pieces of debris fall, he imagined that more would follow, the wall would shake loose stones, then rocks, then boulders. All of which would bury Victoria alive, if they didn't crush her fir —

"*Jamie!*" He gazed at Sam, barely focused on her until he noticed that her indigo eyes were wide with shock as she stared at him as if he had committed a heinous crime.

He blinked and turned his attention to Victoria, who had slid down to the floor on the other side of the room, her skirt puffed up around her, she stared at him with fearful eyes, which made him hate her more. "It's her fault!" he yelled.

Sam jogged across the room and helped Victoria to her feet. Jamie could see tears falling from her eyes and down her cheeks, the sight of which made him feel guilty, and yet more angry with her at the same time. *What right did she have to be upset?*

"I'm sorry," Victoria said, her bottom lip shaking as she spoke. "I'm sorry about the time I tried to kill you, but you get to live forever now so it's okay, right?"

Jamie stared at her for a moment. "You *murdered* my family."

Victoria whimpered. "I'm *sorry.*"

Jamie turned his back to her, no longer feeling he could look at her and *not* hurt her some more.

He heard Sam let a heavy sigh. "Walk straight through that tunnel," Sam ordered, pointing straight ahead. "I'll walk back here with Vikki."

Jamie didn't question that Sam used a nickname to address Victoria, he assumed it was because they knew each other. And why wouldn't they? Sam had said that she'd lived here for a short time as a child. Jamie didn't speak at all, he simply moved forward with Sam following behind him with the girl he'd made cry.

Outside, he could hear that a storm had started.

# CHAPTER 38

*Y*ou *killed his family?>* Sam thought to Victoria, while simultaneously projecting a map of the tunnels into Jamie's head. He walked at least ten steps ahead of them, not turning back, or even asking Victoria if she was alright.

*<I thought I killed him too>* Victoria thought back, as if that was justification. *<It was so long ago . . . do you think he'd feel better if I said sorry again?>*

*<I really don't think it will help>* Sam thought. *<I've never seen him look so angry, I think he's trying as hard as he can to not kill you right now>*

*<I won't tell Aleczander he pushed me>* Victoria assured. Sam was glad that she'd brought it up first. Aleczander could be the nicest person you'd ever met . . . until the moment you said or did anything to hurt Victoria, who was practically like his younger sibling. Sometimes even so much as a sideways glance in her direction was enough to set him off.

*<Thanks>* Sam replied.

Victoria let a sigh and pulled the pink wig from her head, her long auburn hair spilling down over her shoulders in messy waves.

"Why are you dressed like that anyway?" Sam asked aloud, knowing that this was a conversation Jamie wouldn't be hurt by overhearing.

"I was at a party with my friends."

Sam looked at Victoria curiously. "I didn't know you had friends outside of here."

Victoria nodded her head. "It's a recent thing. I met them about two years ago. Anyway . . . one of them just turned nineteen, so we had a party. We broke her out of her room and brought her out to a nightclub . . . and we all wore these costumes," she laughed. "Because it's always fun to play dress up."

"Okay . . . *why* did you have to break her out of her room?" Sam asked curiously, wondering what kind of parent grounded their kid on their birthday.

"She's in a sort of witness protection thing, and her bodyguard is very strict about her coming into contact with people he doesn't know. You should have seen the look on his face when he tracked us down." She giggled again. "He was not at all impressed." She frowned and muttered more to herself than to Sam, "I had to stay with a coven 'til sundown."

"Witness protection?" Sam asked incredulously. "You know someone in witness protection?"

Victoria sighed. "*No* . . . I said it was sort of like witness protection. There's some guy who's pissed at her dad and he's trying to kill her or something, it happens to her a lot, but her dad kind of over reacted, so he's hidden her away somewhere. I mean *really*, it's not like she can't handle it herself. People try to kill her all the time . . . she's kind of like you," she added thoughtfully. "Except nicer to be around."

"*Thanks,*" Sam mumbled, trying not to be offended.

"So what are *you* doing here?"

"Aleczander wanted to see Jamie."

Victoria tilted her head to the side, and gazed at her curiously. "Why? Did he do something wrong?"

"No," Sam said with a laugh, wondering why Aleczander hadn't told Victoria about Jamie. "Aleczander is his Sire, and Jamie—"

"Wait, wait . . . *what?*"

"Aleczander Turned Jamie."

"*When?* Was this *before* or *after* I tried to kill him?"

Sam winced and stole a glance at Jamie who had stopped walking. He was clenching and unclenching his hands by his sides.

"I'm not sure," Sam admitted. Feeling slightly guilty that she'd never bothered to ask Jamie how he'd been Turned. She knew it was Aleczander who did it, but not how it happened.

"While you had me here," Jamie replied as he started walking again.

Victoria spoke quietly. "Have you ever had your heart broken and smashed into tiny little pieces by someone you loved more than anything?"

Jamie looked back over her shoulder, his expression curious. "Someone hurt me . . . " she continued. "And then I heard that Kraven wanted you and your family dead . . . so I said I'd do it."

"Because someone hurt you?"

"Yes," she said. "Someone who cared about you more than anything. And I wanted to hurt him by hurting what he loved."

Jamie opened his mouth to speak, but was interrupted by a man who stepped out through one of the doors that lined the walls.

"Ah," the man said. Sam looked at his face and recognised him immediately. She could tell by the fearful glance he sent in her direction that Claudio recognised her too. "He's waiting for you through here." Claudio stepped aside, allowing Jamie space to walk past him. Jamie looked back at Sam for a moment, a silent invitation for her to follow.

Sam looked at Victoria for a moment. "Later."

Victoria smiled and nodded, before she waved goodbye to Jamie—who completely avoided looking at her—and continued making her way down the hallway.

Sam followed Jamie into the room, ignoring the fact that Claudio flinched away from her as she got closer.

It didn't matter. Fear was something she was used to.

Most other supernatural beings only had two feelings towards her, either they hated her or feared her. The rest were completely indifferent and the ones who liked her hardly counted because they were such a small minority.

# CHAPTER 39

$\mathcal{J}$amie stepped inside the room slowly, feeling an immense amount of relief now that Victoria was gone.

The door closed as soon as Sam entered behind him, he looked back over his shoulder to see if Claudio had followed.

He hadn't.

Which was to be expected given the way he'd looked at Sam when he'd seen her. He stared as if he were looking into the face of a grim reaper who was reaching out with a skeletal hand.

Jamie didn't understand it.

Sam was Sam.

Yes, she had Power, a *lot* of Power. He knew that better than anyone, the traces of it had burned through his veins for days after he'd tasted her blood. At first it hurt, but now it was nothing more than a dull electrical current that had mingled with his own blood and subsided to a point that he could barely notice it anymore.

But even with the amount of Power she had, she was nothing to fear . . . not in the way Claudio seemed to anyway.

He'd known her for long enough to know that she wasn't cursed as Claudio and some other people believed she was.

She was simply Sam.

Sam placed a hand on Jamie's shoulder and urged him forward. He moved slowly, with some reluctance. Over the past few months his desire, as well as his need, to meet his Sire had slowly worn down. This meeting had taken so long to organise that he was now at a stage where he felt there was no real reason for him to meet Aleczander.

And what would he even say to the man?

Jamie eyed him carefully; he was right there, sitting at the head of a very large table. Around it there were at least thirty chairs. He looked exactly as Jamie remembered. He was still pale, so much so that blue veins were visible through the skin on his neck. His hair was still the same copperish blonde colour, it was cut shorter than Jamie remembered, but was still long.

"Jamie?" he asked. Even his accent was the same as it had been before. Jamie would have thought after so long the Germanic accent would have become diluted, but then, if Aleczander spent most of his time away from humans there was no one for him to adjust his speech to.

Jamie nodded his head. "I apologise for leaving you as I did," Aleczander started. Sam pulled Jamie forward as she walked over to the table. She pulled out the chair beside Aleczander and nodded at him. Jamie reluctantly sat down, and Sam took the one beside him. "You were supposed to be killed," he continued. "And if anyone knew you had not been, both you and I, and even Victoria would have suffered for it."

"Why didn't you just let them kill me?" Jamie asked. He hadn't wanted to come for apologies or explanations, but now that he was here, and the subject was being discussed he couldn't help asking the thing he'd been wondering about since the moment he'd awoken as a Vampire.

Aleczander let a sigh and looked away as he seemed to think about his answer. "I did not and do not know why they wanted you dead, usually I would not have interfered . . . but when I saw how you struggled against the Vampire tricks, how strong your will was to be able to resist . . . I am not sure. I suppose I felt that someone who was fighting so hard to survive should be given the chance to live. And I thought that someone with a will like yours would have the ability to navigate the world alone."

Aleczander smiled at him. "And I was correct, for here you are, alive and well."

"More or less," Jamie said with a shrug. Forcing an attitude of nonchalance as he'd come to the realisation—from what had been said to him today—that people had wanted him dead for longer than just the past few months. And that knowledge disturbed him more than he cared to show.

Aleczander leaned forward in his chair, his hands clasped on the table in front of him. "Claudio told me that you had not come into contact with a single Vampire since you left here."

Jamie nodded his head.

"He also said you lost the one you Sired?"

Jamie felt Sam look at him in surprise and he realised that he'd never told her about the ones he'd lost . . . but it wasn't as though she'd asked to know anything about his life either. Again, he nodded his head.

"My condolences."

Jamie laughed slightly. "It was a very long time ago . . . it hardly matters anymore."

Aleczander nodded. "So was there anything specific that

you wished to discuss with me, or did you simply want to meet?"

"Um . . . " Jamie ran a hand through his hair. "There *were* some things I wanted to know, but Sam pretty much explained everything to me already, so . . . " He shrugged.

Aleczander nodded his head and smiled kindly. "So, at this point, whether we had met or not would not have made much difference."

Jamie smiled, and nodded. "Sorry."

"Apologies are unnecessary," he said, his eyes shifting over Jamie assessingly. "I see you have an amulet."

"Oh." Jamie looked down at the ring on his right hand. "Yeah . . . Sam gave it to me, then she pushed me into the sun."

"I didn't push, I opened the curtains." She turned to Aleczander. "You should have seen how fast he got under the table."

Aleczander's mouth twitched slightly as he regarded the ring. "They are against the law."

Jamie looked at his ring, then to Sam who was smiling proudly. "I'm immune to everyone's laws," she said. "Witch Law, Coven Law, Demon Law, Vampire Law . . . the laws of physics."

Aleczander laughed slightly.

"Do I have to give it back?" he asked Aleczander.

He regarded Jamie for a moment. "We do not allow them to be owned by Vampires because it can cause problems with daylight attacks."

"Really?"

"It has been known to happen. But if it comes down to laws, and whether or not you need to abide by them, the question becomes a matter of allegiances."

"Allegiances?" Jamie gave Sam a questioning glance, before

he turned his attention back to Aleczander. "Are you at war or something?"

"Not currently," he said, his expression serious. "Though it is not military allegiances I am speaking of. *This*," he directed around him, "is the Vampire Kingdom. Here, I am currently in rule of over three thousand Vampires."

"Wow . . . " Jamie let a breath. "That's a *lot*."

Aleczander smiled. "It is only two thirds of the Vampire population. The idea of this place is for us all to unite as one force, if we stay together we are safer. Safe when it comes to those who wish us harm, such as Vampire Hunters. In return for the protection of the group, all that is asked is abiding by the laws. Those who are not allied with me, are alone, and they are usually found and harmed quite easily."

"So then soon," Jamie said, "when all the ones alone are killed off, you're in control of everyone."

Aleczander smiled once more. Seeming amused by Jamie's words. "Not at all. There are always more being made, they are alone, or allied, or they form groups of their own."

"So if I agree to be allied with you, I have to give up my ring because it's against the law?"

Aleczander nodded his head.

Jamie looked at his ring for a moment, then at Aleczander. "Who are your allies? Apart from the other Vampires."

"We are a neutral party," Aleczander said. "We are allied with all sides, and with none."

"Okay, so if I'm allied with you and a Warlock or someone attacked Sam, I couldn't do anything helpful?"

Aleczander looked at Jamie in confusion, then at Sam, then back again. "I do not understand."

"You're a neutral party, so if someone were to attack Sam, or declare war on her, there's nothing you could, or *would* do to help. And if I were to be allied with you, I could do nothing to help or it would be like claiming that we're on her side."

"The good of the many," Aleczander said carefully. "Although I care a great deal for Sam, there would be nothing I could do to help her. Not outright."

"Then no thanks," he said with a smile. "I think I'd rather be immune to Witch Law, Coven Law, Demon Law, Vampire Law and the laws of physics."

Sam grinned widely. "It's the best way to be."

"And besides, I'm pretty much the only friend she has anyway."

Sam scowled, then stuck her tongue out at him. Aleczander chuckled. "Sam has a great deal more friends than she is even aware of," he said. "We are neutral, yes, but should there come a time when war breaks out again, she would be surprised," he turned, and looked directly at Sam, "just how many people, us included, would follow her willingly into battle."

Jamie jumped slightly at the sudden sound of a knock at the door. The sharpness of it reverberated through the mostly empty room. He turned to look at it curiously. The door opened slightly and Claudio peered inside. "Pardonnez-moi," he said, eyeing Sam anxiously before he continued speaking. "Ishani is here to see you."

Aleczander sighed, dropping his head momentarily. "Of course." He looked at Jamie. "You have made your choice then, but should you ever wish to reconsider, Sam can give you my telephone number."

Jamie nodded. "Okay."

Aleczander stood, and Jamie followed suit, walking a step behind with Sam as they moved towards the door.

"Tell Eva I said hi," Sam said as they reached the door, about to step through it.

Aleczander smiled slightly. "You could tell her yourself."

"Mmm," Sam looked thoughtful for a moment. "I *would*, but I should really get home."

He laughed slightly. "Why is it that I seem to be the *only* person who can bear to have discussions with my wife?"

Sam shrugged. "Maybe it helps that you get to see her naked."

Aleczander almost choked on his laughter. "Blunt as ever."

She gave him a mocking salute. "I remain forever constant."

"Actually—" Jamie started his disagreement—Sam was anything but constant, her personality and her attitude changed more frequently than the weather—but he was cut off by Sam shushing him.

He looked up as a tall, slender woman walked towards Aleczander, pausing momentarily when she saw there were other people with him. "Aleczander," she said. Jamie noticed that she spoke with a thick Indian accent.

"Ishani," he replied. "This is Jamie, a fledgling of mine, and of course, Sam." He turned to face Sam. "Ishani is helping me with some negotiations."

Sam raised an eyebrow. "Still doing Lycanthrope stuff?"

Jamie watched the woman carefully. Wondering how it was that Sam had determined she was a Lycanthrope. She looked perfectly human to his eyes . . . but then, so did Aleczander and Sam and Claudio. Even after all this time, he hadn't learned how to recognise other non-humans.

Ishani scoffed. "Situations like this one do *not* resolve simply, it takes a lot of time."

Aleczander moved away from the door, leaving room for Ishani to step through. "Mao should be here shortly," said Aleczander as Ishani brushed past Claudio, stepping behind Aleczander into the room that Jamie and Sam had just left.

"We'll leave you to your business then," Sam said as she started moving down the hallway.

Aleczander turned to Jamie for a moment and regarded him solemnly. "Be careful," he whispered. "Just because you have survived this long does not mean you will survive indefinitely."

"I don't—"

"Do not trust easily, and do not act without first thinking . . . Sam has my number should you ever need it, even if you do not wish to be allied, it is my duty as your Sire to assist you with personal matters should you ever require it."

"Um . . . okay."

Without another word, Aleczander turned and walked into the room. Closing the door behind him. When Jamie glanced back around, Sam was already gone.

# CHAPTER 40

*I*t was barely past nine a.m. by the time Sam got home. She and Jamie took the portal from the Vampire Kingdom back to the portal in her basement. Once they came through she was sure to deactivate it, she didn't want anything sneaking through while she wasn't home.

Jamie was quiet for most of their walk through the Kingdom; she'd offered him a tour of the castle, and asked him if he wanted to climb down the mountain and view it from the forests. He declined, seeming as though he was only half paying attention to begin with.

He didn't speak when they reached the basement, or while they walked up the stairs. The only words he'd spoken to her was when he said 'goodbye' before he walked to the door and let himself out.

For a moment, she simply stood in the hallway and watched the door, wondering if she'd done something wrong, or if he was still upset about seeing Victoria. Somewhere in the back of her mind, she knew that she should probably follow him out, ask him what was wrong and get him to talk about it. But by the time that thought had even come into her mind it had been too late. He would have been halfway home.

So instead she simply walked up to her room. Finding Jade awake and dressed, lounging on Sam's bed with a magazine in her hand.

"Are you *ever* going home?" Sam asked with a smile.

Jade scrunched her nose up, as if the idea of returning home repulsed her. "No," she said. "I live with you now."

"Everything okay?"

"Yeah," said Jade, waving her hand dismissively. "Usual stuff, bitch being a bitch. Been creeping me out lately, so I figure I'll steer clear for a while."

"Wha—"

"I'm thinking about getting my hair cut," she announced out of nowhere, completely changing the subject. Jade put a hand to her long brown hair, a self-conscious expression on her face.

Sam smiled slightly. "Didn't you *just* have extensions put in?"

She walked over to the bed and sat down next to Jade, who pulled her legs in tightly, resting her elbows on her knees. "That was like a *month* ago. I'm bored of long hair . . . I want something new and awesome."

"What were you thinking?"

"How did I look as Cleopatra?"

Sam laughed. "That's about half the length of your hair . . . and you *never* have bangs."

"I know," Jade said. "But I looked good in that wig, right?"

"You looked amazing."

"It's settled then." She clapped her hands together, and gave Sam a devious smile. "Do it."

"Wait, you want *me* to do it?"

Jade gave her a sideways glance. "Who does your hair?"

" . . . I do," Sam answered carefully. " . . . With Magic."

"Then do mine."

"I've never done that on another person, what if I ruin it forever?"

"Then you better find a really good hiding place 'cause I'd have to *murder* you." She laughed. "You are the almighty Sam . . . so stop being a bitch and fix this mess!" She pointed at her hair, which was as far from a mess as a hairstyle could get.

"*Fine*," she said with a dramatic sigh.

Jade grinned, showing her teeth, and closed the magazine she had been flicking through so she could scoot herself forward. "Okay, work some Magic."

Sam sighed and stepped forward. "I need you to picture what you want it to look like *really* clearly. Like, form a picture of it in your head and think it loudly."

Jade nodded her head and closed her eyes. Sam placed both of her hands on her; one on her forehead, the other on the back of her head. Sam closed her eyes and reached into Jade's mind, taking the image that she was forming inside and pulling it into her own thoughts, projecting it forward with a small amount of Power. For most projects, Sam had to let it out with force, but for cosmetic Magic, the gentler her projections, the better they worked.

That was something she'd learned quite a while ago.

She felt the image in her mind, and the Magic on her fingertips, travelling along the hair and willing it to form as Sam wanted it to.

After a moment, she stopped, opened her eyes and looked down at Jade who had her eyes shut tightly, her face in an expression of excitement and apprehension.

"Is it done?" she asked, keeping her eyes closed.

Sam stood for a moment, admiring her handiwork. Before Jade's hair had been a dark chocolate brown colour and was so long it touched her waist. Whereas now, it was jet black and just about an inch past her shoulders. As well as that, she had a bangs cut straight across her forehead resting just below her eyebrows.

"It looks weird," Sam said, and Jade's eyes shot open, her expression filled with fear. Sam held back a laugh. "Weird because it's different. But good . . . it suits you."

"Let me see!" Jade jumped off the bed and ran into the bathroom, leaving the door open as she admired her own reflection. "I *do* look good!" she said with a proud smile.

"You're welcome."

"You should open a salon," Jade said, running her fingers through her new hairstyle. "Seriously, you'd make a *fortune*."

"How has she been creeping you out?" Sam asked, as she leaned against the bathroom's doorframe.

Jade looked towards Sam in confusion. "What?"

"You said you don't want to go home because your mom's being creepy."

Jade laughed, though to Sam it sounded slightly forced. "Oh . . . *that?* No, it's nothing, you know?"

"No." Sam shook her head. "No offence, but your mom is a creep. I've felt something off with her for a while, and you know I've never trusted her."

Jade watched Sam as she spoke, her expression completely devoid of emotion.

Sam continued, "I'm not around her enough to notice if there's any major changes with her, but you are—"

"I'm *not* Magic," Jade said, her tone seeming slightly irate. "I don't *sense* things."

"Everyone senses things," Sam said. "You don't have to

have Magic to have instincts."

"She's my *mom*," Jade said finally, her eyes pleading, almost as if she thought Sam would do something to harm Hayley. The thought *had* crossed her mind, but she would never betray Jade like that.

"I'm not going to hurt her," Sam said, trying not to show how offended she was by Jade's implication. "But if there's something wrong, maybe I can help. But I can't do anything if you don't tell me what's going on."

Jade sighed and shook her head. "Forget about it," she said. "It's better just to leave her alone for a while."

"Bu—"

"Just drop it!" she yelled. "Not *every* problem can be solved by Magic!"

Sam's mouth snapped shut, the action cutting off her words before she even had a chance to speak them. Jade may have been human, but her mother wasn't. Therefore, whatever was going on with Hayley was most likely something to do with Magic. Instead of arguing the point like she probably should have, she kept her mouth shut, and allowed Jade to go on believing that her mother would be fine if she gave her some space.

Jade was basically the only friend that Sam had left. The only one who had refused to leave her side for the past two years. She wasn't sure if Jade realised just how important she was, and it was because of her importance that Sam decided to say nothing and not aggravate her by pushing too much.

Even though she *knew* that things would get worse for Hayley if she didn't do anything.

# CHAPTER 41

$\mathcal{B}$ethany leaned over him, pausing only momentarily before sinking her teeth into the soft flesh between his neck and his shoulder.

It didn't hurt as much this time, but he supposed that was because she was inside his mind, whispering lies about how he wanted this and felt no pain. Scott *knew* it was a lie. He wasn't a complete idiot. But for some reason, even though he knew the words in his mind weren't his own, he did nothing to push her away. His body lay complacently as she kneeled over him, her legs on either side of his waist.

She pulled away from him for a moment, and got *that* expression on her face again.

Her face, which still looked beautiful despite the fact that her mouth was covered in blood — *his* blood — and her teeth were razor sharp, would be the cause of many of his nightmares. That was something he was sure of.

Being fed on by a Vampire wasn't something he was soon

to forget. The fact that Vampires were even real was something that had sent his mind reeling. Even if she forced him not to remember that there were things going bump in the night, the thought would be somewhere in the back of his mind.

His mother was a shrink, so he knew what kind of damage this kind of experience would cause. Even if it was pushed to the bottom of his subconscious he was in for a lifetime of nightmares and expensive therapy to figure out the cause of them.

"Tell me what you are," she whispered as she nuzzled against him, burying her face in his neck, kissing the skin she had torn through with her teeth.

That was a question she'd been asking him all night. *'What are you?'* She'd first asked it when she met him outside the bar when his shift had ended. He'd simply stared at her in confusion, not sure what it was she was talking about. And he'd told her as much.

She'd seemed amused by his answer, which he assumed was why she was keeping him alive right now.

Amusement.

"What do you think I am?" he asked, meaning it to sound sarcastic, but he hadn't the strength to manage it. Instead his voice came out quiet.

She leaned back and looked at him, her head tilted to the side as she seemed to regard him with confusion. "I don't know," she muttered thoughtfully. "Your blood is human . . . but that smell." She inhaled deeply. "There's something non-human around you."

"Maybe it's you."

She smiled slightly. "No . . . " she said. "It's not the scent of a Vampire, it's a lot stronger than that, and it lingers on you. Are either of your parents magical?" she asked casually.

Scott tried to laugh, but his lack of energy made it difficult. Casually, he wondered if she planned to kill him, and right then that thought didn't frighten him as much as it should have. "No," he said.

She came closer and inhaled again. Scott flinched instinctively. "Do you have a girlfriend? Perhaps —"

"No," Scott said, his mind immediately forming an image of Sam. She wasn't his girlfriend anymore, but even so, he still thought of her as such, still loved her and held out hope that one day . . . maybe.

Sam *was* extraordinary . . . but magical? There was no way.

Bethany sat back and huffed, folding her arms across her chest as she sulked. A thoughtful expression on her face as she, apparently, tried to figure out what he smelled like.

# CHAPTER 42

The boy was being difficult.

Originally she'd just liked the idea of using him as a distraction. That was until she caught the unmistakable scent of Power rolling off him.

She'd tasted his blood so she knew that it wasn't him, meaning there was someone in his life—that he had regular contact with—who was a non-human. An immensely powerful one.

And she wanted to know who it was.

She pushed her way into his mind. It wasn't very difficult considering that it wasn't the first trip she'd taken in there tonight. Though she hadn't been looking for anything before.

Now she had a vague sense of what it was she was searching for. She pushed her way inside, and began sifting through his memories. The boy, Scott, wasn't old enough to have too many, so flicking through them didn't take Bethany too much time.

One face that kept popping up in both his memories and his thoughts was that of a blonde haired girl, someone he'd once been with and was still in love with. It was all quite sad, that he should still be so completely infatuated by her when, from what she could see in his recent recollections, that she no longer returned his affection.

Bethany stopped and pulled back, watching Scott intensely. He was barely conscious, leaning back against the pillows, half sitting. There was something missing from his memories. The unmistakable gap where something had been taken from him.

She smiled slightly.

He must be quite important for someone to want to clean his mind.

She dug in deeper, attempting to restore what had been removed. Which turned out to be nothing more than a waste of her strength. Whoever had taken Scott's memories was strong. Strong enough that there wasn't the slightest trace left for her to rebuild.

Bethany searched through the faces in his mind once more. If she couldn't find the memories, perhaps she could find the face of someone who would be able to take them in the first place.

More images of the girl with the blonde hair, Sam . . . not that Bethany was particularly interested in the girl's name. There was nothing overtly special about her. As far as Bethany was concerned, she was just as plain and uninteresting as every other hum —

She let a gasp when she saw *his* face, floating around in Scott's head with an immense amount of jealousy and distrust around him.

The Vampire.

Of course it would be him.

Since she'd come to this town she hadn't found a single other non-human, so who else would have the ability to erase the boy's memories but him?

She dug in deeper, attempting to find more images of him in Scott's mind. If Scott knew where to find him it would make her job extremely simple, she could be done with this town in a day.

Bethany had never cared for this Vampire, not *really*, but even so, she felt—while watching him laugh and smile with *Sam*—as though she were watching someone take something that was hers. Something which she was the only one with a rightful claim to.

And it made her furious.

So much so that a high pitched scream of frustration escaped from her lips. Scott's body twitched with fright, his eyes went wide and he stared at her, obviously confused by her outburst.

"The man with the dark hair!" she yelled. "The one you hate!"

"Who are you—"

She let an irate sigh; the noise came out as a half growl. "He's always with the blonde you pine for."

Bethany could tell by the way his expression went still that Scott knew precisely who she was talking about. "I don't know what you mean."

She smiled coyly. "I've been inside your head. You know exactly what I mean, and who I'm speaking of. Don't worry . . . I have no interest in harming your pretty little girlfriend."

"She's not my girlfriend." Scott spoke the words as if they caused him physical pain.

"Would you like her to be?"

Scott looked at her curiously, his head tilted slightly. He

didn't speak, not that speech was necessary. Bethany could tell by the expression he wore on his face that he was intrigued by the prospect.

She smiled. "I can make it happen."

"*How?*"

" . . . Magic."

He let a derisive snort and he watched her dubiously. "I'm being perfectly serious," she said. "I can make her love you."

He chewed his lower lip as he appeared to consider what she had said. "But . . . would it be real?"

"I couldn't make it so, if she didn't already have feelings. I can't build upon nothing."

Slowly, he nodded his head. "And . . . what would you want me to do?"

Bethany smiled slowly, barely noticing how he flinched at the sight of her teeth. "I'm so glad you asked."

# CHAPTER 43

The school was open again.

After the fire in the chem lab they'd closed it for a day—meaning a three day weekend for the students—to assess the damage and repair what they could. As Sam walked along the corridors she could see that the building itself was mostly undamaged. The fire had completely destroyed the chem lab and three other classrooms along that hallway, as well as half of the cafeteria.

Meaning that a lot of classes had been redirected to the gym while they spent the next week fixing what they could.

"Do we actually have to do PE?" Jamie asked, only half paying attention as they walked through the school's back door and out into the cold air.

Sam shrugged. "We're supposed to just have regular classes, but I overheard some people saying that the gym teacher was making all the extra students join in while the teacher they were supposed to have went off somewhere.

They think he was probably getting drunk."

"So . . . is that a yes or a no?"

"Um . . . " Sam thought for a moment, as they followed the concrete walkway towards the gym building. Sam walked in first, pushing the door open with one arm as she peered inside. She let a sigh when she saw some very unimpressed looking students from her history class making their way towards the changing rooms. "It's PE."

Jamie let a loud groan. "But it's too early for movement!"

"Did you even get yourself gym clothes?"

"Gym clothes?" Jamie paused abruptly. Sam pointed to a boy who wasn't from her history class. He was wearing a grey t-shirt with the school logo on it and a pair of deep red shorts.

She turned to look at Jamie. He was staring at the boy with a stupefied expression on his face. "*I* . . . " he said as he turned to look at Sam, "do *not* wear *shorts*."

Sam laughed at the way he stared at her. As if she were completely insane for having suggested it. "Why?"

"*Because!*" he said slightly louder than necessary. "I am not a lady of the night, nor am I a sixteen year old girl who's run away from home and looking to get back at her parents by dressing inappropriately! Ergo . . . I do *not* wear shorts!"

Sam winced as the air was pierced by a high pitched whistle. "Okay!" yelled Mr Jones, the world's most unfit looking gym teacher/basketball coach. "Everyone from Ms Hall's music class and Mr Walker's history class, go change into some gym clothes, please." He rolled his eyes and sighed tiredly when half the people in the room raised their hands to ask a question. "If you don't have any gym clothes with you then please remove your shoes if they don't have a flat sole, and take anything you may have in your pockets and put it into your bag. You can leave your bags in the changing rooms with your coats. Also, please don't forget to remove all jewellery, if anything gets lost or broken I will not be held responsible."

There was a unified groan and a few protests from people who were, much like Jamie appeared to be, not at all pleased with the prospect of having to do an extra class of PE. Mr Jones blew on his whistle again, causing a lot of the students to grumble or cover their ears. "No excuses!" he yelled. "The only people who will be excused from this class are injured people, anyone with asthma or serious illnesses and girls wearing dresses or skirts with no gym clothes to change into."

Sam threw her bag down on the floor at her feet, and shrugged off her coat. She had gym clothes with her, but they were in her locker and she didn't feel like walking all the way back to get them, so she'd do PE in the clothes she had on now. She rolled her jacket up and put it into her bag, checking her pockets to make sure there was nothing of value inside. Once she was sure they were empty she pulled her amulet over her head and placed it carefully on top of her coat before she zipped her bag shut tightly.

"Boys changing room is that way," Sam said, pointing to her right at a door on the far end of the gym. "Go leave your stuff."

"I'm not doing PE," Jamie said stubbornly, shaking his head.

"Don't be such a lazy bastard," Sam said before she turned and walked towards the girls' changing rooms, with her bag slung over her shoulder. Inside there was an extremely large group of students, only a small portion of whom were actually changing. The others were gathered together in groups, talking and laughing about things that Sam didn't pay much attention to.

At least not until she walked further into the changing room and overheard something that caught her attention.

The mention of *Elliot's* name.

"It's not funny," said Kami. "I'm really worried. He hasn't called or texted me in three days."

"Relax," Madison said. "Boys don't always call when they say they will. That's a fact of life."

"You don't get it," Kami said with a frustrated sigh. "Last time I saw him there was . . . something just wasn't right."

Sam left her bag on one of the benches within the rows of lockers, next to the pile of bags and coats, hoping that the conversation would stick to a subject she was interested in, and feeling herself longing to groan in frustration as Madison changed the subject to discussions of the winter formal . . . which wasn't for another month and a half and also wasn't an interesting or relevant topic.

Sam left the changing rooms, since they no longer held anything useful to her and walked out into the gym, looking around for Jamie, and pausing slightly when she saw him standing beside Mr Jones, having a conversation with him.

" . . . autoimmune haemolytic anaemia," she heard Jamie say as she got closer.

"I have no idea what that is," the coach said, giving Jamie a dubious glance.

"It's a blood disorder. I keep it in check, but I am prone to weakness and dizziness, sometimes it just comes out of nowhere. I don't mind doing PE," he said. "I just thought you should be aware so that no one panics if I collapse or pass out."

"Is that likely to happen?"

"It's been known to."

The coach nodded his head. "You'll sit out for today, though for future reference you'll need a doctor's note."

Jamie nodded his head, and walked over to the bleachers where some other students were sitting, mostly girls who were wearing skirts despite the fact that it was winter, and some guy with a broken arm.

Jamie looked up at her once he'd taken a seat a little bit away from the other people and gave her a victorious smile. She shook her head disapprovingly and mouthed the word 'liar'. He only smiled wider.

# CHAPTER 44

*J*amie sat on the uncomfortable wooden benches as he watched Sam play what the teacher had declared '*the largest game of dodgeball, ever*'. It was fascinating to watch her move.

He'd never noticed before, but she moved with a seamless grace, winding her way through the crowd of people on her side of the hall, catching the ball with one hand when it came near her, which eliminated the person who'd thrown it, and throwing it back at the other team with a swift movement that caught someone in the shin every single time.

She never went out of her way to participate in the game, but whenever the ball came near her the students on her team stepped aside and allowed her to deal with it. Which was a smart move on their part, because none of them could move like her.

Jamie was so captivated by watching her play that he physically jumped with shock when she suddenly froze and allowed the ball to hit her in the hip. The students on her team groaned, and looked at her as if she'd committed the ultimate act of betrayal. She shrugged at them and moved away. At first he thought she was walking over to the benches where he was, but instead she turned and walked towards the girls' changing rooms.

Jamie stood as he watched her move away. Her face set in an expression of determination. She paused at the entrance to the girls' changing rooms and turned to look at him over her shoulder. She pointed out to the crowd of students, then at him, then continued to make confusing hand gestures, which he was sure to her mind made perfect sense, but to his eyes . . . she was just waving her hands around like a crazy person.

She looked at him expectantly for a moment, and he shrugged, wondering if she'd honestly expected him to understand what she was signalling for. Obviously she had, because she sighed, and repeated the gestures, this time mouthing the words, *'Make them blind'*.

*Oh,* Jamie thought, replaying her actions in his mind, thinking that they made sense now that he knew what she'd meant. He wondered briefly why she hadn't spoken to him psychically; surely it would have been a simpler form of communication.

He sent out a wave of energy which blanketed every mind in the gym, giving him the ability to move across the room and into the girls' changing room without being seen.

Sam led the way, and he followed without question. Knowing that if she had allowed herself to be taken out of the game she must have had a good reason. So he followed her through the rows of lockers, past the showers to the open fire door at the back of the room, where she paused and put a finger to her lips in a silent hush. Jamie stood behind her,

206

keeping himself pressed tightly to the wall inside the changing rooms.

He leaned his head back against the cold brick wall, now able to clearly hear the conversation that was going on outside.

"Elliot!" a girl called. She sounded half angry half happy. "Where the hell have you *been*?"

"Busy," was the reply.

"Oh . . . too busy to use a phone?"

"Just busy!" he yelled. Jamie could only imagine that the girl who had been speaking to him appeared upset by his raised tone, because Elliot sighed, then spoke softer. "Kami, I'm sorry I haven't called you. There's just a lot going on right now, and I don't want you to get involved."

"What's going on?" Kami asked, her tone demanding.

"I can't tell you . . . you've just got to trust me."

"Well . . . will I see you later?"

"No."

Kami let an irate sigh. "Will I see you *ever*?"

"Kami . . . " Elliot's tone was pleading, as if he were willing her to understand. Jamie didn't know Elliot all that well as an individual, but he knew *that* tone. It was the tone you used to attempt to reason with someone you cared about.

"No!" she yelled. "If you don't want to see me just say so, you don't need to lie to me."

"I *do* want to see you, it's just like I said —"

"Oh, right. *Things* and *stuff*."

Elliot let a frustrated groan. "I'm not a good person," he said out of nowhere. There was a moment of silence before he continued. "I'm not, it's a fact. And there are some things I *need* to do, and they're not good things."

"Elliot —"

"You wanted to hear it, so I'll tell you. I've done bad things, and I'll probably be doing more bad things and I'd rather you weren't around me when I did. Because I may not be able to stop myself from doing something bad to you. So just *please*, stay away from me."

"But you don't need—"

"Yes," he interrupted. "I do."

Jamie looked at Sam as they listened carefully for any more words, but there were none. All Jamie could hear from outside was a singular set of lungs breathing in and out. After a moment, he heard footsteps. He opened his mouth to ask Sam what they should do, to find out if they should hide, question her, or if he should blanket her mind like he had everyone else's.

But before he got a chance to speak, Sam silenced him by pressing her lips to his. She wrapped her arms around his neck and pulled him close, leaning her body in to his.

And he let her . . . too shocked to do otherwise.

"Oh my God you guys," Kami said. Sam moved away from Jamie quickly, as if she hadn't expected them to be interrupted. Kami stood there looking at them with an expression of mild disgust and amusement. "Get a room!"

"Um, excuse you," said Sam, placing both hands on her hips. "But we *are* in a room."

Kami scoffed and rolled her eyes. "Whatever." And then she walked away. Sam watched after her with an expression of interest.

"You heard what I heard, right?" she asked.

It took Jamie a moment to realise she'd spoken; he was still mentally reliving the sensation of having Sam kiss him. "Um . . . heard? Right . . . yeah. No . . . " he sighed. "I'm sorry, what?"

Sam rolled her eyes. "Can you keep up please? Elliot, the guy we're pretty sure is possessed just said he was going to be doing some bad things?"

"Yeah . . . No . . . Wait . . . Yes, I heard that part."

Sam shook her head. "You're an idiot."

"Why am I an idiot?" he asked, more confused by her sudden declaration than he was offended by it.

She shrugged, and didn't respond. Out in the hall Jamie heard the sound of a whistle being blown, and the teacher yelling at the students to go get changed. Followed by the sound of footsteps moving in their direction.

Jamie looked at Sam and smiled widely. "Should we kiss so they don't see us?"

"No," she said, taking a moment to look at him quizzically as though she was unsure as to why he would suggest such a thing. "Use the door." She pointed to the fire door at his back. "I'll get my bag and meet you outside."

"My bag is still on those benches."

Sam looked over her shoulder towards the approaching voices. She placed her hands on his chest and shoved him. "*Go*," she ordered. "I'll get your bag too."

Jamie nodded and left the girls' changing rooms through the fire door. Outside, there was a track field surrounded by a mesh wire fence. He walked around the fence slowly, keeping an eye out for Elliot, half expecting him to still be in sight somewhere.

*<Jamie!>*

He physically jumped at the mental intrusion of Sam shouting inside his head. *<Yes?>*

*<My amulet is gone>*

Jamie stopped walking and turned his attention back towards the gym building. He turned on his heel and walked swiftly back to it, while simultaneously projecting a psychic shield around himself and then, as he got to the fire door, Sam.

At the door, he paused for a moment, noticing as soon as he entered that the room was filled with semi-naked girls. They continued to change from their gym clothes while he stood there, invisible to their eyes. After a moment in which he was too stunned to move he began to walk forward, his eyes cast down at the linoleum floor.

Sam was at one of the benches within the rows of lockers, furiously looking through her bag, the contents of it spilled out on the bench as she searched through the objects individually, then turned her empty bag upside down and shook it, as if she expected the amulet to simply fall out.

She threw the bag down on top of her things, and let a noise of frustration and anger which sounded halfway between a sigh and a growl. "It's gone," she said as Jamie approached her.

"Would someone have stolen it?"

Sam shrugged. "It's charmed," she stated. "Humans who see it have no interest in possessing it, so why would they steal it?"

"What about non-humans?" Jamie asked, thinking about Elliot, who *had* been outside the girls' changing room.

Sam looked at him as if she'd already had that thought, but dismissed it. "It's a family heirloom," she said. "Why would he want it, it doesn't even *do* anything."

Jamie raised an eyebrow in confusion. "It doesn't do anything? I always thought it was a protection amulet."

Sam shook her head. "I thought so too when I first got it, but it's not. It doesn't do anything. It's made with Magic, yet it's completely non-magical. It's just a necklace, the only value it has is sentimental." When she looked at him he saw that her indigo eyes were wide and shimmered with tears waiting to be shed.

And once he saw that, he was suddenly furious with

whoever had dared to steal something that meant so much to her. "Was it your grandmother's?" he asked. He'd heard about how her grandmother had been the leader of the Coven before Hayley, so he could only assume, that since she and Sam seemed to be the only members of the family who embraced the idea of things that weren't human, that the amulet must have been hers.

Sam shook her head while chewing her lip. "It was my mom's."

"But, I thought you never met her."

"I haven't," Sam said, tears flowing silently down her cheeks. "I don't even know what her name is. That amulet was all I had, and now it's gone."

Jamie clenched his hands into fists at his sides, the only thing that could stop his arm from reaching out as he ached to wipe away her tears. Sam took a breath and let a resolute sigh, her expression turning to one of determination as she wiped away her tears. "We need to deal with him," she said, as she began putting all of her things back into her bag.

Jamie nodded his agreement. "Jack is still doing surveillance on his house."

"We're going there now."

"What about school?" he asked, despite the fact that he had no desire to remain. He was only here because Sam insisted on attending, and he had been charged with the task of being her shadow.

Jamie quirked a smile at his own thoughts. He had never considered it before, but he *was* Sam's shadow. And he was protecting her *from* Shadows.

He was a shadow who fought Shadows. The thought of that amused him.

"Fuck school," she said, answering his question, waving a dismissive hand as she turned and led the way through the locker room and back out to the main hall. "We have better things to do."

# CHAPTER 45

Elliot finally managed to get rid of Kami, turning his back to her and walking away, refusing to look back as he strode towards his car.

Because he knew without even looking that she was just standing by the gym's emergency door making sad eyes at his back.

And he knew that if he turned around and actually *saw* her making the sad eyes that he'd have to go back and hug her or something. Because if he didn't go back to her after they both knew he'd seen her sad eyes then Kami would just think he was a total dick.

Eventually he reached his car and crammed himself inside, slamming the door shut and taking a deep breath.

He leaned his head back on his chair, his skull hitting the leather headrest. "Fuck," he said through heavy breaths.

He closed his eyes to try calm himself.

But it didn't help to ease his troubled mind.

He could still see it.

It didn't matter if his eyes were open or closed, he could still see the thick blood covering every inch of his living room. And the bodies — God, the bodies . . .

His eyes shot open and he stared straight ahead, his hands gripping the steering wheel so tight that his knuckles turned white.

"Fuck."

His mind drew him back to the images that Kon had shown him. A world of nothing but an all-consuming chaos. Absently, his hand went to his pocket and wrapped around the amulet, a low pulse of energy humming from the object making it slightly warm to the touch. Before he even knew what he was doing it was in front of his face and he was staring at it with disbelieving eyes.

Sam seemed to believe that this amulet was nothing.

Not special in any way.

That bitch couldn't have been more wrong.

Elliot could hardly believe what he had in his possession right now. The things it could do, how important it was, and what the puppet-master clearly wanted it for.

It was too much.

Too much power in his hand.

Too much responsibility.

There was absolutely no way he could pass this thing on when he knew the evils it would be used for.

It wasn't that he gave a fuck about the world really . . . for so long he'd thought that he wouldn't even blink if someone wanted to come along and burn the whole universe to the ground. He would gladly just sit by and watch the flames as they left behind nothing by ash.

But now that he was faced with the prospect of the end actually coming to pass, he found himself too attached to the idea of living to want to take part in the world's destruction.

He swiftly pocketed the amulet and started his car, steering it off the school grounds, rocketing down the street leading to the centre of town.

There was nowhere he could go, nowhere he could really hide.

He was tainted by the Shadows; they were a part of him and he a part of it. There was nowhere he could go that they couldn't get to him.

But he could easily make himself a safe place to stay for a while.

He couldn't exactly go home ever again, not after what happened there, so his hotel room was the only place he could go.

Behind him there was a very loud crash, he absently glanced in the rear-view mirror to get a look at what had happened. Behind him small wafts of smoke billowed up from two totalled cars. Within seconds the drivers were out of the car and beating the shit out of each other.

Pretty soon after that, some passersby joined in the fight.

All around him people were losing their minds, all with the shortest of fuses awaiting the one tiny spark that would set them off.

He'd been seeing things like this all week.

There had been almost ten car accidents outside of his hotel this weekend alone and more than just the drivers had been hospitalised by the brawls those accidents turned into.

And he knew without question that it was all because of him.

The taint within him was seeping from his soul and infecting anyone around him. He'd only spread the infection on purpose once at the school, just to try to freak the Witch out a little.

If he'd known then that he wouldn't be able to stop it from happening all the time he would have resisted the temptation to mess with her.

Elliot drove faster, breaking the speed limits as he tore down the streets towards the parking lot by the hotel. Almost crashing his car as he turned into the lot, spinning the vehicle in such a way that he could hear the metal creaking in protest.

Once the car was — more or less — parked he jumped from his seat and out the door, hurrying through the lot, across the hotel lobby and bolting up the stairs.

The door to his room banged shut behind him, rattling the walls from the force.

Wasting no time he slammed his fist into the mirror by the entrance to his room, shards of glass exploding across the floor as it shattered. He picked up one of the larger pieces and used it to slice open his hand. Biting his lip and wincing at the pain as the skin parted and blood began to pour from the freshly open wound.

The next few minutes were spent using his blood to draw runes on every available space of wall. By the time he was done his room looked like it belonged to a serial killer, bloody symbols dripping down the walls and ruining the fancy hotel decor.

When the last of the symbols had been painted on the wall Elliot took a step back and whispered, "Tcetorp dleihs edih, tcetorp dleihs edih, tcetorp dleihs edih."

The symbols glowed faintly and the blood suddenly dried, setting the Magic into place.

The cacophony of sound that usually filled his mind was suddenly silent and everything within him was still. For the first time in his life he was completely cut off.

It was just him.

A puppet with no strings.

For the first time in forever he was alone.

Exhausted and terrified, Elliot could do nothing but fall on his bed and sleep.

# CHAPTER 46

*S*am was outside the school, waiting for Jamie who was currently in the process of breaking into the principal's office, getting *another* copy of Elliot's address; they had given the only written copy they had to Jack, and neither of them had thought to memorise it.

The plan had been to wait for Jack to report back to them. He was watching Elliot's house, getting to know everyone's routines so he could give them a time frame for when the house would be empty long enough for them to look around.

But circumstances had changed, and she wanted to deal with Elliot as soon as possible. The sooner they either killed or de-possessed him the easier their lives would become.

Sam looked over her shoulder when she heard the front doors open, and immediately sighed, wishing she was anywhere else.

"Oh, hi Sam," Scott said, as he walked down the front steps, over to where she was leaning against the wall. "Are you ditching?"

She shrugged. "Three of my classes are damaged, and I don't feel like doing PE all day."

"Yeah," he said with a smile. "That's fair I guess."

Sam forced a smile and nodded. Scott was one of those people she used to give a lot of thought to. She used to spend a lot of her time thinking about him and the two years they'd been together. But for the past few months she'd been thinking about him less and less. And in the past week, well she hadn't really thought about much of anything pertaining to her life as it was before.

It was like when she woke up after the regenerative coma she'd been in, she'd opened her eyes as a partly different person.

Though she could tell, by the way that Scott was watching her now that his thoughts of her hadn't lessened over time. And now that she had seen him, for the first time since she'd woken up, all the thoughts that she'd had *before* came flying back to her mind.

"I'm glad I ran into you," he said. "I've had the strangest, most insane weekend of my life and I found out some—"

They both looked up at the door as Jamie emerged and jogged down the steps, pausing halfway when he noticed Scott standing with Sam.

Sam pushed herself away from the wall, and was about to tell Scott that she had to go and would talk to him some other time, when he stood in front of her holding his arm out to the side to keep her behind him. "You stay away from her!" Scott yelled at Jamie.

Jamie just looked at him for a moment, clearly confused. Then he turned his head in Sam's direction, his eyes searching her face for an explanation, though she was just as confused as he was.

"Scott," Sam started, attempting to calm him down.

"Sam." Scott looked at her over his shoulder. "You're not safe. He's a monster!"

"What?"

Jamie took a step towards them, Scott turned his head back quickly. "Stay *away!*"

"What makes you think I'm a monster?" Jamie asked, his tone sounding more curious than anything else.

"I know *what* you are!" Scott said. "I don't know what you want with Sam but I won't let you hurt her!"

"I'm not going to hurt her," Jamie said, and took another slow step towards Scott.

"What do you think you know?" Sam asked.

"I don't *think*," he said, looking at Sam for a moment. "I *know*."

"You look a bit pale," Jamie said as he got closer, glancing sideways at Sam, as if willing her to see whatever it was he could. She turned to look at Scott, and noticed that Jamie was right, his naturally tanned skin was slightly paler than it should have been. Almost as if he was sick. "It almost looks like you've lost a large amount of blood recently," Jamie said.

Scott took a few awkward steps away from him, keeping Sam shielded behind his body, pushing her back with him.

"Tell me about your strange and insane weekend," Sam said, her eyes shifting between Scott and Jamie, then back again.

"What?" Scott seemed confused by her question.

"You said you had an insane weekend, what happened?" she asked, her tone more demanding than it had been before. "Were you attacked by something?"

"Attacked?" He spoke the word like he didn't fully understand its meaning, and for a moment while he thought of an answer, Sam saw that his eyes seemed slightly glazed over.

"He's been attacked," Jamie said to Sam. "As far as I knew there were no other Vampires in town. The blood bar is the only place I've met any and that's two towns over."

Scott's head snapped in Jamie's direction at the word 'Vampires'. "You admitted it!" he declared triumphantly.

Jamie shrugged nonchalantly. "No point in pretending . . . I can just erase your memory and you'll never remember I said it."

Scott gave Jamie a sideways grin. The expression was unfamiliar, the kind of smile Sam wasn't used to seeing on Scott's face. But then, two years of not talking and a Vampire attack, who was to say he was the same person she used to know?

"You can't mess with my memories anymore," Scott said, grinning. He reached his hand under the collar of his t-shirt and pulled out a leather string with a black stone tied around the end.

Jamie let a dramatic sigh. "*Where* is everyone getting those from?"

Sam recognised it as black obsidian, the perfect gemstone for protecting against psychic attacks. She let a sigh. "Scott," she said, he looked at her over his shoulder. "I am so sorry about this, but we have a *lot* to deal with already, and we really don't have time for this right now."

Scott looked at her in confusion. "You knew?" he whispered, then spoke again, his voice louder than before. "You *knew* what he was, and you . . . you don't care!"

"No Scott," Sam said impatiently. "I don't care. Vampires are nothing compared to the shit I usually have to deal with." She turned to Jamie. "Hold him."

Scott turned to Jamie just in time to let out a half scream, as Jamie wrapped one arm around his waist, locking his arms by his sides and the other covering his mouth to stifle his screams. Sam reached up and grabbed hold of the stone at Scott's throat, wrapping it up in a bubble of her energy and suppressing its protective properties. For a moment, he looked at her with an expression of betrayal. Sam clenched her jaw, knowing that she was only doing what was best for him.

Slowly, the expression on his face evaporated, and turned to one of blankness. Jamie took his hand from Scott's face first, then slowly backed away from him. Sam let go of the amulet, letting it rest against the fabric of Scott's t-shirt. He stood there looking slightly dazed, as if in a trance. Jamie walked forward and grabbed onto Sam's arm, dragging her away from Scott before he could come to and remember they had been there.

"Did you see who it was?" Sam asked as they made their way down the street.

Jamie shook his head. While he had been inside Scott's mind he saw a lot of things. More or less every memory he'd had in his entire life. He was young, only eighteen years old, it had been easy for Jamie to view all of his memories quickly. However there *were* two places his memories were incomplete, where they had been messed with by other people. The first was obviously when Jack had done what he'd done to Scott's memories. And the second, was the past two days.

The *entire* weekend was missing from Scott's memories.

The boy had spoken of the past few days, so he obviously had some recollection of what happened, but for some reason his memories were blocked. As if someone had gone inside his head, found those memories and thrown them into a locked chest to which only Scott and whoever had moved his memories had a key.

"Nothing at all?" Sam asked incredulously, as if she didn't believe him.

"Someone blocked them," he said. "They weren't erased, just blocked. I couldn't see them."

Sam let an irate sigh, and mumbled something about how she would have gotten more results if she'd done it herself. Jamie didn't pay much attention to her; he was too preoccupied thinking back on the things he'd seen in Scott's head.

He'd always assumed that he and Sam had been together at some stage, though he'd never asked and she'd never spoken of it. As it turned out, he had guessed correctly. Not only had she and Scott been together, but they'd been together for over two years. And despite the fact they were no longer a couple and hadn't been for almost as long as their relationship lasted, Jamie felt overcome with jealousy when he'd seen Sam and Scott together in his memories.

They'd talked about everything. She hadn't had any problem speaking to Scott about things; when she and Danny had fought, how she had mourned the death of her parents, how she had seen her grandmother killed. She'd openly shared her feelings with him, held his hand in public, kissed him in public and in private they'd done much more.

It wasn't so much the physicality that bothered him, it was the openness. How she hadn't minded when he'd asked her questions, and how she'd asked questions about him.

Whereas, despite the fact that Sam wasn't his girlfriend, Jamie felt as though he was always treading on thin ice when it came to conversation. He never quite knew what subject would cause her to shut him out. And he found himself jealous of the mortal boy for how easy Sam had found it to confide in him.

They walked in silence down the streets, Sam casting worried glances at the sky every five minutes, as if she were encouraging the clouds to hold onto the rain until she got to somewhere with shelter.

Jamie took the Post-It out of his pocket and glanced at the address, checking to make sure they were heading the right way.

"Do you realise," Sam spoke suddenly, while glaring at the clouds, "that you have been super quiet since Saturday?"

He looked at her curiously. Having not expected her to notice or to comment on something such as his silence. "I have?"

She nodded, taking her gaze from the clouds to look straight ahead as they walked. "After we talked to Aleczander I offered to show you the entire dimension, and you refused. Which was surprising since you always seem to take any excuse to spend time in my general presence and that tour would have taken at *least* four hours. Then you didn't talk to me on the walk to the portal, you left as soon as we got back. You were nowhere to be found all weekend, you didn't talk to me on the walk to school, and you're not talking to me now." She let a breath and smiled. "Are you trying to imply that you don't want to talk to *me* anymore, or that you just don't want to make sounds in general?"

"I'll be honest," Jamie said without returning her smile. "I'm surprised you noticed . . . or that you even," he shrugged, "you know, *care*."

"I *noticed*," Sam said defensively. "I guess . . . since I don't like to talk about personal stuff, I forget that other people *do* like to talk and I forget to ask. And I guess it makes people think I don't care."

"And when did you come to *this* realisation?" he asked out of curiosity.

"Saturday," she said. "After you stormed out of my house, I was just standing there thinking, and I realised that you were probably upset, and I should probably follow you out and ask. But by that time, well . . . with how fast you run you could have been home already. So I left it thinking that you'd be back later anyway. And then you didn't come anywhere near me until it was absolutely necessary, and you didn't ask about my weekend either."

He laughed despite the fact that he didn't necessarily find what she'd said amusing. "Is there any point?" he asked. "Asking you questions when you either answer them vaguely then move the subject along, or get angry and stop speaking altogether?"

"I don't *always*," Sam protested.

He arched an eyebrow as he stared at her, and decided to test her by asking a simple personal question. "What's your middle name?"

Sam stopped walking and looked at him as if he'd lost his mind. "What's *your* middle name?"

He smiled. "Michael."

"I don't have one," she said, keeping her tone light and conversational as if to prove him wrong. "Or if I do, it's lost along with my real surname."

"Have you ever tried to find out what it might be?"

"What my real last name is?"

Jamie nodded his head. "Or your mother's name, or your father's."

Sam glanced over him assessingly. As if she were deciding, in that moment, whether or not it would be alright to tell him something about her life. She let a sigh, and nodded her head. "It's one of those things I think about a lot, finding out. But then I think, what's the point? Knowing about the past can't change it, so why is it so important?"

"Because knowing is better than not knowing," Jamie said.

"Is it?" she asked. "Do you think it would be better for me to get a megaphone and stand in the centre of the town and say 'Hey everybody, guess what? I have super powers, Jamie's a Vampire, that guy who pops in every now and then is a Ghost, monsters are real, there's a war going on, and oh yeah . . . the town is secretly run by a coven of Witches!'" She inclined her head and gave him a dubious glance. "Is knowing what's real better than the blissful innocence of not?"

"That's different," Jamie said. "We both know that humanity as a whole couldn't handle finding out they're not alone. What we're talking about is you, and whether your life would be better if you knew. I don't know if your life would be better, or even if it would be changed in any way, but I do know that if you knew where you came from you'd find out more about yourself, and then there'd be things you wouldn't have to dwell on anymore."

"You're right," she said with a smile. "If I knew, I could have a whole batch of *new* things to dwell on."

Jamie laughed. "Have you ever actually *tried* though?"

Sam smiled fondly at her own memories. "When I was thirteen," she said with a smile. "I was going to go on a quest."

"A *quest*?" Jamie tried not to laugh.

"Yes," she said stubbornly. "A quest. People don't quest enough. I think questing should have a comeback, like leggings, they've had their comeback, it's quest's turn."

Sam shot him a glare when he snorted in an attempt to stifle his laughter. Then slowly her expression softened and she laughed along with him. "I was *thirteen*!" she said. "I just read a load of fantasy books . . . I thought there was a possibility for dragon battles and I was like, 'dragon slaying, yay!'"

"What made you think there'd be dragons?" he asked, then his laughter sobered and he stared at her, his eyes wide. "*Are* there dragons?"

Sam shrugged. "I was a kid, and not as far as I know, though that doesn't mean there's not. If there are, I call dibs, you heard it, I was the first one to call dibs on the dragons."

Jamie was so lost in their conversation that he hadn't noticed they'd already walked past Elliot's house. He only *did* realise when Jack appeared in front of them, causing both Sam and Jamie to jump with fright.

"You can't call dibs on dragons, Sam," Jack said with a roll of his eyes.

"Can too," she retorted. "And I have two witnesses to say I did."

Jack smiled. "What are you two doing here?" he asked. "This is *my* surveillance operation... am I being fired? Because you know I'll steal all the office supplies on my way out and sell them on the black market."

Sam rolled her eyes. "There are no office supplies."

"It's a non-traditional office," said Jack with a shrug. "But it's full of supplies nonetheless."

"We think Elliot stole Sam's amulet," Jamie stated.

Jack eyed him incredulously, then turned his gaze to Sam. "It's missing?"

"I put it in my bag at PE, after class it wasn't there. In between we saw Elliot outside the girls' changing rooms, so he's either a perve or a thief."

"Nothing says he can't be both . . . The amulet doesn't really do anything," he said, his expression thoughtful. "Though there *was* once a rumour that the previous owner put all of her Power inside it, but we all know that's not true."

"Would he think it was true?" Sam asked.

Jack shrugged. "It's possible."

"Is he home right now?" Jamie asked.

Jack shook his head. "He hasn't been home since Friday."

Both Sam and Jamie shared a questioning glance, before turning their attention back to Jack. "He's been gone for the whole weekend?" she asked.

Jack nodded. "His mother went in around three, his father came home at six, and the kid strolled through the door, completely plastered, around two a.m., then about a half hour later the garage door opened and he drove off. Still drunk by the way, if I hadn't been invisible and already dead, I would be now . . . Dead, not invisible."

"And he hasn't come home?" Jamie asked.

Jack glared at him for a moment. Jamie flinched slightly; the expression reminded him of the conversation they'd had last week, when Jack had given him the same glare he was wearing now and asked 'what are you accusing me of?'. "That's what I *said*, isn't it?"

"What about his parents?" Sam asked. "Are they out or are they home?"

"Well, I didn't think anything of it until this morning, and I was going to come get you guys after school was over . . . "

"What?" Sam asked, her tone indicating that she knew she was about to hear something she didn't necessarily want to.

"They haven't been out of the house since Friday."

"So . . . " Jamie said, glancing back at Elliot's house. "He left on Friday, and his parent's haven't been seen since?"

Jack nodded.

Jamie turned without hesitation and walked to the house. Jack and Sam followed behind him. "You don't waste time using thoughts," Jack said when he was standing next to him. "Do you?"

Jamie paused for a moment and stared at him. "What do you mean?"

"Well, there could be traps, did that cross your mind?"

Jamie nodded. "Of course."

Jack looked slightly taken aback. "And if there are?"

Jamie shrugged. "I'll deal with if it happens."

Jack smiled approvingly, then shook his head. "See, that's why I like you better than her last boyfriend."

Sam groaned and rolled her eyes. "He's *not* my boyfriend."

Jack waved his hand dismissively. "Semantics."

Jamie approached Elliot's house with none of the hesitation that Jack appeared to believe he should feel. As he drew closer, he couldn't help but think of what Elliot had said outside the changing rooms, *'I'm a bad person, I've done bad things . . .'*

It made him wonder, if Elliot knew there was something wrong with him, knew there was something not right with how he was, why wouldn't he try to stop it?

Obviously he felt *something*. He was a human possessed by a monster, so why wouldn't he do something to help himself or at the very least aid the people he could potentially hurt?

Unless of course, he didn't *know* there was something wrong.

Jamie remembered, more vividly than he wished, when he had been possessed. Watching himself through blurred vision as he attacked and almost killed Sam. He remembered everything about it, the sounds she made as she struggled to breathe, the look in her eyes as her spark of life ebbed out, the taste of her blood and, more than anything, how it *hadn't* felt wrong.

There was a chance that Elliot didn't *know* he was possessed, perhaps he thought that his actions were his own, perhaps he truly did think that he was just a bad person doing bad things.

As they approached the front door Jamie glanced sideways,

momentarily checking the windows. Though it turned out to be a waste of time, the view was blocked out by the curtains. He pointed to the windows, and saw Sam and Jack turn towards them, then back to him, their expressions confused. "Have the curtains been closed all weekend?" Jamie asked.

Jack frowned thoughtfully, then shrugged. "I don't really remember, could've been."

Jamie let a breath. He was sure at this stage that if his heart could beat normally it would have been pounding. Perhaps the fact that it couldn't was the reason why he felt no fear as he reached his hand out and found the door to be unlocked.

He walked in first, already knowing what he would find inside.

The image of two dead bodies flashed in his mind, and he inhaled sharply, catching his breath in the back of his throat as the bitter stench of rotten blood assailed his senses. He looked around the hallway, standing just inside the doorway as Sam and Jack stepped in behind him. He peered over his shoulder at Sam, gauging her reaction to the house. By the look on her face though, he couldn't tell if she felt anything at all. There was no sign of horror or apprehension, just a grim determination displayed by the harsh set of her jaw and the straight line of her mouth as she shoved past both Jamie and Jack and ventured further into the house.

Jack pushed the front door open all the way behind him, casting the dim grey light of midday through the hallway which was actually a lot cleaner than Jamie had expected.

He'd imagined blood sprayed in all directions, an impossible amount of it spattered across the walls, the ceiling, pools of it on the floor and two bodies torn to shreds.

Instead, what he saw was completely normal. Which was why it felt so *wrong*.

Jamie followed behind Sam as she crossed the hallway into

the living room where it was empty and once again clean. Cushions lined up neatly on the sofas, which sat in a neat position, the leather completely uncreased. Although Jamie had never before seen the layout of the house and therefore couldn't know for sure, none of the furniture *looked* out of place. Everything in this room was neat and tidy, appearing completely undisturbed.

He followed Sam into the kitchen, when he heard her groan in frustration as once again the room was completely undamaged in anyway. In fact, the only sign of the house having any inhabitants was the white pastry box which sat on the countertop with its lid askew. Jamie could see, that half the contents were missing from the box.

When he walked forward and lifted the lid to peer inside, he saw that what was left in the box had half hardened half turned to goo. He scrunched his nose and let the lid fall.

"What do you sense?" Sam asked him. She turned her head away from the kitchen window, which was covered by a roller blind.

Jamie let a sigh and ran his hand through his hair. "I can't *feel* anything," he said. Sam nodded along, indicating that she couldn't sense anything either. "*But* there's blood —"

"Where?" Jack interrupted.

Jamie shrugged. "It smells rotten, days old, but I can't tell where it's coming from."

"Upstairs?" Sam asked.

He shook his head. "I'm not sure. It smells like it's everywhere. Here, the hallway, the living room. It's *everywhere*, but . . . there *is* no blood."

Sam let a sigh and looked towards Jack for a moment, her eyes making it appear as though she were speaking to him in codes. Jamie turned to Jack just in time to see him nod, then vanish. Before he could open his mouth to ask what she had said to him, Jack returned. "He's right," he said, as he appeared between Sam and Jamie. "There's no blood, no bodies, no nothing."

"Basement?" she asked, seeming half hopeful.

Jack shook his head. "Checked it. Nothing."

Jamie frowned. "He killed them," he stated. "We all know it. I can smell the blood, so they were killed *here*. And he left in a car so *how* could the bodies just vanish?"

Sam looked to Jack expectantly. "Did you see *anything* else over the course of the weekend?"

Jack looked at Sam steadily for a moment, before he shook his head. "Nothing," he said. Sam sighed, her shoulders sagging in disappointment.

Jamie stared at Jack, watching as he placed a hand on Sam's shoulder and muttered words of comfort. Jamie watched him because he could do nothing but.

There had been a moment, a flicker in Jack's eyes before he answered Sam, something that she didn't notice but Jamie did.

And it was in that very moment, that Jamie *knew* Jack was lying.

He didn't know exactly what came over him, but out of nowhere Jamie blurted, "I want to see the basement."

Jack turned to him slowly, clearly unimpressed by his words. "I already checked there," he said, his jaw clenched as he spoke.

"I know," Jamie said with a smile, trying not to make it look or sound as though he was second guessing Jack. "It's just that . . . well, I can sense blood a lot better than either of you, so I'll know it's there, even though you couldn't see it."

Jack's expression softened. "Oh," he said simply.

"Why the basement?" Sam asked, her expression confused.

Jamie ran his hand through his hair as he took a moment to

think of his response. "Well, so far that's been where murders happen."

Jack shrugged. "It's worth a try," he said as he walked past him and out of the kitchen, towards the hallway where there was a door. When he opened it, Jamie saw a flight of stairs leading down. With a sigh, Sam followed Jack down the stairs and after a moment's pause, Jamie stepped through the door behind them.

As he walked down the stairs the first thing he noticed was the smell. The stench of rotten blood filled the air mixed with the chemical fumes of bleach. "It seems pretty clean down here," Sam said, as she walked to the centre of the room and looked around assessingly.

"Blood under bleach," Jamie stated, trying to minimise the words he spoke to avoid having to inhale too much. "A *lot* of bleach."

"So it's been cleaned," Jack muttered thoughtfully.

Jamie walked into the room. Inside it looked like any other basement. The entire room was filled with boxes and old items of furniture covered in dust. The walls were made of bare grey brick and the floor was unfinished cement. The walls were clear of symbols, something that Jamie had thought they might find after he remembered the scene in the library basement. And on the floor there was nothing. No blood stains or candles.

He sighed in defeat. "Sorry," he said. "I'm just wasting our time."

Jack placed a comforting hand on Jamie's shoulder. "Don't apologise," he said with a smile. "Any ideas are welcome, especially if it helps up find something."

Jamie gazed down at the floor, trying with all of his strength to think of something useful. It wasn't until he finally gave up, that his eyes registered what he was looking at. He hunkered down and placed a hand on the substance that stained the floor. It was solid, and when he took his hand away, there was nothing on his fingertips. With his thumb he scratched at it, a smile forming on his lips as he realised what the substance was.

"Over here," he said, looking up as Jack and Sam gathered around him. "Candle wax . . . not usually the sort of thing you'd find on a basement floor."

Jack smiled. "No . . . it isn't."

Sam let a sigh as she looked towards the staircase. "We need to search the house," she said. "Every room . . . I want to know where Elliot is, and what exactly happened here."

# CHAPTER 48

Bethany stood outside the redbrick building, staring at it curiously through a light sheet of rain. The sky was a dark navy turned murky by the orange cast from the streetlamps. The ominous glow of the night sky causing the redbrick to look sickly.

The building itself was not overly impressive, but she stared none the less.

She had never been to school before, never in her life. As a child she was educated in her home, a place that was no more than a shed compared to the places she'd lived since.

And as a female she had been schooled in things such as sewing, cooking, cleaning and other womanly duties. From the moment she could walk she had been prepared for her role in life.

That of a woman who would one day be a wife and mother and nothing more.

But then, when her family had been slaughtered by a rogue

Vampire, she had the good fortune to be saved and brought into the ranks of Hunters, who gave her a more useful purpose.

They taught her to track, to fight and defend, the ways of Vampires and the ways of Hunters. If she'd ever had children, they would have been raised to be Hunters too, both the boys and girls.

The fact that she had never been traditionally schooled was something she had never mourned over, but now that she was staring at the building she found herself curious.

"What are we doing here?"

Bethany inclined her head slightly, looking to the side where Lucy stood, her arms wrapped around herself as she shivered against the cold.

Bethany let a sigh of irritation. She didn't enjoy being questioned, and she found that after spending the weekend with Lucy and her endless stream of queries, she was losing her patience with the human.

"We are following a trail," she said, her voice dripping with the annoyance she felt.

"Who's trail?" she asked.

Bethany let a low growl, and turned swiftly, swinging her arm out and backhanding Lucy across the face. Lucy's head snapped to the side with a crack, and she raised a hand to her reddening cheek, before she turned to face Bethany and stared. Her mouth half open with shock.

"You will desist with the questions," Bethany snarled, as she turned her back to the school and began to follow the scent of the boy she had spent her weekend with, knowing, rather than hoping that through him she would find who she was looking for.

# CHAPTER 49

*B*y the time Sam got home night had fallen.

They had spent the afternoon in Elliot's house, scouring every inch of it as best they could to find a trace of something—*anything*—to assist them in their search. However, after hours of tearing the house apart, then carefully putting it back together, their search had turned out fruitless.

There was nothing to be found, no trace of where Elliot could have gone, no trace of where the blood-scent was coming from, and no bodies.

With a sigh, Sam had declared that they give up the search and try something else. But what else they could try she hadn't been clear on, she would need time to search through her books at home before she could come up with a viable plan.

Jack had left them then, declaring that he would go check his sources for information.

As they left Elliot's house, Jamie had offered to walk Sam home and assist her with the research, she however, declined, stating that she wanted some time to herself.

So Jamie had ended up walking home alone.

And twenty minutes later Sam wound up at her front door, staring at it with blind eyes as she let herself inside the house.

The heat from the house hit her like a wave as she stepped inside, most of the lights were on and when she looked, she found Danny sitting on the couch in the living room, his head bent down as he looked over something she couldn't see.

She let the door close behind her. Danny's head shot up as it banged, and he looked at her curiously for a moment. Then, when his brain finally registered that it was her, his expression turned to one of stone.

Sam stared at him impatiently, wondering what was wrong with him *now*, when he held up his hand, showing a white page with handwritten words scrawled across it and gazed at her with eyes filled with accusations.

"You didn't read them," he said, his voice coming out softly, his tone tinged with hurt.

Sam let a sigh, as she shook her head. "I figured you'd have guessed that when you didn't get any replies."

Sam could see that he clenched his jaw as she spoke, something which she knew from when they were kids, was a sign of anger. Or more specifically, a sign of his anger with *her*. She'd never witnessed him be angry with anyone else.

"Jack came to see me," he said. "He came to me every week and relayed your *message*."

Sam stared in confusion. "I never gave him any messages."

"Yeah," he said as he stood to face her. "I got that." He let a sigh as the letter slipped from his hand to the coffee table, where there were at least a hundred other un-opened envelopes. "You really are a selfish bitch," he said.

Sam replied with a glare.

"I took time, every week to write to you, and you never even read them! Didn't you care?"

Sam tilted her head slightly. "You didn't."

He stared at her for a moment, his face twitching with an expression of pure anger. "*I* don't care?"

"No," Sam said. "You don't . . . you left me and wrote me a stupid letter to make *yourself* feel better, so don't you dare try to make it out like you sent those for me. I wasn't going to help you feel better for abandoning me. You left me because you hate me and you think it's *my* fault they were killed!"

For a moment Danny simply stared, the expression on his face was one of someone who was lost for words. A bubble of anger rose up through Sam like fire burning in her veins, and before Danny had a chance to speak in his defence, she yelled, "See! I *knew* it!"

"Sam—"

"No," she said, cutting him off. "I was right, I can tell by the look on your face. You don't give a fuck about me or about anybody, everything you did you did for yourself. If you hate me so damn much why would you even bother to come back at all!"

"Sa—"

"NO!" she yelled again, turning her back to him as she rushed towards the door. "Just don't fucking talk to me!"

Without waiting for him to respond she threw the door open and rushed outside, slamming it shut behind her. She heard the door open, but she didn't turn to see him standing there. She ran into the darkness, her heart pounding harder with each step she took.

Her thoughts buzzing through her mind in a frantic jumble, one memory repeating itself, the only thing that stuck out through the haze.

*She stands scared behind a door, watching her adoptive parents beaten bloody through the gap. The room is dark and Demons surround them. A tall man steps forward and asks, "Where is your son?"*

# CHAPTER 50

They walked down a residential street. Bethany looked left and right at the identical houses as they walked. Despite the fact that everything on this street was more or less a mirror image of what was on the other street. She recognised the area from within the memories of Scott.

These were streets that he walked along frequently, though they weren't the ones that led to his home. She paused as she came close to the house she had been looking for. Lucy stopped behind her. Bethany could feel the tension in the other girl as they stood staring at the rows of houses.

"So—"

"Hush," Bethany interrupted, holding up a hand to silence her.

She stared across the street, not at the house she had originally come for, but at the car parked just a little down the road from it.

A black car with darkly tinted windows, a little dusty as if no one had cared to wash it for quite some time. Usually a dusty car wouldn't have piqued Bethany's interest, but there was something odd with this particular one.

For some reason, there appeared to be people sitting inside it.

Slowly, Bethany took a step towards it, she pushed her senses outwards, enveloping the car in a wave of energy, and inside it she felt the unmistakable pulse of non-human Power.

A smile slowly spread across her face, she looked over her shoulder at Lucy. "Wait here."

Lucy opened her mouth, about to protest, but before she could get a word out Bethany moved away, heading quickly towards the car. She heard the engine start as she got close to it; she ran the rest of the distance to the car, and grabbed hold of the handle, pulling the back door open and rushing inside before the car started moving.

"Fuck!" the driver swore a moment later, and stomped his foot down on the brake. The door slammed shut as the car came to a sudden stop. Bethany smiled from the back seat.

"Hello boys," she said.

Both men turned to face her. One of them had blood coloured marks on his skin, swirling patterns up to his jaw line, the other had no visible marks on him, but she could tell by the feel of him that he wasn't human.

"What do you want Vampire?" the driver hissed, he seemed severely annoyed at the sight of her.

"What do I want?" Bethany asked, thinking through the situation momentarily. She smiled. "I want to speak to your leader."

# CHAPTER 51

There wasn't a moment when Sam stopped to think about where she should go, or a moment in which she questioned why she should go there.

In fact, in her mind there was very little thought at all.

She was just running through the woods, allowing her legs to move her on instinct. She only realised where she was when she arrived on the front porch. For a moment she simply stood there, breathing hard as she leaned her head against the wooden door.

Slowly, she reached her hand up and knocked.

She pushed herself back on her heels as the door swung open. Jamie stood on the other side, seeming surprised to see her standing there despite the fact that she was the only person who was able to get this close to his house without an invitation.

Sam didn't know what kind of expression she had on her face, but she assumed she appeared distraught, because after studying her for a moment, his expression grew concerned.

"Sam? Are you okay?"

She said nothing in response. There were no words she could think to say. So instead, she acted on impulse.

As she always did.

Sam gave him no warning, and that was why Jamie, paralysed with surprise, fell to the floor as soon as her body hit his.

Giving him no time to recover, Sam pressed her lips to his. Feeling a brief sense of satisfaction as he let a gasp, his body frozen with shock beneath her.

For a moment he was still, lying on the floor, unmoving, as Sam kissed him. Her lips moving lightly over his, waiting for his reaction before pressing harder.

He didn't move to push her away, but he didn't react either. With a sigh Sam placed both of her hands on the floor either side of his shoulders, about to push herself away, but when she tried, he wrapped one of his arms around her waist, resting his hand on the small of her back and pulled her closer. Pressing her body to his.

Sam placed her hands on either side of his face, before tangling her fingers in his hair. He sat up as they kissed, still holding her close to him, with her sitting across his lap. She wrapped her arms around him, pulling him in tight. Slowly she ran one hand down his back, pausing for a moment before it came to the end of his sweater. Then she gripped onto it and started pulling it up.

She felt Jamie freeze. Then he pushed her away from him. She let her hand fall and stared at him in confusion. "What?" she asked.

He looked at her assessingly for a moment. "I don't know what's happening right now."

Sam rolled her eyes. "Take a guess," she said sarcastically.

He let a frustrated sigh. "No," he said. "Last time this happened I thought I knew what was going on, I was wrong, and now I have *no* idea what's going on ... Am I being used?"

Sam half felt like smiling at his question, but resisted the urge. She shrugged. "I suppose," she answered honestly, which seemed to upset him.

He gently pushed her back, then stood, Sam sighed and got up too, not wanting to sit around on the floor alone. "I don't want to be used," he said, his tone serious, his expression hurt.

Sam let an exasperated sigh. "Do you need a proclamation of love from *everyone* you're with?"

For a moment he glared, his lips pressed firmly together. "No," he said through his teeth. "I don't need a proclamation of love from everyone — "

"Well then!" Sam interrupted. "Why do you need one from me?"

"Because I love you!" he roared. "And if you don't love me too then I would appreciate it if you wouldn't kiss me. There is no in-between. So make your mind up, either you do or you don't."

Sam turned her back to him, waving her hand dismissively as she scoffed. "Whatever," she said, managing just one step towards the door before she felt his hand wrap around her wrist, holding her in place.

"Not whatever Sam," he said, his voice quiet. She looked at him over her shoulder. "I can't force you to tell me how you feel, but I would like it if you could at least be consistent. It's okay if you want to be my friend and nothing more, but I can't know what you want from me unless you tell me, or at the very least refrain from kissing me after more or less telling me you don't care for me like that."

Sam took her gaze away from his face, feeling as though she were about to cry. After the day she'd had, this speech was the very last thing she needed. She took a breath, swallowing her emotions and putting on a mask of indifference, turning a glare to his hand on her wrist. "Are you done?" she asked.

"No," he said, with a kind smile as he slowly took his hand off her. "Why did you come here?" he asked. "Because I'm almost sure it wasn't just to attack me."

Sam shrugged. "I was running and I kind of just ended up here."

He looked at her curiously for a moment, then walked past her and closed the door, which Sam had left open when she'd come in. He turned to face her, his hands behind his back as he leaned against it. "Why were you running?"

Sam thought for a moment. "Exercise?"

He gave her a sideways look and a half smile. "So, at . . . " He paused, leaned forward and glanced to his right, Sam followed his line of sight to the wall where she saw a set of glowing red numbers. " . . . Nine thirty p.m., in the dark, you decide to go for a run through the woods?"

"Yeah . . . *obviously*. If I run through the woods in broad daylight I might get attacked by serial killers."

His mouth twitched as though he was trying not to laugh. "Serial killers in broad daylight?"

"It's a thing," she said defensively, folding her arms across her chest.

"Okay," he said. "So you don't want to talk about it then?"

Sam chewed her lip as she turned her head to the side, staring with unseeing eyes at the bookshelves next to where he stood. Momentarily remembering the time she blew it up.

She turned her attention back to Jamie when she heard him sigh.

He ran his hand through his hair. "Do you want me to walk

you home?"

Sam shook her head. "No," she said, her tone sounding more brooding than she had anticipated. But she couldn't help it, the thought of returning home, where she knew Danny would be waiting for her, was not an appealing one.

"Do you want to stay here?"

Sam half shrugged and shook her head at the same time. She wouldn't mind staying with Jamie, despite the fact that she felt slightly embarrassed by how she'd greeted him. But the main problem with him was that he always asked questions. And right now, she didn't really want to talk about anything.

She was in one of those moods where she wanted to either sulk, or indulge in a distraction.

Jamie looked around the room thoughtfully for a moment. "Do you want to watch a film?" he asked, almost as if he could read her thoughts and was offering her a PG version of what she actually wanted.

She smiled despite her efforts not to, and shrugged.

Jamie laughed slightly, pushing himself away from the door and walking over to the TV, which held the frozen image of some kind of cartoon. She paused for a moment, staring at it with a slight sense of bemusement. She'd never thought of Jamie to be the sort of person to sit around watching cartoons; in a way she'd always thought him too old for that sort of thing. But then she remembered what Jack had said about Vampires, and how no matter how long they lived they would always mentally be the same age. Looking at Jamie now, standing in front of his TV, gazing down at the shelves and stacks of DVDs and games, she could see it. Despite the fact that he had been around for two centuries, he would forever be a kid. Just as she was now destined to be.

With a momentary smile, she walked over to the couch and

sat herself down. Leaning back and placing her feet on the edge of the coffee table. "What are you watching?" she asked.

Jamie looked at her over his shoulder. "Nothing," he replied. "I was just flicking through the channels."

She picked up the remote which sat on the seat next to her, and twirled it around in her hand. "You paused your channel surfing?"

He smiled and shrugged. "Something good might come on . . . I didn't want to miss it."

Sam pointed the remote towards the TV and pressed play. The screen came to life and the scene moved, showing Sam some recognisable faces. She smiled widely. "You were watching *The Simpsons*."

Jamie looked as though he was trying not to smile. "It amuses me," he said, as he leaned forward and snatched the remote from her hand, pointing it at the TV and pausing the show once more. "So what would you like to see?"

Sam shrugged, taking a moment to think through all of the things she enjoyed watching and had a vague interest in seeing now. "Buffy," she said with a smile.

Jamie looked at her for a moment, seeming slightly unimpressed by her choice. "Buffy," he repeated. She nodded her reply. "Buffy the *Vampire* Slayer."

Sam smiled and nodded again.

Jamie sighed, then smiled. "Are you trying to give me nightmares?" he asked, though his question sounded both rhetorical and sarcastic.

She shrugged. "It *amuses* me."

He laughed slightly. "You find amusement in witnessing the slaughter of my people . . . " He shook his head. "That's just cruel."

Sam laughed.

"*Fine*," he said with a dramatic sigh. "Would you like to see the TV show or the film?"

Sam gave him a questioning look. "There's a film?" she asked.

He nodded. "Came out over . . . fifteen years ago I think."

"So, it's super old then?"

He gave her a sideways glance. "It's younger than you are."

Sam glared at him, then stuck out her tongue in retort. "Don't imply I'm old."

"You call me ancient all the time."

"That's because you *are*."

The smile he gave her seemed slightly maniacal. "And one day you will be too."

Sam scowled and folded her arms across her chest. "Yeah well . . . just remember, that no matter how ancient I get, you'll always be ancienter."

"Ancienter?" he asked, his expression amused.

"It's a word!" she yelled defiantly.

He laughed and mumbled, "It's not a word."

Sam was about to reply, when he interrupted. Turning to face her fully. "So, Buffy . . . TV or film?"

Sam shrugged. "Movie," she said. Deciding she'd rather see something she hadn't before. "Do you actually have it?" she asked, leaning to the side as she looked past him to the stacks of DVDs. Although he did have a lot of them, she hadn't assumed that he'd have access to whatever she'd suggest they watch.

He nodded his head. "That's not even close to a fraction," he said, using his thumb to point at the shelves. "I've got quite a collection of films, most of them are in storage though."

"Oh," Sam said, wondering briefly where it was he kept his storage items. From what she'd seen of his home, there didn't seem to be an attic or basement. Downstairs there was just this room and the kitchen, and upstairs was just the bedroom and bathroom. There were no other doors in the house at all . . . perhaps he had another place he kept things.

He hunkered down next to the shelves and pulled a bunch of them out, seeming to know exactly where everything was despite the fact that she saw no evidence of them being organised in any specific way.

He pulled a DVD from the back of the shelf, and threw it over his shoulder. With a bounce, it landed next to Sam. She picked it up off the chair and held it in her hands, squinting her eyes in confusion at the people on the cover.

"This isn't Buffy," she said, as Jamie placed all the DVDs back on the shelf.

She heard him laugh. "It came out before," he said. "The TV show was a remake."

"Huh." She held the DVD out to him and he took it from her, turning away to the TV, kneeling down in front of it. He pressed the power button on the DVD player, jumping back with a start. Sam looked at him curiously as he shook his hand, glaring at his DVD player as if it had committed an act of betrayal. "What's wrong?" she asked.

Jamie looked at his hand. "Nothing," he said with a sigh. "The electricity here has been a bit iffy lately," he laughed slightly. "I keep getting electrocuted."

"How often do you get electrocuted?" Sam asked curiously, watching as he squeezed his hand into a fist and released it, before quickly pressing the open tray button on the DVD player. She smiled as she heard him curse under his breath, he turned to look at her, smiling timidly.

"Sorry," he said. "It's starting to get a bit annoying. Any time I touch anything that's plugged in I get . . . *zapped*."

Sam sat forward. "Every time?"

He nodded, taking the disc out of the case and putting in into the DVD player, pulling his sleeve down to cover his hand before pushing the button to close the tray. Jamie stood, holding his hands out in front of him, wiggling his fingers as he stared at them. "I should get some rubber gloves."

Sam laughed. "*Or*, you could call an electrician."

Jamie waved his hand dismissively. "I don't *need* an electrician," he said. "I can fix it myself, I just don't have the time."

"I don't believe *any* of what you just said."

"I can fix it," he said defensively, picking the remote up and sitting beside her. "And I don't have the time. I'm very busy."

"Doing what?"

"You know," he said while changing the channel. "Things . . . and stuff."

Sam smiled and shook her head. "You don't have things and stuff to do."

Jamie looked at her, his eyes lighting up in a smile. For a moment, she stared at him. Remembering the first time she'd seen his eyes, how she'd thought they were a pretty shade of ice-blue, the colour cold yet simultaneously filled with feeling.

Right now the blue was more vibrant than it should have been, the colour seeming almost saturated, the shade more electric than ice.

And for a moment, as she stared, she could have sworn that she saw what looked like small veins of energy move beneath their surface. But when she looked again, they were completely gone.

She shook her thoughts away, turning towards the TV as Jamie pressed play.

# CHAPTER 52

The idea of staying in Sam's house all day with Danny while Sam and Jamie were out doing whatever it was those two spent their time doing did not really seem like the most entertaining way for Jade to spend her day.

It had been different at the weekend when Sam had been around and they were able to hang out together. But it felt weird to just lurk around her friend's house alone all day with only her friend's older brother for company.

That was why Jade had opted to spend the day at her own house.

It was the first time she'd spent more than just a few minutes there in the past few days.

It was a weird feeling.

As per usual her mother was locked in her room doing God only knew what. She didn't care to ask, and her mother didn't care to tell.

Jade's dad left them a few months ago and it seemed that

253

ever since then her mother had been behaving strangely. She spent a lot of time locked inside the house, inside her room, and didn't really take much time to talk to Jade or anyone outside of her coven. She barely ever saw her mother really, and the times that she did she was met with either a cold indifference or a burning hot anger.

It hadn't always been that way, not that Jade could remember at least.

Or perhaps her mother had always been this way and she just hadn't noticed it until it was just the two of them. No longer with another person to shield her from the seemingly psychotic mood swings.

It didn't really make that much of a difference though, Jade would be out of this place soon enough and she would never have to deal with her mother ever again if she didn't want to.

With a sigh, Jade turned her attention back to the medical journal she was flicking through.

Not exactly study material, but she liked to read the new issues just to keep up to date, thinking perhaps it would make her feel not so far behind when she finally made it to college next year.

She was halfway through an article on the recent progressions in transplantation when the room became unusually cold. Jade looked up just in time to see the air by her closet begin to shimmer.

Swiftly she pushed herself up off the bed and rushed to the door, not sticking around long enough to see who or what was making its way into her room.

She never made it to the door.

Jade's feet had just hit the floor and started moving in the direction of freedom when the intruder smashed her over the head with something incredibly hard.

She felt the blow reverberate through every bone in her

body. The pain swelled in her skull immediately and blood dripped down her forehead.

Her eyes became so tinged with red and her body became so weak that she couldn't tell if she actually hit the floor or passed out before the impact.

# CHAPTER 53

When Jack got home Sam wasn't there. He let a sigh, not needing to think too hard to know where she would be. He didn't try to find her for a variety of reasons, one being that he didn't want to disturb her, another being that he liked Jamie, and didn't want to walk in on anything that would make Jack not like him anymore.

He stepped out of Sam's room and walked down the stairs where he found Danny sitting on the sofa, his body slumped forward.

"What's wrong?" he asked, his tone filled with impatience. Unable to help his feeling or the tone he used to show it; he was sick of Danny and Sam bickering over nothing, and more than that he was sick of Danny living in a state of denial.

Danny looked up at him slowly, chewing his lower lip. "You lied to me," he said, his voice sounding hurt despite the fact that he spoke so quietly.

Jack stepped further into the room, where he saw a stack of

unopened and torn envelopes. He let a sigh and sank down to the sofa next to Danny. "I tried to get her to read them," he said. "She didn't want to, and I didn't want you to feel like she didn't care."

Danny scoffed. "She fucking doesn't care."

Jack pressed his lips together firmly. Despite what everyone seemed to think, he wasn't actually blind, he knew all too well about Sam's faults, however, it still angered him to hear other people speak about her in an unflattering way. "She does," he said firmly. "She cares too much."

Danny rolled his eyes.

Jack felt himself fill with rage. "You don't fucking know what it was like once you abandoned her!" he yelled. "You weren't here, *I* was. And you have some fucking nerve coming in here, treating her like you have after everything she's been through and everything that's happened because of *you*."

"What about what she's put me through?"

"What exactly has she put you through?" Jack asked.

"My whole damn family is dead because of her!" he said, his eyes watering slightly. "*Everyone* dies because of *her*."

"People die," Jack said. "It's a fact of life, people die. They're always going to die, there's nothing that could have been done—"

"They could have left her with the Vampires, in the world she belongs in. Mixing her with regular people was a mistake."

"The *only* mistake that was made was giving her to *your* parents," Jack said, looking Danny directly in the eyes as he spoke. "Your mother was a Witch," Danny huffed and shook his head. "She was a Witch!" Jack yelled, hoping the extra volume would help the message seep in. "And so are *you*."

"No—"

"Yes," Jack said. "Your mother was wrong, to tell you the things she did. There is nothing wrong with what you are, and there was nothing wrong with what she was. She had this idea that being human meant being better, but that's not true. You are what you are and you need to accept it. The reason you dislike Sam is because she accepts what she is, the *only* reason she tries so hard to be human is because she wants to feel like you love her."

"She knows—"

"No," Jack cut him off. "She doesn't. She knows you blame her for what happened, and she knows you hate what she is. And she feels like you hate her, so she tried to be normal for you. If your parents had allowed her to embrace her Powers sooner, and if your mother had used hers when they were attacked, the odds are they would be alive. Did you know that Sam tried to save them?"

Slowly, Danny shook his head. "She, a twelve year old girl, ran at a group of fully grown men to try save them. Your mother told her not to, that it was better to die a human than to live as a freak."

"She didn't say that," Danny whispered. "She wouldn't."

"I was there," Jack said. "She *did* say that. And because of it, they died, and Sam was taken. All because she *didn't* use her Magic."

Danny turned his face away, letting his head fall to his hand. "What am I supposed to do?" he asked.

"You could start by not yelling at her so much, try smiling, and cut down on all the 'Magic is wrong' bullshit."

He let a sigh. "She ran off," he said. "Probably gone to that Vampire."

"He has a name," Jack mumbled.

Danny rolled his eyes and folded his arms across his chest. "I was going to go after her," he said. "But I didn't realise she could run so fast."

"Of course she can run fast," Jack said with a proud smile. "She was trained by the greatest Jack in the world."

"I didn't realise Jack Nicholson could run," Danny said with a smile.

"Don't be an asshole," Jack said. "It's why Sam ran away."

Danny sighed, then checked his watch for the time. Jack watched him curiously as he stared at it in confusion. "Where's Jade . . . I thought you told her she was supposed to hang out here?" he asked.

Jack shook his head. "Sam probably called her and told her she wouldn't be home."

Danny stood, stretching his arms above his head. "You know how to get to the Vampire's house?"

Jack nodded. "Again . . . he has a name."

Danny walked to the hallway and pulled a jacket from the coat rack by the door. "Lead the way."

# CHAPTER 54

$\mathcal{L}$ucy had heard of The Underworld before, but she had never seen the inside of it herself. She had imagined something different from where she was now. From what she'd heard, the 'Demons'—as they called themselves— mainly operated from underground. She'd imagined dusty tunnels that had been converted into a military base and living quarters. However, the place that she and Bethany had been brought to was a small cabin outside of town.

Lucy had been made to wait outside while the discussions were going on beyond the door. Apparently she didn't rank high enough to be present. At first she'd been annoyed, but her anger had been lessened when Malachi, who was Kraven's second in command, had also been told to wait outside. Apparently, *no one* was a high enough rank to be allowed inside.

She watched him curiously as they stood on either side of the door. He was leaning back, with one foot pressed against the door frame, his arms folded across his chest and his head resting back on the wall. He stared upward, seeming lost in concentration. "Can you hear them?" she asked.

He glanced sideways at her, and nodded his head.

"What are they saying?" she asked.

With a sigh he unfolded his arms and held one of his hands out to her. She stared at it for a moment, then cautiously took his hand in hers. He closed his fingers around her hand, and she gasped, suddenly able to hear voices in her head.

Bethany looked around the room with a vague amount of interest, only briefly wondering why everyone had been sent outside.

"Why have you come?" Kraven asked, eyeing her warily from across the room.

"I was curious," she replied.

Kraven huffed in annoyance, folding his arms across his chest. "I haven't the time to alleviate your curiosity," he said harshly. "Why did you ambush my men?" he asked. "Did you track them down purely out of curiosity?"

"No," she said with a smile.

"So I was correct in thinking you tracked them down for less than reputable purposes."

Bethany shook her head. "I was tracking a Vampire, and I just so happened to find your people outside his girlfriend's house." She smiled as Kraven's eyes widened. "I was curious as to *why* you had people watching a human girl."

He seemed to smirk at her for a moment. "That's not your concern," he said.

"So I was correct in thinking you want her for less than reputable purposes?" She repeated his words with a smile. "I want her out of the way anyway," she said. "I just came to make sure that's what you were doing, her being one of your recruits isn't good enough."

"I can assure you," he said, "that I have no interest in recruiting her."

"Good," Bethany said with a clap of her hands. "In that case you can leave me where you found me."

Kraven smiled. "The human you brought with you —"

"Lucy," Bethany said. "She's got potential, but she wears on my patience . . . I was planning to kill her."

"She," he started, "would be a fine recruit."

Bethany rolled her eyes. "Oh, *alright,* you can have her."

With a scoff, Lucy pulled her hand out of Malachi's, not wanting to hear any more of their ridiculous conversation. He looked at her, his mouth quirked in amusement. "That's not how it works you know," he said. "We don't kidnap people and hold them against their will. You'll be offered the choice to stay here, and if you don't want to, no hard feelings."

Lucy folded her arms across her chest. "I'm a *Vampire Hunter,*" she said, emphasising the words. She knew what she was and had no real desire to be anything else.

"You're bait," he said with a smug smile that made her want to punch him. "Not a Hunter, and what were the odds you ever would have been?"

"They trained me how to fight!" she said defensively. "Why would they train me un —"

"Protecting their investment," he said simply. "Vampire Hunters are humans with little sense of the universe. They see what they want to see and ignore what they don't, and they are incredibly sexist when it comes to who gets what jobs. The young, the pretty and the female are the bait. And when you're not young, or pretty anymore . . . well . . . " He shrugged. "There seems to be an awful lot of 'Vampire attacks' on people they no longer have use for." The air quotes he placed around the words *Vampire attacks* made Lucy feel slightly queasy.

"You're lying," she said, even though she wasn't completely sure that he was.

"Why would I?" he asked. "By the way, the girl who was being watched —"

"Never seen her," Lucy said. "I didn't even know why we were there, Bethany just kept saying we were following a trail."

"The Vampire's?"

Lucy nodded. "He was a weird one, begged me to kill him when he thought he killed his girlfriend," she shrugged. "Guess she was al — wait . . . is this a blonde girl?"

Malachi smiled. "So you *have* seen her."

"She's not human," Lucy said in surprise. "Bethany thinks she is."

"And it's best if she keeps thinking that," he said with a meaningful look in her direction.

"Well I'm hardly going to tell her, am I? She's probably already gone."

He nodded his head. "She is. Kraven is in there thinking of a strategy to attempt to get you on our side," he smiled at her. "Though I would say I've just about talked you over."

She scowled. "Says who?"

"Should I give you a description of the benefits? First there's cake."

Her mouth quirked in amusement. "Are you really trying to bribe me with cake?"

"It's pretty good cake," he said. "And you can have some whenever you want. Second, we provide you with a home, though for the first two years you'll have to stay in the common area at our training facility. The rooms are pretty big though, and they have private bathrooms. You'll learn how to fight and to use Magic—"

"Magic?" she asked in disbelief. "You do realise I'm *human*, right?"

He smiled. "So was I two centuries ago. And now I'm an immortal Warlock. Which is another benefit, immortality is not mandatory, but it's available if you want it. Also, the fight skills are for your own protection, you don't *have* to actually participate in fighting. There are many careers, and also, it's a ten year contract to begin with, then after you sign up for five years at a time. It's like a job, when your contract is up, you're free to leave, but your memories will be wiped of any important information you may have gotten."

"So, not killed?"

"God no," he smiled. "Despite what our enemies say, we're not actually the bad guys."

Lucy took a breath and gave Malachi a measured look, folding her arms across her chest as she did. The offer *was* tempting . . .

"Pay?" she asked.

"On a weekly basis starting at four hundred a week, double when you finish the training years. Which is way more than you'd make as a *Vampire Hunter*." He spoke the last two words slowly, his tone mocking.

She responded with a glare.

"Food?"

"Provided free of charge for as long as you live in the common area, if you move out you do your own shopping."

"Uniform?"

"Isn't one, though if you're working outside, dark colours are preferred for camouflage purposes."

Lucy nodded. Just as the door opened. She looked at it warily, expecting to see someone standing there.

There wasn't.

She looked to Malachi, who walked past her into the cabin, glancing back only to indicate for her to follow.

She stepped inside, Malachi closing the door behind her, and looked to the brown leather sofa where Kraven sat. He stood when she entered, looking at her with a serious yet friendly expression. "I'm sorry," he said. "What was your name?"

Malachi smiled and answered before she had a chance. "Lucy," he said. "Didn't get a last name, but she's already agreed to sign up."

Lucy placed her hands on her hips and looked accusingly in Malachi's direction. "I never said that."

"It was implied," he said, waving a hand dismissively in her direction.

"No it wasn't," Lucy said.

"You were going to say okay before the door opened."

"I was," she admitted, "but there was a sentence to follow."

"Conditions?" Kraven asked. She looked at him, he seemed amused. "That's rare ... People don't usually have conditions."

Lucy shrugged. "Well, I do. So I'll agree under one condition."

"Is it that Malachi has to stay away from you?" he asked, seeming genuine in his inquiry. "Because that is a complaint I've heard before."

"My advances never come unwelcome," Malachi said defensively.

Kraven smiled. "Then why do I get so many requests for you to be moved?"

Malachi shrugged. "My advances are welcomed, but it gets awkward for some afterwards."

"That wasn't my condition," Lucy said. "But it's part of the deal now."

Malachi sulked, and folded his arms across his chest while mumbling about how he gets no appreciation for the work he does.

Kraven smiled at her. "What is your condition?"

"Bethany . . ." Lucy said. "I want to kill her."

# CHAPTER 55

$\mathcal{J}$ack looked on with a sense of amusement as Danny suddenly stopped moving at the line of trees that surrounded Jamie's house. He looked down at his feet in confusion, most likely wondering why they had suddenly stopped working. Jack smiled. "It's warded," he said.

Danny sighed and rolled his eyes. "How do I get in?"

Jack walked up to the house at a quick pace, pausing halfway there when the door opened. Jamie stood on the other side, looking between Jack and Danny in confusion. "You can come in," he said to Danny.

With a less than gracious attitude, Danny stormed forward, walking straight into Jamie's house and almost pushing him down in the process. Jack sighed as he followed.

Jamie closed the door behind them and Jack looked around, expecting to see Sam, but she wasn't there.

Danny, after apparently noticing the same thing turned a glare in Jamie's direction. "Where is she!" he demanded.

"Upstairs," he said. Before Jamie had a chance to say anything else, Danny turned and stomped up the stairs. "She's asleep," Jamie said, called after him, looking back a Jack for a moment to see if he was following.

With a sigh Jack followed. "Please tell me she has clothes on," he mumbled.

The expression Jamie gave him seemed slightly amused. "Why would I steal her clothes while she's sleeping?"

"Don't be a smart arse."

At the top of the stairs there was just one door at the end of a short hallway. Danny was already standing in front of it, his hand hovering on the handle. He looked over his shoulder at Jamie, his expression set in one of anger. "Is she dressed?" he asked.

Jamie let a sigh. "She fell asleep while watching a film," he said. "I put her in bed so she'd be comfortable. I didn't touch her, and I haven't stolen her clothing."

Danny opened the door and stepped inside, Jamie followed and Jack came in behind. The room was quite large, and very neat. The only thing that littered the floor were Sam's boots which lay on the floor at the foot of the bed, where Sam was lying unconscious, one arm under her head, her hair spread across the pillows.

"See," Jamie said with a smile. "Fully dressed."

Danny grumbled, and Jack grinned.

"Now," said Jamie, folding his arms across his chest. "Do either of you want to tell me why Sam showed up here after running around through the woods for an hour?"

"No," Danny said, at the same time Jack said, "Danny started a fight."

"She didn't tell you?" Danny asked, eyeing Jamie curiously.

Jamie shrugged. "She didn't want to talk about it."

Danny snorted. "Some boyfriend you are. If you saw she

was upset you should have made her talk."

"I'm not her boyfriend," Jamie said, his voice sounding slightly irritated as he spoke. "And forcing her to talk would only upset her more."

"He's right," Jack said. He knew better than anyone what Sam was like, and how if she didn't want to talk to you the worst thing you could do was try to force her. Forcing her to share would just push her away and make her less likely to acknowledge your existence.

"Whose side are you on?" Danny asked with a glare.

"Sam's," Jack stated.

Danny let a sigh and turned around to face the bed where Sam was sleeping. He stepped forward and placed his hand on her shoulder, shaking her harder than he needed to. Jack scowled at the back of his head, trying to project his contempt in such a way that Danny would feel it without turning around.

Sam's eyes flew open at the same time she sat up. She blinked as if dazed, then slowly her expression turned to one of confusion as her eyes met Jack's, then she turned to glare at Danny. "What are *you* doing here?" she asked.

"I came to take you home," he said. "I tried calling you earlier bu—"

"I threw my phone off a cliff."

"Bit dramatic," Jack laughed. "But I like it."

Sam sighed and rolled her eyes. Which was the response he usually got from her, so he wasn't surprised or offended.

"Why did you let him in?" she asked, turning an accusing glare in Jamie's direction.

He shrugged. "It's cold outside, and I didn't want to get the blame for him catching the flu."

"Smart move," Jack said. "He does like to blame people for things that aren't their fault."

"That he does," Sam said, folding her arms across her chest as she eyed Danny.

He simply sighed, then turned towards Jack and Jamie. "Do you two *have* to be here?"

"Well, it's my room," Jamie said. "So I feel like I do have to be here."

"If Jamie gets to stay I get to stay," said Jack. "It's only fair."

Danny groaned and turned to Sam. "I'm sorry," he said. She watched him, her expression kept carefully controlled. "There, we're good now."

"Do you even know *why* you're sorry?" she asked.

"Because I upset you, and you won't come home otherwise."

"Ooh . . . " Jack let a low whistle.

Jamie shook his head. "Even I can tell that's the wrong answer."

Jack was expecting Danny to yell at them, but to his surprise it was Sam that spoke. "If you two aren't going to be helpful you can leave!"

"I'm always helpful," Jack said defensively.

"I don't know what happened, so how can I possibly help?"

Sam dropped her head and rubbed her eyes with the back of her hand. "Don't apologise unless you know what it's for," she said softly.

Danny took a breath and let it out slowly. "I'm sorry for everything," he said. "I know I can be an ass, and that I give you a hard time, but it's just because . . . " He let a sigh as he seemed to struggle to find the right words. "I don't really understand this stuff and I get *scared*. I don't know what's going to happen, I don't know if you're going to die, or if I'm going to die . . . I don't actually hate you or anything."

Sam let a sigh, and smiled slightly. "Okay," she said. "I forgive you just this once."

Danny smiled.

"Now hug it out," Jack said.

Danny raised a hand and let it fall on Sam's head, he ruffled her hair before he stood.

Jack half smiled. "Close enough."

Sam pushed the duvet off herself and swung her legs over the side of the bed. "Where's Jade?" she asked.

Danny looked to Jack in confusion, then back to Sam. "You didn't call her and tell her to stay home?"

Slowly, Sam shook her head. "*Please* tell me you checked she was actually home before you came here."

Danny gave Jack a worried glance. "We assumed —"

"Are you kidding!" Sam jumped up off the bed, grabbing her boots from beside it, she put them on one at a time, balancing on one leg as she did.

Jamie ran his hand through his hair. "There are evil spirits on the prowl and neither of you thought to check?"

"Did *you*?" Danny asked.

"Not only do I not have her number," he said, "but she was supposed to be at *your* house."

"Stop fighting!" Sam yelled as she walked past them and pulled the door open. "It won't get us anywhere."

Jack turned and followed Sam out of the room and down the stairs, watching her as she drew a portal on the inside of Jamie's front door with expert precision. It flashed into existence with a bright glow. Sam looked back and indicated with her head for everyone to step through. Both Jamie and Danny did as commanded, but Jack could tell they were uncomfortable with using a portal. Though neither of them argued about it.

Once they were gone Jack followed, knowing that Sam was with him as he heard the portal close.

# CHAPTER 56

$\mathcal{J}$amie stepped through the portal hesitantly, his stomach feeling as though it was upside down within his body, as it always did when they used this form of travel. He met Danny on the other side, and after sharing a glance of contempt, they both turned to watch the portal. Jack was the next one through, followed by Sam.

Before Jamie had a chance to open his mouth and ask what exactly it was they were about to do, Sam dashed past him, running—in the dark—towards the staircase, the wood creaking loudly under her weight. Without wasting a second Jamie was behind her, followed by Danny and Jack. "Sam," he said as she swung the basement door open and ran into the hallway. "What's the—" Jamie paused when he noticed they weren't in Sam's house. He looked around curiously at the darkened hallway.

It was only when Sam called for Jade that Jamie realised where they must be.

She ran through the hallway and Jamie followed her as she ran up the stairs, looking back towards Danny and Jack, he asked, "Should we really have bar —"

Jamie was cut off by a green flash that whipped past his head at a frightening speed. He cried out in alarm, and it took a moment for him to identify what it was . . . a blast of green Magic. He stared as it flew to the wall by the front door where it hit the frame, leaving black scorch marks on the wood. He turned his head quickly towards the top of the landing where Sam stood with her back pressed to the wall after apparently narrowly avoiding being hit with the magical blast.

Hayley stood at the top of the stairs, looking down at them through half-lidded eyes, a slow smile creeping on her face.

"What are you doing?" Danny asked, sounding outraged as he stormed up the stairs behind Jamie, stopping halfway between him and Sam. "You could have killed her!"

Hayley tilted her head slightly to the side, giving Danny a look of innocence mixed in with a hint of confusion. "You broke in," she said. "And you brought the Vampire . . . I don't like the Vampire, he doesn't respect me as a leader."

"Are you drunk woman!" Jack asked, peering at her from between the banister. "Because you sound like you're either completely hammered, or completely mad."

"Are you disrespecting me Hunter?" she asked, turning her head slightly in Jack's direction. Though her tone sounded more inquisitive than angry or threatening. "After what I did for your Sam?"

"Hayley," Jack started. "I've never had respect for you . . . I tolerate you because I'm fond of Jade. Now tell us . . . " The gleam in Jack's eye made him look somewhat menacing. It reminded Jamie of the look on the face of the Hunter as he'd lunged at Sam. "Where the fuck is Jade!"

Hayley smiled, showing her teeth, which seemed too white

in the darkness of the house. "She's gone," she said calmly.

Sam pushed past Hayley and ran towards the room that Jamie knew to be Jade's. "It's a mess," she called as she walked back out into the hallway, marching straight up to Hayley and staring her down.

Jamie had never given much thought to how tall Sam was, but as she stood now, her chin at level with Hayley's forehead, her eyes glaring down at her, she looked more than imposing, and completely terrifying, though her stance gave her a somewhat regal appearance. And at once, he thought of Jack, and how he'd worn the same expression moments ago.

"Where is she?" Sam spoke through her teeth, making her words sound not like a question or request, but a demand and a threat.

Hayley sighed and let her eyes flutter closed, seeming half amused and completely bored.

Sam's arms shot out, and Jamie stepped forward, thinking that Sam was about to strike the woman, but he stopped in his tracks when Hayley flew back, hitting the wall with a dull thud. Sam raised her arm up high, causing Hayley to slide up the wall, the top of her head pressed to the ceiling, her neck bent slightly to the side.

Despite the obvious fact that Hayley was being held at an uncomfortable angle, she was laughing. As though she found the situation to be amusing.

For a moment Jamie simply stared, unsure as to how he should react. Watching Hayley laugh like a maniac made him feel uncomfortable. There was obviously something wrong.

Even though he didn't really know Hayley and the one time he had spoken with her had been strange at best, he *knew* that there was something about her that wasn't right.

She was behaving almost as though she were possessed.

"There's something wrong with her," Danny said. Only by

his thoughts being voiced by someone else did Jamie realise that they all must have been thinking the same thing.

In front of him he could sense Sam shaking, and when he looked up at her, for a very brief moment, he saw an expression of fear and panic reflected in her indigo eyes.

He could tell that she was struggling, deciding whether she should spare Hayley whatever pain she would have to be put through or exact whatever tortures she was considering to find Jade.

And it was that momentary look in Sam's eyes, the expression of anger fuelled desperation that broke Jamie's heart and filled his veins with a feeling of rage towards the person who had caused her to look that way.

Before he fully realised what he was doing he charged forward and caught Hayley by the throat, holding his hand firmly across her neck. "Where is she!" he yelled. Thinking that if she didn't like him, he would give her a better reason than the one she had.

He didn't need to look behind him to know that everyone was staring at him in shock. He could feel their surprise as if it were his own, and could feel their eyes on him. He pressed harder against Hayley's neck. She let out a whimper, but smiled all the same. "You'll *never* find her," she sang. "She's going to die."

Before Jamie had a chance to speak, Sam yelled, "Tell me where she is or I'll cut your fucking throat!"

Jamie stared at Hayley for a moment as she smiled. With more force than was necessary, he pulled her down so that she was at eye level with him. He glared at her, his eyes staring directly into hers, her iris's swimming with Shadows. He spoke calmly. "Tell us."

She gripped onto his arm, which was still at her neck and said nothing. She simply smiled her eerie smile.

Jamie clenched his jaw in anger and pushed harder against her throat. She let a gasp. For a moment, as he watched that smile once again spread on her face, he imagined the various ways he could wipe it off.

He imagined perhaps taking a knife, and with it he could slice tiny cuts along her skin, pushing the blade in harder the more she refused to cooperate, he was sure that pain was all the incentive she would need.

He imagined taking the blade to her face, slicing it across her temple where there wasn't much skin to cushion the pain and bringing it across, blood would flow from it, dripping down her face until it made its way to her eyes.

He hadn't realised his fangs had extended until he heard Hayley scream. "Stop!" she pleaded. "Stop it! Get him off me!"

"Tell us!" Danny said, his tone making him sound as though he was genuinely concerned for Hayley's safety. "Quick or he'll kill you!"

"Warlocks!" Hayley yelled. "I gave her to the Demons . . . I don't know where they took her!"

Jamie let her go, half expecting her to stay floating in the air, but she fell to the landing floor with a thud. At some point Sam must have released her from the spell.

Jamie stepped away from her, feeling at his teeth curiously. It was then that he noticed the blood on Hayley's face.

"Let's go," Sam said, walking down the stairs and towards the front door. "I have an idea."

Without questioning what exactly Sam's idea was, Jamie followed her outside.

Jack turned to him as they walked out of the house, using the front door this time instead of a portal. "You know, it usually takes Vampires *at least* half a millennia to learn that. And most of them never accomplish it successfully."

Jamie looked at Jack curiously. "What are you talking about?"

"Psychokinesis," he said with a smile. "I didn't realise you'd mastered it."

" . . . I haven't."

# CHAPTER 57

$\mathcal{S}$am glanced over her shoulder when she heard the front door to Hayley's house slam shut, she let out a breath she hadn't realised she'd been holding.

Hayley was possessed by one of those Shadow things, she'd seen it in her eyes as Jamie had threatened her, but there was nothing they could do to help her right now. Not only did Sam not know how to depossess someone, she didn't have the time. Jade had been taken, that was their priority.

She unclasped her hand and gazed at the item inside. A scrunched up corner from a page within a medical journal with splashes of semi-dried blood on it.

"What's that?" Danny asked as he came closer to Sam.

"It's Jade's blood," she said, not taking her eyes off her hand. "I got it from her room. I was thinking we could use it to scry for her."

"Is that your plan?" he asked.

"What plan?" Jack interjected as he got within earshot.

"Sam's going to scry for Jade."

Sam shook her head. "That's not the plan," she said. "That's part of the plan, I'll do that after I talk to Madison."

"Why Madison?" Danny asked, at the same time Jamie asked, "Who's Madison?"

Sam rolled her eyes. "Half-Warlock," she said. "Am I the only one who always thought it was strange to have a half-Warlock in a Witches coven?"

"Is there really that much of a difference?" Jamie asked.

Jack shook his head. "Not really," he replied. "But Witches are notoriously racist, and won't allow anyone who's not a full blooded Witch in their covens . . . Warlocks are half-breeds, mixed Magic, not pure like the Witches believe they are. It's all complete bullshit if you ask me though. Magic is Magic, and the more it's mixed the stronger it gets."

"I think Madison is a spy," Sam said casually, as if she were stating something that would be mentioned in everyday conversation.

Everyone was looking at her strangely though, as if they thought she was insane for having come to that conclusion.

"Sam." Jack gave her a kind smile, the kind that was usually followed by a hand on the shoulder and him saying something like 'you're stressed', 'you need sleep', or 'you've completely lost your mind'.

"I have a *feeling*," she said. Knowing as she said it that the feeling wasn't hers. She'd known Madison since she'd come to this town. They'd been friends — best friends — and never had she thought that Madison's reason for being her friend was anything unscrupulous.

Even now she didn't think that Madison had done anything outright evil, she wasn't capable of it. But there was a nagging thought in the recesses of Sam's mind that told her there was something *wrong,* and that Madison had information she needed.

"What kind of feeling?" Jamie asked, watching her curiously. "Is it like a premonition?"

Sam shook her head. "Still not psychic," she stated. "But . . . it's like those dreams I had, they were in my head, but they weren't mine . . . and every time I had one, they were right. So . . . "

"So you should talk to Madison," Danny said. He reached out and took the crumpled piece of paper from Sam's hand. "Me and Jack can make an attempt at scrying."

Jack looked at Danny, his eyebrows raised in both confusion and surprise. "We can?"

Danny shrugged. "I know how," he mumbled defensively.

"Okay," Sam said, too tired and glad for the help to bother arguing. Even if Danny didn't really know how to scry, Jack — as a trained Bounty Hunter — did.

"I'll go with Sam then," Jamie said. "Should we set a time to meet back? How long does scrying take?"

With a sigh Danny rolled his eyes and started walking towards their house, Jack followed behind him.

"We all have phones," Sam said, grabbing hold of Jamie's arm by the wrist. "If anyone finds anything important, they'll send a text."

# CHAPTER 58

When they had started walking through the vacant residential streets, Jamie hadn't been sure how long it would take them to get there. He remembered walking with both Sam and Jade to Madison's house on Halloween night, but he hadn't been paying much attention to the twists of the streets, or the appearance of the houses, he'd been too preoccupied by his feeling of elation at being invited along to a party. Even in his human life, he was never the sort of person that was invited to parties, or *anywhere* really.

They arrived at Madison's house within fifteen minutes, which surprised Jamie, because he had remembered the walk being shorter last time. Though that could have been because the last time he'd walked this route, he, Sam and Jade had been caught up in conversation and laughter. Whereas this time, he walked a pace behind Sam in complete silence.

Jamie looked up at the house they had stopped in front of. All of the windows were dark, and from what he could tell, it appeared as though everyone was asleep. "So . . . " he said, turning to Sam. "What's the plan?"

"You keep the parents unconscious," she said. "It might take a bit more focus than usual because her dad is a Warlock, so pay close attention to him, if you feel him stir even just a little, push harder."

Jamie nodded his head to indicate his understanding.

"I'll deal with Madison."

Sam opened the front door as if it wasn't even locked, she looked at Jamie over her shoulder, and he took that as his cue to keep the parents in a state of unconsciousness. He pushed out with his mind, with all of the strength he could muster, and sent out a psychic wave, directed towards the room where he could feel two heartbeats.

"Jamie!"

He opened his eyes when he heard Sam yell, as soon as he did he saw the lights in the house dim before switching off completely. Sam stared at him open-mouthed. "What did you *do?*"

Jamie gazed upwards in confusion. "Nothing," he said. "I just did what you told me to do."

"Well *I* didn't do that," she said, pointing up. "Is her dad awake?"

Jamie didn't have to reach out too far to find out, he could still sense the sleeping couple he'd wrapped up in a psychic bubble. He shook his head.

Sam let a sigh and folded her arms across her chest. "*Madison Parker!*" she yelled up the stairs, like a mother who was about to scold a child. "You get your ass down here *right now!*"

Upstairs Jamie heard the distinct click of a door pulling away from its frame as it opened. That sound was followed by a soft thud, the first in a series of hesitant steps. At the top of the stairs, Jamie saw Madison's familiar face peak out from behind the wall. "Sam?" she asked, looking down in confusion before she came out from her hiding place and walked down the stairs. "What are you doing here?" she asked. "Why did you mess with the lights?"

"Jade got kidnapped," Sam stated bluntly.

Madison stopped, suddenly still as though she was being held in place, though Jamie knew she was simply stunned. "What?" she asked. Looking to Sam, her eyes clearly confused and concerned.

"She was taken by Warlocks," Sam continued. "From her house . . . I don't know when, but it was sometime today. And when I heard that I just thought, hmm . . . now why would Warlocks want Jade? And then I thought, who better to ask than the spy?"

"What?" Madison's eyes were wide. "I'm not a spy! Why would you even think that?"

"Two reasons." Sam counted them out on her fingers. "One, I'm not an idiot, and two, I never said I thought *you* were the spy."

Madison looked from Sam to Jamie, then back again. "You don't really think that I had something to do with Jade —"

"No," Sam interrupted. "I don't think you had anything to do with taking Jade, just like I don't think you have any part in the plot against me . . . I do however think that you're a spy and that you work for Warlocks . . . like your Halloween date for example, he looked like he'd been around a while, and he seemed surprised that I was getting weak. Do you know what that says to me?"

Madison shook her head.

"To me, that says that he thought he was in charge of taking me in alive, and someone else, who works for him or whoever his boss is, has a different plan . . . one where they kill me and take whatever Power they can."

"He doesn't know who's behind that!" Madison interrupted. "And neither do I!"

Sam smiled.

"So she's right," Jamie said, looking at Madison. "You're one of the bad guys."

Madison shook her head and sighed in frustration, closing her eyes tightly as if she were fighting a headache. "*No*, I'm not a bad guy."

"Your boyfriend?"

Madison half smiled. "A, my boss. B, not the type to be anyone's boyfriend. C, *also* not the bad guy."

"You wanted me to meet him, why?" Sam asked, her expression seeming genuinely curious.

"Because, he wants you on his side. There's a bigger picture, there's a war —"

"Not my problem."

"It is!" Madison yelled. "It's everyone's problem. Yours, his and mine. Anyone who is alive and not human ... it's *everyone's* problem. You want to be left alone? That's what everyone wants. You get it by fighting. I've picked my side, and I chose it specifically because I know who I can trust, and who I can't. I know the overall plan of both sides, and I chose the one that wants you, alive and well, on their side. The side that wouldn't resort to kidnapping and killing your family and friends."

"Looks like you chose wrong," Sam said, her hands clenched by her sides.

Madison let a sigh. "You have to look deeper," she said. "There's something *wrong*, can't you feel it?"

Jamie looked at Sam; her hands were shaking by her sides, as if she were trying with all of her strength not to lash out at Madison. He could see the expression of hurt and betrayal behind her eyes, her lips parted as if she were about to reply.

"Where would they have taken Jade?" Jamie asked, saving Sam the trouble of speaking and continuing a conversation that was only causing her turmoil.

Madison looked to him, her eyes seeming both tired and sad. "I don't know," she said. "I don't know where they would have taken her."

"The Under—"

"Not there," Madison said, interrupting Sam before she had a chance to finish. "Like I said, there's something wrong, anyone going against the main plan wouldn't risk doing it at the base, they'd go somewhere else. And I don't know where, if I did, they would be dead by now."

With a sigh Sam turned her back to Madison. "You can let them go now," she said to Jamie. "It doesn't matter if they wake up anymore." Without another word, Sam walked out the door.

"Wait." Madison moved past Jamie, stepping outside. "Let me help. If Jade was taken by Warlocks I want to help."

Sam whirled on her, her eyes blazing with barely contained fury. Jamie took a hesitant step towards her, half preparing for the possibility of having to stop her from attacking. "I don't want *your* help!" she yelled, before storming down the driveway.

Jamie followed her, briefly looking over his shoulder at Madison, walking back to her house, her head hanging low. For a moment it appeared as though she was crying.

"Sam," Jamie said, placing his hand on her elbow to keep her from walking away from him. "I don't think she mean—"

"You don't *know*!" Sam yelled. "You don't know anything, so don't act like you do!"

# CHAPTER 59

Scott had gone to his window when the lights flickered.

He scrambled out of bed and ran to the window just in time to see the lights in all of the houses—and all of the streetlamps—switch off.

The entire neighbourhood was plunged into darkness.

Curiosity getting the better of him, he opened his window and leaned out. After a few seconds he heard an electrical buzzing sound and then the streetlamps came to life.

For a moment, Scott simply stared at them, wondering why the lights were behaving as they were. He scanned the neighbourhood, looking to see if anyone was out. That was when he noticed that the front door to Madison's house was open.

Scott chewed his lower lip as his mind wondered over all the possible explanations. Most of which consisted of burglars, serial killers and all manner of horror movie monsters.

Quickly, he dashed from the window over to his bed where his shoes were lying on the floor. He shoved his feet into them and laced them up before he ran down the stairs to the front door. Briefly wondering if he should wake his parents for help.

He didn't.

When he came to the door he paused at the sound of Sam's voice.

His hand itched to reach forward and yank the door open so he could run to her. And he wondered, as he always did, why he felt as he did. Why did he feel so compelled to be near Sam? The thought that he may not get a chance to be in her presence filled him with a sense of dread, a feeling that he might die if he didn't get to be near her soon.

Instead of running to her, he walked to the living room window, pulling the curtain aside just enough that he saw Madison — safe and well — walk inside.

A moment later Sam stormed off, followed by the new kid. The one that Scott had an immense amount of dislike for.

He huffed as he let the curtain fall back into its place. Annoyed by the fact that Sam allowed that guy to go with her when she did nothing but brush Scott off as though he meant nothing to her.

He wondered where exactly they would be going in the middle of the night.

And with a resolute sigh, Scott walked to the door, deciding that *tonight* he would get his answers.

# CHAPTER 60

$\mathcal{S}$am pulled Jamie's ringing phone out of her pocket. "Where is she?" she asked before Danny had a chance to speak.

"We tracked her to the beach," he said. "But Sam, it—"

Sam hung up.

She didn't want, or need to be told any more. She knew where Jade was, and she had already decided what she was going to do to the people who'd taken her.

Gripping Jamie's phone tightly in her hand, she swung her arm back, then brought it down hard, throwing the phone to the pavement, watching with grim fascination as it smashed.

"Sam!" Jamie stared at her, his eyes wide with shock. "That was *my* phone!"

"I'll get you a new one."

Before Jamie had a chance to speak she took off. Running through the streets as fast as she could. Not needing to look back to know that Jamie would follow.

The beach was not a place that Sam came to frequently.

White sand that shone a pale blue in the moonlight, a rocky shore where the bottom of the cliffs met with the sand, and trees lining the road leading up to it. On sunny days it was capable of looking beautiful. But Sam had never felt drawn to it, not like she did the cliffs.

As she ran down the hill towards the beach, with Jamie behind her running at what would be a slow pace to him, she saw a dark shape emerge from the water.

She slowed in her tracks as she stepped onto the sand. Squinting her eyes as she saw that the shape was a man, and that he wasn't alone. The man slumped down to the sand, dropping whoever he was holding. She looked to Jamie, knowing that he could see better in the dark than she could. When she saw the look of recognition sweep across his face, she surged forward and Jamie followed.

Though unlike him, she never made it to Jade. She stopped moving when the man looked up; her body freezing in shock as she recognised him.

Jamie fell to the sand next to Jade, his hands going to her neck to check for a pulse. "There's no heartbeat," he said to Sam.

The man looked at him. "I tried to save her," he said. "I couldn't—"

"Get away from her," Sam said through gritted teeth, her hands clenching and unclenching at her sides.

The man looked away from Jamie, turning his gaze on Sam. A slow smile crept across his face and Sam saw that his eyes were filled with Shadows.

# CHAPTER 61

*J*amie stood, obviously sensing the tension in the air. Sam didn't pay much attention to him though, she was staring at *Kraven*. She knew that was his name despite the fact that she didn't know him. But she remembered.

The face of the man who murdered her family was something she would never forget.

"Sam?" Jamie sounded concerned.

"I said, get *away* from her!" Sam yelled. She felt the Magic boil in her blood as it mixed with her fury. She tried as best she could to keep it contained, but she was tired and agitated, and when her emotions mixed with her Magic . . . especially when she was close to nature like this . . .

She heard the waves start crashing loudly against the rocks in the distance, and she didn't need to look up to know that a storm was starting.

Slowly, Kraven stood, never taking his eyes off Sam. Smiling as he did as though this was a part of his master plan and she had walked right into the trap he'd set for her.

Without taking her eyes away from him, or making any physical move, Sam cast out a psychic net, scanning the area for any other people. Though she found nothing but sleeping animals and two running people. She didn't need to push too hard to know who the people were.

Jamie stayed by Jade's side, watching them both curiously and cautiously.

"Bring Jade closer to the trees," Sam ordered.

Jamie complied without question.

Kraven didn't move to stop him from leaving, though he did turn his head to watch them go. Sam stared at him, her brain calculating what the best way to proceed would be. She knew that she should be smart about it, but her mind felt frantic. She was filled with anger. Anger for the family that he killed, the friends he'd caused her to lose, the life she could have had . . . all of the things that this man had taken from her.

Without much more thought, she ran at him, her body colliding with his. She slammed him to the ground and, while pinning him down with her body, punched him in the face. Putting all of her force into her fist as it struck him.

Bone cracked beneath bone and her fist came away bloody.

Though despite the fact that he was obviously feeling pain, he laughed an insane, crazy, maniacal laugh, that reminded her of the cackle that had come from Hayley.

She leaned back, and he lay there laughing, his arms spread over his head. They were free enough that he could easily fend her off if he wanted to, but he didn't.

Sam watched him curiously for a moment. Staring at the gleam in his black eyes and the smile on his face, all of it screaming *do it*. He wanted her to fight . . . and for some reason he wanted her to win.

She brought her hand down—the mark on her wrist glowing softly with unshed Power—and placed it palm first on his chest. For a moment he looked at her in fear, as if she wasn't doing what she was supposed to. She sent a surge of Power into his body; she felt as the current ran through his veins and straight to his heart, which pounded quickly as it was struck by Magic. He cried out in pain, his eyes squeezing tightly as his body began to writhe and spasm beneath her.

Sam scrambled to her feet, not understanding why, but going with her instincts as they told her to move back. As she hit the sand by Kraven's feet a plume of what looked like black smoke burst from his body, through his mouth, his nose and his eyes.

For a moment after the Shadow escaped, his body twitched, before he was finally still.

Sam looked to the black cloud that had formed above him. It was different than the Shadows she had grown accustomed to, it appeared more corporeal in form as it grew and began to take on a sickly shape. It looked like the sort of thing that Sam would have imagined a *real* demon to look like. With a sickly rotund body, and pudgy arms that grew claws as they formed.

Unlike the Shadows, this creature, when it had come to a complete form, didn't look like black smoke. It looked as though it was made of tar, its body slick with ooze that came off it in drips as it slowly made its way towards Sam, not seeming to notice that it was climbing right on top of Kraven's motionless form.

Sam heard Jamie yell at her to move, though his voice seemed far away, and she didn't turn to look at him. She hurried to her feet, stumbling back a few steps as the creature advanced. It moved slowly and awkwardly, so Sam knew that if she ran it wouldn't be able to catch her.

But she couldn't bring herself to run.

That thing had come *out* of a person.

If it climbed inside another one . . .

Sam stopped moving and stood her ground, allowing the Magic to build in her veins. Just as she was about to strike, she stopped, realising that the creature was too close for her to attack. She jogged backwards, not allowing it to get close enough to touch her. She didn't know what this thing was, and she didn't know what would happen if that *goo* got on her skin and she didn't particularly want to find out.

When she stopped for a second time, she noticed that the creature had started moving faster. As though it had eased out whatever kinks its body had developed by being cramped inside a being half its size.

Fear rose up in Sam and she let out a scream, something she hadn't done since she was a child, and was embarrassed for it right after it happened, not that the feeling lasted long as she was fully focused on the creature as it continued to move towards her.

She stumbled back as the creature drew closer, tripping backwards as it suddenly fell to the sand.

Sam looked on in confusion as a pair of arms wrapped around the creature from behind. "Blast it!" a voice yelled, and Sam realised that Jamie must have tackled the monster.

Without wasting a moment, Sam threw a bubble of energy around the creature, yelling at Jamie to get out of the way before she sealed it off. The creature was pushed forward, its body slamming against the bubble Sam had created, leaving black smudges on the shield. Jamie rolled out of the way, and scrambled to his feet, his clothes covered in black ooze. When she saw that he was far enough out of the way, Sam closed off the shield, encasing the creature in a bubble of purple energy.

Slowly, she pulled the shield tighter and tighter. The

creature screaming in agony as the bubble condensed to a point too small for it to survive. With a shaking hand, Sam squeezed her fist closed, bringing the bubble to a point where it disappeared and popped, leaving nothing behind but a black stain on the sand.

Sam let a relieved sigh, before she remembered why she was here in the first place.

She ran to Jade, noticing for the first time that Danny and Jack were already kneeling by her; she briefly wondered when they had arrived, and how much of what had happened they had witnessed.

Danny knelt beside Jade with his hands on her chest. A cloud of sand blew into the air as Sam fell to her knees. She placed both of her hands on Jade, next to where Danny's were, she could feel that he was trying to feed her energy. "Will blood help?" Jamie asked.

Sam shook her head; Jade was past the point of needing blood, she was dead. She'd been dead for at least fifteen minutes, forcing Vampire blood down her throat would do nothing for her. She wasn't alive enough for it to be absorbed.

What she needed was an energy transfer.

So that's what Sam was doing.

With a sigh she backed away from Jade's body. "Danny," she said, "take one of Jamie's hands."

For a moment Danny looked at her curiously, then reluctantly, he took one of Jamie's hands in his. Sam took the other, interlinking their fingers, then she placed their intertwined hands onto Jade's body. After a moment's pause, Danny did the same.

Sam concentrated, pulling energy from both Danny and Jamie and pouring it—along with her own life force—into Jade.

She felt a stirring from within Jade, and opened her eyes to identify the source of it.

Her breath caught in her throat as she gazed down at Jade, who was surrounded by a bright glow the colour of emeralds. Slowly, Sam took her hand away and saw that Jamie did the same. The light around Jade ebbed and faded. Sam looked on in anticipation, waiting for the moment that Jade would wake up.

Jade's eyes didn't open.

Her body spasmed, and she coughed, water spilling from her mouth.

Before Sam had a chance to do anything to help, Jamie grabbed Jade and held her in a sitting position, her back leaning against his chest. He wrapped his arms around her and squeezed, holding his arms around her torso below her breasts. She coughed louder and more water spilled out.

Sam let a relieved sigh as Jade's eyes flew open and she fell forward, her hands slamming into the sand to break her fall. With his hand, Jack leaned forward and patted her on the back, helping to rid her lungs of the water.

Sam smiled widely, her eyes stinging with tears as she realised that Jade was alive.

Though the smile quickly vanished, when she heard a cough that hadn't come from Jade. She looked up to find Kraven stumbling to his feet.

He gazed around slowly, until he found Sam, and looked at her with clear golden brown eyes that watered with unshed tears. For a moment, Sam felt sorry for him, then slowly that feeling faded when she remembered all of the evil things that he'd done.

His eyes moved to Jade, his expression filled with remorse. "I'm sorry," he said, his voice coming out raspy, as though he hadn't spoken in a while. He coughed again, and moved slightly forward. Sam sprang to her feet, putting herself between Kraven and Jade, her hands balled into fists by her sides.

Kraven looked at Sam, as tears fell from his eyes, though he didn't seem to notice or care.

"Thank you," he said, taking shallow breaths as if he were finding it difficult to breathe. "That *thing* . . . it's been years since I've—"

"How long have you been possessed for?"

Sam turned her head to find Jamie getting to his feet. Jade was breathing, but half unconscious; she was sitting up, her head resting on Danny for support in staying upright.

Sam clenched her fists tighter.

"Since the war started," Kraven said, then he laughed humourlessly. "Not that it was ever much of a war."

"*You* started the war," Jack said. "And that was over thirteen hundred years ago."

Kraven nodded, biting down on his shaking lip. "I never let it latch," he said, his whole body was shaking now. "I'm not the only one . . . everyone, there's one inside everyone. The more chaos the stronger—" He broke off in a coughing fit. Sam saw that the hand he had used to cover his mouth was now covered in freckles of black tinged blood.

He looked to Sam again, this time he smiled. "Thank you," he said again.

Sam stared at him for a moment. Her body felt light and her head was filled with just one thought. She spoke quietly. "You killed my family," she said.

Kraven's eyes flashed to Jack, then back to Sam. "I'm sorry," he said. "It wasn't *me.*"

Sam took a step towards him, and he took one back as she did. "It was you!" she yelled. "You remember it . . . it was *you!*"

He shook his head, his eyes pleading with her to

understand. "I didn't—"

"Shut *up!*" Sam threw a blast of energy at him, the Magic hit him and sent him tumbling through the air before he crashed to the sand.

"Sam *don't,*" Jack warned, reaching out a hand to stop her, but she moved away from him. Her attention focused on Kraven, who was now getting to his feet.

"Fight me," she said, stepping closer to him. "You wanted to fight me, so fight me!"

Kraven shook his head, using his hand to wipe the blood from his face. He looked at her with eyes filled with a millennia's worth of sadness. "No," he said quietly. "I don't want to fight you."

Sam screamed in frustration and ran at him, knocking him back down to the sand, where she pinned him down and hit him.

She hit him again and again and again.

*"Fight me!"*

"No," he repeated, lying there unresponsively. Allowing her to beat him and biting his lip through the pain. "I won't fight you, you're needed."

Sam screamed again, about to bring her fist down when arms wrapped around her, pulling her off Kraven. She struggled, her arms and legs flailing as she fought for her freedom. "Let me go!"

"Sam," it was Jamie, "I can't let you kill him."

"He deserves it!"

"No he doesn't!"

Jamie threw her, for a second she flew through the air, skidding across the sand before she was caught by Jack. She looked to Jamie in shock as she regained her footing. He stood in a defensive position in front of Kraven, who was staring at Jamie, seeming just as surprised as everyone else.

"He was possessed!" Jamie said. "I know what that's like, you have *no* control, he couldn't have stopped if he wanted to."

"Get out of the way," Sam said, shoving Jack away from her.

"No," Jamie said. "If you blame him for what he's done than you may as well blame me for what happened to you. If you want vengeance you'll take it on me."

"Why are you defending him?" she cried, unable to understand why Jamie couldn't see that he was a bad guy and he needed to be stopped. It wasn't about vengeance, it was about setting the universe right by ridding it of what was evil.

"Because he hasn't done anything wrong."

"*He's* the one who has people hunting the *both* of us! He's the reason you were shot. The reason my parents, Danny's parents and our grandparents are dead! He *tortured* me!"

"He didn—"

"I was twelve!" Sam yelled, her eyes welling up with tears. "And he *tortured* me . . . I *still* have nightmares about it."

From behind Jamie, Kraven spoke, "I'm sorry."

"Shut up!" Sam yelled, putting her hands over her ears to block out the sound.

Jack turned towards where Jade and Danny were staring. "Danny, you take Jade home . . . to your house, not hers."

Sam was distantly aware of Danny getting to his feet, cradling Jade in his arms as he left.

"Jamie," Jack said. "Stay there, and Kraven . . . for the love of the *Gods,* don't speak."

"Sam . . . " Jack placed his hands on her shoulders, she flinched at his touch, moving away so that his hands fell back to his sides.

"She's right," Kraven said, getting to his feet and stepping past Jamie. Sam glared at him as he moved, knowing that if he kept moving as he was she would soon have a clear enough shot.

"Kraven," Jack said in a warning voice.

"No," he replied. The Magic began to build in her veins. "She's right. Samantha . . . " Sam's head shot up as he addressed her. *How dare he speak my name,* she thought as she watched him move and stand next to Jamie. "I'm *sorry.*"

"Just shut up," she said.

"I didn't mean to, and if I could —"

"Shut up!"

With a sigh he stepped in front of Jamie, slowly moving towards her. The mark on her wrist began to glow. "If I could, I would take everything —"

"Kraven!" Jack yelled, his voice sounding alarmed. "For fuck sake —"

*"SHUT UP!"*

Sam released the energy. Shooting it towards him in a blast that looked like a shooting star. For a moment, she smiled at the look of fear on his face, before she saw Jamie staring at her in disappointment. The Magic exploded in a purple shower, the blast so strong that it threw Kraven so far he landed in the ocean with a splash.

Sam turned, and stood facing the water, watching it carefully for several minutes. Dimly aware that Jack and Jamie were yelling at her from behind. She smiled, when after what felt like five minutes of staring, nothing came to the surface of the water.

*I win,* she thought with a giddy feeling of triumph.

Just as she was about to laugh, she heard a familiar voice say, "Sam?"

She turned to find Scott standing by the trees, staring at her as if he'd never seen her before.

# CHAPTER 62

Everyone froze at the sound of Scott's voice. And Jamie thought the same thing he assumed both Sam and Jack were. *How long has he been there? And how much did he see?*

Sam was the first to speak. "What are you doing here?" she asked, stepping forward so that she was between Jack and Jamie, all three of them standing shoulder to shoulder.

Scott took a step towards her, his gaze never faltering. "I saw you at Madison's," he said. "And I followed you."

"Why?" Jamie asked.

Scott turned to him, projecting an immense amount of hatred in the form of a glare. "You got to go with her!" he yelled, his argument making him sound like nothing more than a petulant child.

"How much did you see?" Sam asked, seeming to ignore both what Jamie had said and Scott's reply.

Scott turned his attention back to Sam, his eyes seemed to glaze over as he looked at her and smiled. The expression he wore was one that Jamie recognised, it was one that he had forced onto many people. "I saw everything," he spoke kindly, "It's alright," he added, taking a step towards her. "I still love you."

"That's just pathetic," Jack mumbled, though it wasn't loud enough for anyone but Jamie to hear.

Jamie watched Scott curiously. Watched how he gazed at Sam through half-lidded eyes, a soft smile on his face as he moved towards her, and he realised that Scott didn't really understand *what* he was doing. Jamie remembered how he'd been fed on by a Vampire, and wondered what exactly had been done to him.

"Sam," Jamie said, placing a hand on her arm to stop her from walking any closer.

Scott glared at him again. "Let her go!" he yelled.

"Sam," Jamie repeated. "*Look* at him, can't you see there's something wrong?"

Sam glared at him, her eyes still blazing from the Magic she'd used and glittering with unshed tears. "There's nothing wrong with him," she said. "He just loves me."

"*Sam,*" Jamie tried to plead with her. "We need to erase his memories."

"No," she said. "The bad guy is dead. We win, he doesn't need to forget anymore."

"He's *infatuated,*" Jamie said.

Jack nodded. "We should get rid of that."

"You want him to *hate* me?"

Scott's eyes went wide. "I could *never* hate you."

Jamie and Jack shared an expression, and although they couldn't actually share thoughts, they expressed enough understanding through their eyes that Jack nodded to him, before wrapping his arms around Sam. And as she struggled, Jack dematerialised, taking Sam with him.

Scott looked to the place where Sam had been with fearful eyes. "Where has she gone!" he asked, turning to Jamie and staring at him accusingly. "Where did you send her?"

"Home," Jamie replied simply. Reaching out to Scott with one hand, he placed it on his head to keep him still. Scott fell to his knees, looking upwards as his eyes rolled back in their sockets.

Jamie spent the next few minutes taking away his memories, as well as his infatuation with Sam.

# CHAPTER 63

*J*ack got Sam home within seconds, as soon as her feet hit the floor he let her go. She immediately turned and hit him hard in the chest, right over his heart. A sharp pain shot through him, but Jack ignored it, standing perfectly still as though he felt nothing. His mind repeating his mantra; *You're dead, you feel no pain.*

Sam was crying as she glared at him. "Why did you do that?"

"You're not thinking straight," Jack stated bluntly. "After the night you've had you need rest. So Jamie's going to take care of Scott and I'm going to take care of you. Now get to bed."

"No," Sam said stubbornly, folding her arms across her chest.

Jack let an irate sigh, resisting the urge to smack her for her attitude. "Sam," he repeated through his teeth. "Go to bed."

Danny came down the stairs and stared at them both for a

moment. "I put Jade in the spare room," he said. "Figured I should since she can't go home."

"Where's Hayley?" Sam said, her eyes already looking hungrily at the door, as if she knew another fight lay beyond it.

Jack swore internally, which caused the lights to flicker slightly.

"Gone," Danny said.

Jack relaxed a little. If Sam could calm down now she would be fine, but if she continued the way she was . . . he would rather she didn't tap into the violent part of her blood. It was better that she only used her Magic for defence. That was what he always thought, and after tonight, seeing how the possessed Kraven had lay on the beach and allowed her to beat him nearly to death, he knew that a violent Sam was what the enemy wanted.

She let a sigh, as her body seemed to relax a little.

"I'm going to sit outside," she said, sniffling as she wiped tears from her eyes. "I need fresh air."

Jack nodded. "Fresh air," he repeated. "Good idea."

Sam opened the door and stepped out.

When the door shut behind her, Danny looked to him and asked, "What happened?"

With a sigh, Jack explained what he could.

# CHAPTER 64

*J*amie approached Sam's house with a slight amount of hesitation. He knew what he was about to face, and after the night had started off so well he didn't think he could deal with it. His body felt charged, but he was emotionally drained.

Sam looked up as he approached, her eyes filled with accusation and annoyance and—what stung Jamie's heart the most—hatred.

"Why?"

Jamie sighed and took a step closer to her. "Because someone had to."

"You didn't *have* to do that!" Sam cried. She looked up at him, her eyes red and wet from her tears. "Don't pretend you did it for him, we both know why you really did it."

Jamie pressed his lips together firmly. Resisting the urge to get overly emotional with her. "And why, pray tell, did I do it Sam?"

"You wanted him out of the way!" Jamie bit down on his tongue so hard he tasted blood in his mouth. "You messed with his head, you made it so that he wouldn't love me anymore just because you wanted him out of your way."

"Stop behaving like a spoiled child," he said as calmly as he could.

Sam looked at him, her face twitched in a moment of confusion before she gave him the most venomous expression. Clearly, no one had ever said anything like that to her before. Which was why Jamie knew he should keep talking.

"Not everything is about you, you know. And do you really think that after the way you've treated me, that I just sit around, pining after you coming up with ways to make you mine?" Sam opened her mouth to speak, but Jamie didn't give her the chance. "No. I don't. You know how I feel about you, and you only care about it when it suits you. You're a user Sam. You use people."

Jamie nodded his head in the direction of her house, where he knew Jade, Danny and Jack were. "They all know it and so do I, though for some reason they give you the benefit of the doubt and say that you don't even realise you're doing it. But I know you Sam, I know you better than you think, which is how I know that you *do* realise it. You're fully aware of what you can do to people and you use it. You're a manipulator. That's what you do. And that's what you've been doing to Scott for years."

Sam stood up and turned, about to walk inside, Jamie ran in front of her and blocked off the door. He wasn't going to allow her to leave. Not until he had said all he had to say to her.

She didn't speak.

She didn't tell him to move.

She just stood there and glared at him, projecting an immense amount of hatred.

"You got inside his head," Jamie stated. "Maybe when you did it, it *was* an accident, but you *knew* you were in there. You knew this whole time that you had a hold on him. You told him to go away, to leave you alone, that you didn't want him. But you kept your hold on his mind. Making him pine for you. Making it so that he would love you forever."

"I love h—" she interrupted.

"No Sam, you loved him once. If you still cared about him at all, you would have taken away his infatuation. But you didn't, and that wasn't fair. So *I* did it, because it was the right thing to do."

Jamie felt a hard push against his mind, he closed his eyes against the pain.

*<Go find Scott and undo what you've done!>* Sam yelled inside his brain. Her words echoed around in his head, repeating themselves again and again until the message sunk in. Latching itself onto his subconscious. Making it appear as though the thought was his own.

"Go," Sam said, taking a step back to let him pass.

Jamie looked at her in disbelief.

After everything he'd said to her, she didn't feel the slightest amount of remorse for what she had done to someone she supposedly loved. "You know, it's moments like this, when you behave so callously towards other living creatures, that I find it incredibly easy to remember that you're not actually the human you try so hard to be."

Sam's eyes grew wide and she looked at him in confusion. She let a panicked breath and pushed against his mind again. *<GO FIND SCOTT AND UNDO WHAT YOU'VE DONE!>*

This time Jamie didn't close his eyes to fight the pain. He stood before her, unflinching as she invaded his mind again and again, repeating the same message and becoming increasingly scared when it had no effect.

"TAKE IT BACK!" she yelled when she realised her Magic wasn't working.

"No. And if you cared about him at all, you wouldn't ask me to."

"I *do* care," she said.

"No, you don't. You don't care about anyone!"

For a moment, she looked at him, then slowly she half smiled, though he could tell that the expression wasn't genuine. "I care about you."

Jamie looked at her in disbelief. He shook his head, knowing what she was trying to do.

"I told you that I loved you and you didn't care. You brushed me off and you act like I'm nothing. You *used* me Sam. Just like you use everyone else. But unlike them I'm not going to stay here and let you use me."

Jamie walked past her, purposely bumping his shoulder into hers, knocking her to the side. He could feel her eyes on him.

"Where are you going?" she asked. He heard her take a step in his direction.

"Home," he answered without turning to look at her.

*<Stay. You want to stay here>* Sam tried once more to manipulate his thoughts.

Jamie stopped walking and turned his head so he could see her. She was standing on the front porch watching him confidently, as if she knew her Magic would make him obey her. Jamie shook his head, and shut his eyes tightly to stop the stinging.

Even after everything they'd been through, and everything he'd done for her, and everything he'd said, to her he was still nothing more than a puppet she could play around with. The realisation sunk into his heart, making his chest clench and his eyes sting. "I'm done with you Sam."

She took a step towards him, her expression bewildered. "What?"

Jamie turned fully, so that he was facing her. "I'm. Done. With. You." He said each word distinctly, filling each one with every ounce of his anger and his pain. Without waiting for a response he started to walk away.

"Get back here!" she ordered.

Jamie ignored her.

*<You don't want to leave. You want to stay>*

Jamie stopped walking, clenching his fists in anger. "I'm impervious to Sams," he said callously, without looking back. "Your Powers don't work on me . . . they never have."

# CHAPTER 65

$\mathcal{I}$t was early after sunset that Jamie awoke from a fitful sleep, plagued by nightmares of a world filled with hungry Shadows.

In the dream there had been so many of them. Everywhere he looked, all of the faces he saw, the eyes were cruel, malevolent Shadows swimming around in the irises. Vindictive smiles, filled with deceit and plotting, aimed at him wherever he looked.

He had been glad to wake up, only realising it had been a dream when he'd opened his eyes to the dimly lit room. He sat up slowly, casting a glance around the room, checking everywhere for anything that didn't belong. Something that had become a regular habit in the past two weeks.

There was something off. He could sense it in the air. At least he thought he could sense it, but he could simply be feeling the lasting waking effects of his dream.

He took a breath, something he did to calm himself despite

the fact that he didn't necessarily need the oxygen. He stood, closing his eyes for a moment, allowing himself to feel the comforting effects provided by the darkness.

Something moved outside.

His eyes shot open and he turned his head in the direction of his window, staring at it despite the fact that the curtains were closed and he couldn't see through them.

Slowly, he slid his hand under his pillow and pulled out the dagger that Sam had hidden there, then he made his way out of his room and down the stairs.

When he got to the front door he paused, listening closely for sounds of movements. The noise of autumn leaves being crushed underfoot sent a feeling of nausea to his stomach. Someone was definitely outside, yet he could sense no heartbeat.

"Jamie!" a woman shouted.

He felt his eyes go wide as he recognised the voice, the dagger slipped from his hand and fell to the hard wood floor with a bang. Slowly, he opened the door and stepped outside, allowing his eyes to see what his ears already knew to be true.

He sucked in a breath as he saw her. Standing at the tree line, her hands clasped behind her back, swaying back and forth, her dress floating in the breeze as she moved. "Bethany?"

She looked at him, a slow smile spreading across her face as her eyes made contact with his. "Husband," she said, taking a step forward before she was stopped by Sam's runes. She smiled kindly. "I found you."

<u>**AND SOME FINAL WORDS . . .**</u>

As this book is self published and I lack the advertising and marketing budget of more traditionally published books, my main form of advertising comes from you guys (the readers).

So please, if you liked, loved, hated, despised or felt/thought anything about this book at all, leave me a review and let me and others know what you thought.

Visit me online for book updates and some of my insane ramblings about life and stuff:

**evilbunnybooks.com**

**The Immortal Souls: Magic & Chaos – Book 3**
**DEMONIC RECRUIT**

Something's wrong with Jamie.

Plagued by nightmares of evil, tormented by memories of a past long since forgotten and overwhelmed by a Power beyond his control.

He's aggressive, his temper is short, he's getting violent and somewhere in the darkness the Shadows are stirring . . .

**COMING SOON!**

www.ingramcontent.com/pod-product-compliance
Lightning Source LLC
Chambersburg PA
CBHW031214120726